Dirty Eddie

Ludwig Bemelmans

DIRTY EDDIE

New York · The Viking Press · 1947

Parts of this book appeared serially in *Town & Country*

Printed in U.S.A. by The Haddon Craftsmen

Ad usum Delphini

The characters in this book, including Dirty Eddie, are fictional, and any resemblance to living persons or pigs is pure coincidence.

Contents

Fifth Part: In the Beautiful San Fernando Valley

Sixth Part: Your Sins Are Forgiven

A Star Is Born

. . . and named with the aid of a golden cigar band. In which we travel to Hollywood and meet the resourceful Maurice Cassard.

1. Talent Scout

"Believe me," she said, "I know how to do it. Lean forward, darling."

The lovely young creature, stretching like a tigress against the satin-striped banquette on which they sat, leaned across behind him.

"Now, swallow hard three times," she said, and she deftly stuck the palms of her small thumbs into the ears of Vanya Vashvily.

He swallowed three times and the hiccoughing stopped.

"You see," she said, "it worked."

And he said, "Thank you, baby."

And that was as much conversation as he had with any of the assortment of dream girls that he wore like boutonnieres every night he went out.

Vanya Vashvily always sat on the first banquette to the right as you enter the Champagne Room of El Morocco. He spilled a salad of varicolored pills next to his glass as he sat down. He looked like a nice neighborhood butcher who had taken off his white coat and straw hat after a hard day's work.

The girls that came with him were like floral tributes that had been sent to the opening of the new butcher shop. As the night wore on, the floral tributes turned, always, into funeral pieces.

Vanya Vashvily would start to breathe heavily. He folded his hands over the fourth and fifth buttons of his waistcoat. His glassy eyes slowly rose up under the half-closed lids. He

nodded for a while and his bald, flat head became the favorite
landing place for the few flies of the elegant establishment.

The Hungarian virtuoso who plays in these intimate and
expensive premises, and who resembles Paul Lukas in his
kindest mood, then came to the table. Taking a mute from
his pocket, he stuck it on the bridge of his Gaurnerius and
embalmed the esteemed client in the nostalgia of Russian and
Viennese melodies.

The pretty and much-sought-after girls sat upright like little
soldiers on guard while he slept and nobody thought it odd
that they were with him. The intimates all knew about Vashvily, and when strangers asked the maître d'hôtel to explain
the phenomenon, they only needed to be told that Vanya
Vashvily was a Hollywood producer looking for new talent.

The patient and resourceful sitter on the night of the hiccoughing, Mona or Puck or Cleatus or Gri-Gri, handed a glass
of water to Vashvily as an added help and said:

"Now drink it down in one swallow, darling, and you'll be
all right."

The concerned maître d'hôtel, who had stood at the table
during the spell, added his suggestion to the girl's therapy.
He leaned forward over the table and said to Vashvily that he
should eat something. The producer nodded.

Later, the girl sat with folded arms and with wonder in her
eyes, as she watched the curious performance of a man eating
a sandwich with closed eyes while the Hungarian virtuoso
played "Mei Muatterl War a Weana Kind."

The music would put the producer completely to sleep and
he would sit frozen with the half sandwich in his hand.

He always awoke refreshed after fifteen-minute-intervals,
and in one of those awakenings he asked for the bill and
signed it.

After the next siesta, he announced his wish to go home and
his departure was organized.

The maître d'hôtel held open the door that led from the
Champagne Room into the corridor. The bellboy kept the
corridor clear. The coatroom concessionaire waited with hat
and coat and then turned the revolving door while Vashvily

went round and round in it, until the doorman outside took
him out and helped him, with his eyes still closed, into the
waiting taxi.

It was snowing heavily that night and the doorman who put
him into the cab asked:

"Where to, Mr. Vashvily?"

"To the Beverly Hills Hotel," said the producer.

"Pardon, Monsieur, but we are in New York," said the doorman.

Vashvily pointed to the girl, and after she gave her address
to the driver they started. She was let off at her home and
then the driver delivered the dead Vashvily into the hands of
the heavily liveried night doorman of his fashionable hotel.

The young woman who ran the elevator that served the
apartments in the tower of the hotel waited for him in the
lobby.

The marble floor, at that hour, was slippery. The mats and
runners had been taken up by the night cleaners and Vashvily
moved over them trotting like a toddler afraid of falling. With
closed eyes he sat down on the petit point upholstery of the
bench that stood inside the elevator. The operator waited until
he was leaning comfortably in the corner of her cab and then
slowly ascended the thirty-two stories up to the floor on which
he lived.

She opened the door there and leaned against it, waiting
until he announced his intention of going to bed by moving,
and then she brought him to his feet and led him into his
rooms. She left the door of the apartment and of his bedroom
open so that she could hear the elevator signal.

She started putting the tired producer to bed, undressing
him, and talking to him, and walking him in his socks to the
bathroom and back. She got him into bed and covered him up
like a child. She left him with his hands folded over the
coverlet and turned the light out as she closed the door, and
then sat in the living room of his apartment, reading until she
went off duty.

Vashvily, who, in spite of his periodic absences from his
surroundings, perceived every offense as well as every kindness

done to him, said one night as she covered him up and the lamp on his night table shone fully in her face:

"Don't move."

He looked at her with completely opened eyes and sat up. "How would you like to be in the movies?" he asked.

"Make me a star," she said, smiling.

Covering him once more, she told him to go to sleep and walked out of the room. He followed her with his eyes.

He awoke the next night again as he sat on the edge of his bed. She was about to pull the socks off his feet, which were as blue as his face.

He studied the shape of her head as she knelt before him in the dark uniform with white collar and cuffs. He looked at her shoulders, her hands, her arms. As she turned, he saw in the tall mirror, opposite his bed, how good and straight her back was.

He knew that her face would photograph well. It had attracted him when he first looked at it the evening he had moved in. She was in body, as in mind, wholesome, healthy, and right. He could tell good material. He had exercised good judgment before. He looked down at her again. The socks were off.

"Thank you," he said and startled her.

She leaned back, supporting herself with both arms in a straight line, placed from the shoulders to the floor. She had grace in all her motions. She was the kind of girl he had looked high and low for. Not exotic, not overbred, but exciting in her own fashion. She was what he called a Serena Blandish type. That's what he wanted and here she knelt before him, scrubbed and unperfumed, her red hair undyed and combed back. A plain, honest working girl with untold possibilities.

He was not given to sudden decisions, but of her he was sure. He wore a pained expression, like a person leaning forward into the wind, for a while as he looked down at her.

"Anything the matter?" she asked.

"I would like to talk to you. What's your name?"

"Marie," she said.

"Marie what?"

"O'Neill—two l's"—and she wrote it on a slip of paper on the desk.

He got up to put on his robe and went to the pantry for two glasses and a bottle of champagne. He offered her a drink.

He got a cigar out of a box and lit it, a large, blunt cigar with a white and gold band, and then he looked at the wide band on the cigar for a while and said:

"Belinda! Belinda would be a good name for you."

He put the glasses on the night table and lay down on the covers of his bed, folding his hands behind his head. He looked at her in the mirror and talked around the cigar.

"Sit down here," he said, motioning to the bed.

"I came east to look for new talent," he began. "I'm casting a picture. I want a new girl for it and I think you might be it. I'd like to put you under contract."

"I know that one," she said, "but you've got me all wrong, mister."

She got up.

"Good night now," she said, and turned to walk out of the room.

"Wait a minute. Come back here," he said, sitting up.

"The elevator's ringing," she said. "What did you want?"

"I just wanted to ask you whether there's anything to keep you here. I mean have you any ties, a family, I mean, somebody . . . Are you married? Could you go any time you want to?"

"No," she said, "I haven't anybody."

"You didn't answer my question," he said.

"Oh, sure, I'll go," she said. "Any time, naturally."

Saying good night once more, she went down in her elevator to the ground floor, where she read the morning papers and never thought of telling the night clerk, the doorman, or the man who always leaned against the wall, of her great fortune.

The next night, as she came on duty, the girl from whom she took over handed her an envelope. She tore it open and there it was in black and white, written on the letterhead of the New York office of the Olympia Studios.

"My God," she said. "The poor guy—he meant it."

Vashvily came into the hotel at three that night, and walked slowly round in the revolving door until the elevator came down and Belinda took him out.

It was not until the twenty-fifth floor that she could find the words to thank him.

"That's all right," he said, sitting in the corner of the cab.

She led him into his bedroom. He opened his eyes and pulled some papers out of his pocket, and then asked for the telephone, dictated some telegrams, and made reservations for two on the train to Los Angeles.

She pulled off his shoes and socks again, and helped him into bed. She had covered him up and thought he would sleep, but he suddenly sat up and said, "There is something I wanted to ask you—" He retrieved the hearing aid she had just taken away and said, looking at her intently:

"How is it that a girl as smart and pretty as you takes a job running an elevator?"

"Oh," she said, turning the pages of a magazine without either reading text or seeing pictures, "it isn't a bad job."

"Just the same," he said, "how does a girl like you get a job like that?"

"Well, would you like to know?"

"I don't want to know if you don't want to tell me."

She turned and braced herself. "A gangster got it for me."

Vashvily, whose story mind was working, fell into the proper lingo and said: "So you can case the joint for him?"

"No," she said, upsetting his scenario of jewel thief and girl placed in fashionable hotel. "You don't understand. He lives here—has an apartment, a duplex, on the two floors right above yours. Joe Malnatti is his name. My father knew him back in Chicago."

Vashvily's face looked like a drawer full of cutlery and he made mental reservations at another hotel for his next visit.

"How do you get mixed up with people like this?"

"I was a kid. We had a place near Cicero—and I got tired— the same street, the same place—I wanted to get away."

Vashvily was impatient with the childhood part of her recital.

"That gangster with the duplex in the tower," he said dryly, "I can't rhyme that at all. He rents all the expensive space. He's got money, he's a big shot—and yet he lets you run the elevator at night. Why didn't he just give you money?"

"I wouldn't take money from him."

"Oh, principles!" said Vashvily.

"Yes, principles!" said Belinda. "He's a nice guy. Why, he's like a puppy . . . wants to bring you a drink—the place is yours—everything he's got is yours. I guess it's only tough when they fall in love with you—you never get away from them except in a cedar box. If you go in for one of those guys, you just sign your life away."

"Does he know where you are now?"

"Who?"

"This gangster who is in love with you."

"Who said anything about love? I was just curious. I liked him. Nothing ever happened. He wouldn't have anything to do with me. He said I was too young."

"They have peculiar standards," said Vashvily, as relieved as a worried father who finds his daughter's honor intact.

"You know," said Belinda, "I'm curious. That's how I get into trouble. I'm always curious to find out things. Before I took this job I worked in Westchester County, helping out with the *Reader's Digest*."

"That gangster," said Vashvily, "you said that your father knew him. What business is your father in?"

"The police business," said Belinda, yawning.

The white temple that Vanya Vashvily had built to receive the statue of Serena Blandish had cracks in the wall and ceiling and wobbled dangerously. He was frightened by the great shadows of suspense and mystery—the very elements he tried hard to put into his pictures.

"I'll give her money and I'll get her job back for her. I'll tell her now," he said to himself, and sat up. He called her name twice but she did not answer. She was answering the elevator bell.

He got out of bed, slipped into his dressing gown, and waited for her, to speak to her in fatherly tones and console her. With all his words ready for the funeral of her career, he sat back facing the door. He was wide awake now.

"No," he said, astonished anew as she entered the room and stood before him. "No, she's all right," he said. "She's—all—right . . ."

He climbed back into his bed and she covered him up.

"You know," she said, "when we get to Chicago, we can go through every traffic light in town with sirens screaming and an escort."

"I bet we can," said Vashvily. . . .

"I am one of the five red-headed daughters of the former Chief of Police," she said proudly.

"*Oh!*" said Vashvily. "Why didn't you tell me?"

"I was thinking of calling up the family to come to the station, but then I figured it would look funny, me traveling alone with an old man, and so I decided to skip the whole thing."

"You're a wonderful girl," said Vashvily, and the temple shone brighter than ever.

2. *Through the Eye of the Needle*

Maurice Cassard, with the top of his car down, the manuscript of *Will You Marry Me?* on the seat next to him, and with his hands in gloves, steered out of his driveway, down Chrysanthemum Lane, and along Beverly Glen Boulevard on his way to the house of his friend Vanya Vashvily, the producer.

On a chair in the modern living room of the producer's house sat Belinda. After Vashvily had made the introductions, Cassard divested himself first of his gloves and raincoat and after that took hold of a curious garment, a kind of knitted muffler consisting of a short bib in back and a longer one in front and an opening to put his head through. It looked like something to wear for the guillotine. He pulled this off over his coiffure so that the black, silky hair was disarranged and stood away in all directions like monkey fur.

During the process of undressing he had crossed and recrossed the living room. He was an extremely articulate and nervous man. He had said "Thank you, thank you" to the offer of tea and cigarettes and of a chair; and in a sagging fashion, with his knees falling forward, he had visited with regularity the four walls that formed the room, as if they were about to fall down and he had to rush to hold them up.

Together with these mannerisms went the destruction of countless cigarettes which he took out of a pack, stuck in his mouth, bent and crushed into ash trays, but rarely lit. The pacing, the heavy breathing that accompanied it, the sitting down on chairs for half a second and then rushing to the collapsing walls, all were signals that he was charged with a new plot or trying to adapt an old one. He was an able, hard-working man of great talent and iron memory. During his séances it was impossible to interrupt him. He told his stories with lucidity and enacted all the roles of the characters, he illustrated moods, and at the end of the recital he would fall exhausted on a couch, throw his arms back, and, with averted eyes while crippling the last of his cigarettes, listen to the reactions to the story. There, while lying on his back, he wearily repaired whatever weaknesses were discovered, argued away criticism, and invented or remembered the material with which he built the bridges that spanned whatever voids existed. These bridges, simply or elaborately made of the most varied designs and stuff, were always adequate to the load they had to carry.

The attacker never got beyond the first words of his doubts. "I know, I know, I know," Maurice would say impatiently to anything that was brought up. And he knew. "Ah, amigo," he would begin. (Amigo was his favorite word of address and the beginning of all sentences addressed to men.) When he began speaking his tongue was bedded on his lower lip for

the "Ah" and the "a" in amigo—he slurred them together into
a sound a second long and in that space of time he thought
up all he would say in the next ten minutes. He was remarkable—and successful.

On this day, after he had laid his gloves on a commode
and taken off his raincoat and the bib and hung them up, he
gave a quick glance at the girl, a swift check on hair, face,
lap, and legs, and then began to stagger through the room.
"Ah, amigo," he said—and there was a long pause.

His friend Vashvily said, "Have you found anything?"

Maurice stopped. "Vashvily," he said. "Ah, amigo—listen—
carefully." He sagged toward the west wall. "Ah, amigo, I am
afraid that you will not like what I have to tell you." He
turned and looked the producer in the face. "Yes," he said,
"yes, I have found something. I have found something extraordinary. I have found, amigo, that this story you have given
me to read is abominably contrived." These were pet words
with him. "Yes, abominably contrived. There is no hope for it.
The money you have paid for it you might as well have thrown
out the window."

"Oh," said Vashvily. "And it took you six weeks at twenty-
five hundred to find that out?"

"I know, I know, I know—but—"

"Yes, but what?" said the producer.

"Ah, amigo, allow me to say in self-defense; amigo, allow
me to say in self-defense that which I must say. Ah, amigo,
when you told me this story I was so enchanted I laughed—
you remember. I agreed to explore its possibilities, and then
I take it home—and read it—and, amigo, it is hopeless. For
six weeks I have sweated. For six weeks I have sat there and
tried to breathe life into this clod of mud, and then I said to
myself: No—you will not do it, you will not let him down,
you will go and tell him the truth. It will hurt, but it is better
than to go ahead and spend more money on what will be a
disaster when it gets to the screen."

"Why couldn't you find that out after a week?"

"Ah, amigo, it is you who are to blame. Yes, you, Vanya—
you are so fascinating in your storytelling, you hypnotize the

listener, you inject a spirit into a plot that makes one suspect scenes that are not there at all. It took me six weeks to overcome that and to convince myself that it is hopeless. I regret it very much, amigo, but I cannot do otherwise. And now, may I wash my hands, amigo?"

"In twenty-five years," began the producer, and then changed the sentence: "The next time some son-of-a-bitch tries that on me, I'll—"

Finally he said to the girl, "What'll you have to drink?" He walked to the small bar at the end of the room and took the ice tray out of the small refrigerator and pried cubes from it.

Maurice came out of the washroom and staggered toward where the girl sat. "Ah, your name," he said. "I didn't hear your name when we were introduced."

"Belinda."

"Charming. American?"

"Yes. Why, don't I look it?" In two years in Hollywood, Belinda had become seven years younger.

"Ah, yes, but there is something about you of the European woman. You are an exquisite creature."

The host shouted from the bar, "What will you have to drink?"

"Oh, I'll have a little sherry," said the girl.

"And you?"

"Ah, amigo, anything you make for yourself," said Maurice, mauling a cigarette while he looked at the girl's hair. He sat down on the couch. "Mademoiselle, you must be tired of being told that you are ravishingly beautiful."

"It's always nice to hear it said again," she said.

He patted the wide expanse of pale velvet next to where he was seated, as one invites a dog to jump up and lie down; he held her hand as she changed places from chair to couch, and when she sat back his arm was there to support her. With the familiarity with which one talks to an old acquaintance he began:

"You are a little young for me. I love chicken done to a turn. I love veal when it is white and roast beef when it is red. As for women, I have never been able to excite myself over girls

of seventeen. I think women are at their best at the age of
thirty to thirty-five. After that there is a brusque descent. You,
alors, for an American girl, are remarkable, you are like a
gazelle when you move, you dress with extraordinary taste,
and you have—walk across the room, darling, and come back
to me—you have everything from the toes to the nose; a little
too much hair on one side." He kissed her hands. "But Monsieur
Chevalier at Elizabeth Arden's to whom I shall send you will
fix that. Have you an agent?"

"No—"

"But what is the matter with them?"

She laughed. "Why don't you write a story for me to act in?"

"Ah, alors," he said, "you must let me do something about
that immediately." Then he said quickly, "Are you fond of
sea food—what is your name again?"

"Belinda. Yes, very."

"Is anyone taking you home?"

"No."

"And you are free for the evening?"

"Yes."

"Ah, alors!" said Maurice, and leaned back with a deep
sigh of relief.

The host brought the drinks. Maurice sipped his, and said,
"You do not mind, amigo, if I make a phone call?" Ignoring
the phone on the table beside the couch, he sagged toward a
small washroom off the foyer, dialed the number. While he
waited he fished for his muffler and raincoat on the chair
outside the door, and when the phone was answered he
dragged them both into the closet after him, closed the door
with his foot, turned to the wall, and said: "Hilda? Ah, my
sweet, I am desolate. I called you to see whether we could
make it another night. What is so bad is, I forgot to look in
my little book when I made this date with you. Now of course
it's too late to do anything about it. I see here in my book that
I have accepted an invitation to dine tonight, and I can't say
no because that would make thirteen at table, and it's Friday.
Besides, I hate doing that. What did you say? Ah, thirteen,
mon beau, may be your lucky number, but that woman is

extremely abergläubig." He held part of his conversation beneath, part through his muffler, and the last words, "Je vous adore, mon beau—à demain," he said with the bib in place and his left arm in the sleeve of his raincoat.

He staggered out of the washroom, dragging the coat after him.

The girl came out of another room, her hair changed.

"Ahhh," he said, and put his arm around her. To the producer he said: "Vanya, amigo, you do not mind if I escort this ravishing creature home?"

"No, no, no," said the producer, "go ahead."

Maurice opened the door of the house, ran out, opened the door of the car, and slipped his other arm into the sleeve of his raincoat. Belinda sat down on the green leather of the deep lavender convertible Cadillac.

"You are sure this will not be too cold for you, riding with the top down?" he asked.

"No, I like it," said Belinda.

He stuck the keys into the lock and started the motor, but got up again and staggered back into the house, leaving the motor running.

The producer sat in a chair, staring at the hopeless script in his hand.

"Ah, Vanya—amigo—you are sure it is all right?"

"What is all right?"

"That I drive her home. I mean, I am not disturbing anything. I mean, it is nothing serious with you?"

"Naah."

"Elle est ravissante!"

"She's all right," said the producer. "She's a wonderful girl. Be nice to her."

"Alors," said Maurice, "we're off."

As they drove along the boulevard toward the Beverly Wilshire Hotel, he thought to himself: I can't take her to my hideaway because my agent is using it. I can't take her to dinner at Romanoff's because Hilda goes there a lot. I'll take her down to the Beach, to Roland's. No, I can't take her to Roland's because I had a fight over the bill there last time.

I'll take her to that little place on the pier off Santa Monica, and after that, we'll see.

To the right of them were the soft hills that look like the humps of sleeping camels. In the small rear-view mirror, the two rows of pale yellow mimosa trees that lined the road ran back into the chrome green of oleander, the dark green of the pine trees, the leather-colored skirts that hang from the tops of the high palm trees; and beyond that and ahead was the dark ultramarine sky set between the hills and edged with vapor clouds. The air at that hour in California carries the fragrance of flowers.

"You are a Californian?"

"No, New York."

"Ah, I adore New York. You are here a long time?"

"No, not very long. That is, time passes faster here than anywhere else."

"Alors, I wanted to ask you a personal question. You do not mind if I ask you a very personal question?"

"No, go ahead."

"I would like to know, my dear—ah—is there anything serious between you and Vashvily?"

"I like Vanya," she said simply.

He turned the radio on and the car surged upward, over a hill, and then in a wide curve came down to a red light at the crossing of Sunset and Sepulveda.

"I meant," he said, looking at her and going through the red light and miraculously missing a furniture truck, "whether there was anything serious beyond just liking."

"Oh," she said, "I go to his house whenever I am lonesome, or sometimes he calls me when he is lonesome. And I sit there on the couch with him and he tells me his troubles, and sometimes we have dinner together. And after that he puts on the 'Serenade in C Major' and we sit and listen, and all at once he lies with his mouth open, asleep. Sometimes he falls asleep during dinner. He's got some kind of a heart condition," she said.

"And a very kind heart," said Maurice.

"He's been very nice to me."

"I am glad of that."

"You know a lot about women, don't you?" said Belinda.

"About women, yes, my dear. Most of my affairs—I might say ninety per cent—have been with European women. I adore, of course, the Americans. They are the most soignée women in the world. Of course, the English are nice too, but they are not soignée, not even as soignée as the Europeans."

"What does soignée mean?"

"Ah, you know, the hair in order, the little gloves buttoned, the little black velvet suit brushed, clever fingers, and the nails so they don't look smeared with shoe polish. And above all, the intimate things—the English, for example, they take a bath twice a day and still they're not soignée. They suffer from an atavistic culture."

"And that's the news up to the minute as presented by the Affiliated Bankrupt Stock Liquidators of Downtown Los Angeles," announced the radio.

He said, "Come closer, darling."

"Gee, mister," said Belinda. "You sure learn a lot when you go out with a writer."

"Please call me Maurice, Belinda."

"Mind if I call you Joe?"

"No, but why?"

"Oh, I'm married to a guy named Joe and it makes it easier when I talk in my sleep."

He looked at her with alarm.

"I was only kidding, Joe," she said.

"Oh, don't do that to me," he said.

The road came to a traffic circle and passed a grove of eucalyptus trees and the Spanish entrance to a Tudor villa. It ran along the adobe wall of a luxurious Mexican ranch house, and passed a rock garden that was planted with hedgehog, organ, and cinnabar cactus. It sank again down toward a sign on which an articulate California real estate corporation announced the name of its development as "Botanical Garden Park."

Opposite the sign are the polo field, the pastures, and the riding fields of the Riviera Country Club. A group of young girls were taking their mounts over a series of brush jumps in the dusk.

"Look, Joe, horses."

"You ride, darling?"

"I'd fall off if I ever got on a horse."

"Good."

"Why do you say that, Joe?"

"Oh, I would be constantly worried that you might fall off and hurt yourself."

He took one hand from the wheel and placed it in her lap. "My darling, with me it's largely a matter of skin. I must have my cheeks against that smooth, soft, velvet skin, or else the whole thing doesn't mean a thing to me. I am so glad you do not ride."

"Are you married, Joe?"

"Ah, yes," he said; and then louder, as if affirming his status, "Yes. The only luxury people have here is a home. I have a wife and two children. Alors, my children, they speak French with an English accent, and English with a French accent. That, among other things, is the price of exile. And as for me, Belinda, the music must play at least six bars before I can tell whether it's the 'Marseillaise' or the 'Star-Spangled Banner.' But that, my sweet, is the only thing about which confusion exists in my mind."

"You're lucky," said Belinda.

Soon the whole of the sea and the sky was open before them. He turned to the left on Malibu Road.

Where is this jerk taking me? Belinda asked herself. She knew the location of every good restaurant by now. The only decent restaurant out this way was Roland's up to the right toward Malibu.

Maurice pointed to a row of oil derricks along the horizon. "Except for that," he said, "it's like Cannes."

Belinda thought that he might have a house along the beach, but after they had passed all the good real estate she decided to ask him. Belinda was hungry.

"Look," she said, pointing at some pelicans that were laboring through the air and going in the same direction as they.

It was twilight and the heavy birds' bellies were almost touching the water. "Look, Joe, see how big a bill he's got. That's so he can put food in it when he gets hungry, and he don't have to go around looking for a restaurant for hours."

"Ah," said Maurice, "I know of a little restaurant at the end of the pier in Santa Monica. I dislike ostentation. I am fed up with places like Romanoff's and Larue's. Always the same menu, always the same faces—horrible people—the same awful faces. I am very fond of this little place. The spécialité de la maison is abalone steak."

"What's abalone steak?"

"That is a species of seagoing Wiener Schnitzel."

"What's a Wiener Schnitzel?"

"A veal cutlet."

"You know," she said, "I'm crazy about men who can talk languages. Now Vanya, he speaks French, and German, and Italian, and Russian."

It got cold and she moved close to him. "What's that picture about you're going to put me in?"

"I cannot talk pictures when I drive. I must be able to walk and explain as I tell the story," he said. "We shall have a few drinks and a quiet dinner, and then we will drive away to a place, and then I shall tell you."

The moon was up—a large irregular disk, almost full, and orange-colored. They drove on the pile-supported roadway of the pier, along a row of amusement concessions, past a blue-and-gray edifice that housed a merry-go-round and a marine museum which was dominated by the picture of an octopus. In the light of an electric sign that said "See the Octopus" he parked the car, led her past a fish market to the end of the pier, and opened the door of a small restaurant.

They entered a low room that smelled of the grease in which fish, French fried potatoes, and shrimp are fried. Anchors, ships' models, puffed fish, and nets with green glass floaters decorated the room. The grease-spattered menu announced today's special as abalone steak and French fries at a dollar twenty-five. The place was crowded, and they had to sit down at the bar, on stools which by California ordinance are chained to the bar so they cannot topple. Maurice ordered two double Martinis.

They turned up after a while, the color of the moon outside and smelling like cheap perfume. Maurice took a drink, and lit a cigarette. Later the solitary waitress showed them to a table which was lit up by red paper lamps.

The middle-aged waitress wiped the sticky table with a moist rag, placed the glasses before them, and said, "Now, what'll you have?"

"Two abalone steaks with French fried potatoes," said Maurice.

He lifted his glass and clinked it on Belinda's. He took a small sip and said, "Excuse me, I must wash my hands." He was gone for a short time, and when he came back he said, "So," sat down, and grinned.

"Aren't you going to take those off?" she said, pointing to the raincoat and muffler.

"Ah," he said, "yes." He hung up the coat and bib and, with his hair disarranged, came back to the table. He sat down and said, "Ah," but jumped up again. "Cigarettes," he said, on his way to the dispensing machine. He came back after he was halfway there. "You smoke what?"

"Anything," said Belinda.

"Ah, have you—" He began going through his pockets, but he found a quarter and sagged to the bar for change, and from there to the machine. He brought back a pack of Chesterfields. He ripped the pack open with impatience; the cellophane screamed.

"Alors," he said. "You know, Hollywood is fantastic, Belinda. Here you are, under their noses, and they don't even know that you are here. Two years—and they haven't seen you! It's like the colors of the flowers in their gardens; they are blind. You must leave, you must go to a place like Salt Lake City, and be a waitress and stand behind a counter in a lunchroom—or worse, you must appear in summer stock in Pennsylvania—and there is a chance that you may be discovered. But here you would become a grandmother and die, unless you had met Maurice Cassard."

Belinda said to herself: I better make something clear to this character, and fast.

But he said, "Allow me to finish. Alors," he continued, and took both her hands in his, "I am very happy I have found you. We understand each other perfectly. We shall have a beautiful friendship. I want to know everything about you."

He emptied the remains of his Martini, and ordered two more. He had to let go of her hands as the woman arrived and placed before them two heavy, chipped oval platters on which were the abalone steaks. They looked like breaded veal cutlets and were surrounded by dark brown fried potatoes, a lettuce leaf on which was a slice of lemon, and a tiny paper cup containing tartare sauce.

The newly lit cigarette had already met its death, and lay crumpled in the ash tray. Maurice nervously disorganized the arrangement on the platter before him. He tore the abalone steak apart and attacked the dish like a starving man. He ate as if he were trying to amuse a small child—with wild grimaces, with food falling or hanging out of his mouth. He was completely unconscious of all this. The thinking-machine in Maurice took precedence over all functions.

They had coffee, and Maurice lit a cigarette again. He blew the smoke upward. "I am not flattering you when I say that you are the rarest kind of woman a man can hope for. Je vous adore. You are the jewel of all creation, a beautiful woman of high intelligence."

"Listen," she said, "I want to explain something—"

Now or never, said Belinda to herself. She had detected in back of his eyes a small dim light of sincerity. The pretty girl sat up straight, pressed her cigarette into the ash tray, and with both hands smoothed the silk of her dress. She reached into her arsenal and drew out of that large grab bag a combination of clever sayings, tough lingo, and gentle accents from the Olympia charm school which she had attended for nearly two years, to let the writer know what she really was.

After Belinda had talked for a while, a curious process took place in Maurice's face. It seemed to be replaced with a

mask, not too exactly made after the original. The nose was
suddenly uninteresting, the eyes dull and tired, the whole face,
which had been alert and eager, was now a study in careless-
ness. Occasionally he looked up at her, he drank, looked this
way and that while she was talking, and at times it seemed
as if he were going to start crying.

"What did you say, Joe?" she asked at the end.

"I said you were smart."

"I'm not smart," she said.

"I didn't mean smart," he said. "I spoke of intelligence."

"I'm not intelligent either."

"I mean, you have—without, if you like, intelligence or
smartness—a sympathy, a spirit . . . I mean there is about
you a mental symmetry which your mind shares with your
body, the balance that is found in great sculpture."

"I'm ignorant, really dumb," said Belinda. "I mean, all girls
are dumb."

She lit a new cigarette.

"Ah," said Maurice, "I agree, most girls are—but not you."

"All women are dumb," said Belinda, "but fortunately men
are even dumber."

Maurice looked at Belinda with different eyes. He said:
"Forgive my interruption, but I suffer occasionally from
terrible awakenings, and I have just had one of them. Sometimes I think I am just a poor blind man groping through life,
tapping ahead of myself with a little stick."

"Yes," said Belinda, "and poking people in the eye with it."

"And you," he said, "who are you?"

"Oh, I'm just a thin little gray kitten." She emptied half
of her glass. Her eyes shone and her cheeks glowed. "Feel
my face, blind man," she said, in the accents of the charm
school. "Am I still beautiful?"

"I still insist," he said—and there was again, deep in back
of his eyes, the flicker of sincerity—"that you are the most
extraordinary creature I have ever met." He lifted his glass
with the awful Martini. "Allow me," he said. "A toast to our
meeting."

She sat back, wary of him now—but Cassard went to work. During six brandy-and-sodas, while she looked at the table and arranged his broken matches in various patterns, he unrolled the story of his life in France and in Hollywood. He spoke of the hopes he had for her, and outlined the scenario he would write. He recited poetry and anecdote, told jokes, none of them off color, and was never dull for a moment. She left the matches alone and let him hold her hand. She looked into his eyes and laughed.

The waitress put the bill on the table. Belinda looked at her watch. "You know what?" she said. "We've been here for five hours. . . ."

It was foggy outside; the water stood around the pier like a solid. The scene was lit up by the milky disks of a row of street lamps, and when Maurice and Belinda went out, vapor blanketed them. As they walked to the parking space in back of the restaurant, it was as if their faces were sprayed with a small-nozzled vaporizer. Maurice, who from the beginning had been the perfect material for a California patriot, began to explain the transiency of the weather. The collar of his coat was up. He walked ahead of her with both his hands in his pockets.

"Joe, you look exactly like Jean Gabin," she said.

"I feel like it too."

They started toward Santa Monica. "Where are we going now, Joe?" she asked.

"I have a friend," he said, "who has gone to New York and—"

"I know," she said, "'and left me the key to his apartment.'"

"Very good," said Maurice, "but stop fooling. Now let's be serious."

"No thanks, Joe," she said. "Tonight I sleep alone."

Cassard shrugged his shoulders and turned to his car. He found the key and started the motor. He found the right button that raised the top, but starting up he almost drove off the pier into the Pacific. He stopped the car at the edge, the fenders up against the ramp, and shifted.

"I'm not going to drive with you," said Belinda.

"I don't even want to drive myself. Leave the car here. You come with me, I'll call for a cab."

They went back into the restaurant. A second lieutenant of the Air Forces was in the telephone booth. "I'm trying to get a cab," he said, turning around. "I'm going to Beverly Hills. Want to share the cab?"

"Why don't you hang up, General," asked the practical Belinda, "and drive us home?"

He hesitated. "I've got to get back and pack," he said. "Where do you live?"

"Beverly Hills. We've got a car outside," said Belinda.

Cassard sat in the back seat, and as they stopped for traffic under the brilliant glass snakes of the neon sign that decorates the arch at the entrance of the pier, Belinda looked into the mirror of the car.

"Gee, I look like I looked this morning. The dame with the eyes just opened. It's like dust at the bottom of a glass. . . . What are you thinking about, General?" she asked as they drove along San Vicente Boulevard.

"Oh, I'm curious," he said. "Just terribly curious."

"You're not born on the twenty-fifth of March, are you, General? You're not an Aries, I hope?"

"How did you guess that's the day I was born?"

"Oh, just guessed."

"Well, we'll never get anywhere finding out things like that about each other all night."

"You Aries people stay away from me—you're trouble. I'm going to turn you over to my kid sister. She has my old Ford, she wears my old clothes, she puts ice in the hot chocolate, and she can have you too. Oh, God, that other guy—the one in the tank—he was an Aries too. I've been trying to fence guys like you for years. How is it that I don't get wise to myself?"

"I didn't want to come in the first place. I'm leaving for overseas tomorrow. I have a lot of things to attend to."

"Ya, ya, ya, I know, you've been leaving ever since you put that suit on. I'll bet I'll see you here for the next six years.

That other guy, the one I was engaged to, he was leaving too, but I decided to call it off. He wanted me to come over after he had freed Holland, but I didn't want to be a thing in wooden shoes. I told him to climb back in his little tank and shut the lid after him and proceed at his own risk—and I'd proceed at mine."

"Do you think that's patriotic?"

"Listen, Joe, don't make with that G.I. stuff. I don't take to that feminine psychology you guys have written down for us: 'All right, you stood by me and I'll stand by you.' That's the psychology—right? Okay, he comes back, and I bet you anything you want, after the first hello is over sooner or later he'll say to me, 'You're not as young as you used to be.' And after I get up to make a telephone call and come back to the table he says, 'And you're getting fat, too.'"

"I'd never say that." They drove for a while in silence. The lieutenant said, "Well, tomorrow I'll be up there in the blue—"

"Cut it out, will you, Joe?

"He loved chartreuse gloves." With the benefit of the charm school, Belinda pronounced chartreuse correctly. " 'I love chartreuse gloves,' he said—and he walks off with my chartreuse gloves and slips me a triple Scotch. And then he sent me a rabbit. He took the gloves with him overseas. Not only did he ruin my Thanksgiving, my Christmas, and my Easter, but a lot of other things besides. I never saw the chartreuse gloves again. He says he uses them for lining his tank helmet. Well, he's welcome. Once in a while when I think of that so-and-so, I take the rabbit and throw him on the floor and step on him."

The lieutenant stopped at the Mocambo.

"I thought you had to pack," said Belinda.

"There's somebody asleep in the back of the car," he said to the doorman of the night club. "Park it in a quiet spot, Ernie. Come on, Belinda," he said, and pulled her out of the car.

Cassard awoke later, alone in the cold, wet car. He oriented himself with some difficulty, wound the muffler tightly around his neck, and then he slouched up through the parking lot

to the Strip, as the part of Sunset Boulevard on which Mocambo
fronts is called. He entered the flamingo-colored lobby and
watched the crowd. He saw Belinda dancing and smiled at
her. Then he went to get some change from the cigarette girl
and got into the telephone booth. It was late, but he rang
up Vanya Vashvily.

.Walter, Vashvily's Negro butler, answered, and Cassard
said that it was most important.

"Amigo," he said, "I have thought about what you said this
afternoon—about the story. Until I saw that ravishing creature
—I confess—I was not interested; but now I know—"

"It's a great story and she'll be great for the part," said
Vashvily.

"Something must be done about it," said Cassard. "I will
pass your house, amigo, and pick up that script again and look
at it once more."

"That's great," said Vashvily.

3. *Belinda's Wedding*

Against the laurel-covered, softly rolling hills that divide
Beverly Hills from the San Fernando Valley, halfway between
Coldwater Canyon and San Ysidro Drive stand half a dozen
asbestos-shingled Châteaux de Normandie. Each one is different from the others, yet part of an over-all plan, and together
they frame, with their bastions and turrets, that delightful
panorama which is known as the "Budapest View of Hollywood."

In the third of these châteaux, the best situated, Number
Ten Avenue François Villon, lived Vanya Vashvily, the kind
producer, with his servant, a Negro named Walter.

The benevolent arrangement peculiar to these communities, a hotel-like service, relieves the master as well as the servant of the drudgery that goes with owning a house. It usually makes for contented, long-staying servants. Vashvily's Walter was the exception.

He barely returned the "Good morning" of the uniformed attendants who came to wash the windows. He completely ignored the man who took care of garbage disposal, a major irritant in the life of the Beverly Hills property owner, a matter covered by some dozen city ordinances and Department of Health directives which demand that wet garbage be separated from dry and wrapped with the care given to Christmas packages. Walter was suspicious of the man who vacuumed the swimming pool, trimmed the hedges, and removed dead foliage from the eucalyptus trees. The workman who leaned his ladder against the château to paint a rusted gargoyle was never let out of his sight, and no Doberman's ears were sharper and more alert to the movement of plumbers or delivery boys once they had gained entrance to the house.

As an added protection, Walter had special and intricate locks put on all the doors, each differing from the others, so that no one in possession of a passkey could enter or open any of the doors in the building or that of his master's wardrobe, or reach into a liquor closet, or into any of the many other caches in which vintage sardines, rare cigars, nylons, record albums, and spare whitewall tires were kept.

In spite of these extraordinary precautions, Vanya Vashvily thought that his liquor bill was high, that the grocer overcharged him, and when looking into his clothes closet he pushed the hangers aside and wondered when his suits would come back from the tailor. He worried most of all about a blue cashmere double-breasted suit made by Domenick Punaro, a garment cool in summer, warm in winter, and very comfortable, a suit he had had made a year before and had grown fond of.

Vanya Vashvily lay soaking in his tub when the telephone rang. The Beverly Hills phone is at the end of a cord some thirty-five feet in length and usually in another room.

The butler, with experienced hand, walking backward with the motions of fishermen and of cowboys, played out the cord, looped it around an easy chair, trolled it through the living room and, after expert casting over the Capehart, entered the bathroom and handed the instrument to his employer.

"Darling," said Belinda, "I wanted you to know before you read it in the papers that I'm getting married. Now—in an hour—and I'll never forgive you if you don't come over. You're the only one I asked outside of a pal of Joe's."

"I thought we were having dinner," said Vashvily with some disappointment.

"Well, we are, darling," said Belinda, "right after."

"Who is it? Not Cassard, I hope."

"No, it's a beautiful thing with wings I met last night at the beach."

"Make that a table for five," said Vashvily to Walter, who took the phone and roped his way back into the pantry.

Through the pantry's clerestory window the last rays of the sun shone on Walter's yellow back. He wore a canary sports jacket, discarded by his boss. He relit the cigar he had left behind and dialed Romanoff's to change the reservation.

In his bath, the producer pondered what he should wear to Belinda's wedding. He climbed out of the warm water and staggered to the marble shower stall. After refreshing himself under the brusque high pressure of the spray, he reached for a towel, dried his two discolored and sagging buttocks and his belly, and then, sitting on a tufted hassock, he reached for his thin toes. After he dried them, he took a new towel and went over his face.

He put on his glasses and walked on his heels over the cool marble. He pushed back the sliding door of his clothes closet and shoved back the three suits he found hanging there. As was his old habit, he looked for the soft dark-blue double-breasted cashmere, but again it wasn't there.

He decided eventually on the next best, a gray serge suit. He carefully took the gray trousers off the hanger and lowered them. He was about to step into the garment when a large bunch of keys fell out of the back pocket. Vashvily bent down and picked them up. He examined them. They were not his. He faced in the direction of the pantry and after a while, he said to himself:

"This is the absolute limit!"

He put the trousers down and rang the bell.

Out in the pantry, Walter shouted:

"Yes, sir. Right away, sir."

He put the half-smoked cigar away carefully.

"How do these keys get into my pocket?" asked Vanya Vashvily as the servant entered the dressing room.

Walter took the keys and looked at them, fingering them individually, and then he said:

"I don't know."

"Are they yours?" said Vashvily.

Walter was carefully folding the gray trousers. He placed them on a hanger and put them back in the closet.

"No, sir!" said Walter in loud protest, adding, "What would my keys be doing in your pocket?"

"I don't know," said Vashvily, "but if they're not your keys I'll take them and I'll just throw them out of the car on my way to Romanoff's."

"Oh, no, don't do that, boss. Let me look at them keys."

Walter studied the keys carefully.

"Let me see," he said, and picking out one key he tried it on the clothes closet, locking it.

"I'll be damned," he said with surprise. "If they're not my keys! Now how would they get into that suit of yours?"

"You explain that to me," said Vashvily.

To dispose of the evidence, Walter put the keys into his pocket. He was about to go and was half out of the door when Vashvily, amplifying his hearing aid, shouted:

"Where's my blue suit?"

Walter came back.

"That old blue serge you gave me?" he asked.

"No," said Vashvily. "You know the one I mean—the dark blue cashmere."

"Oh," said Walter, relieved. "That's the one that's getting a new lining."

"Seems to me you took it a year ago," said the producer.

"Well, the tailor said it would be ready in two weeks. You know how it is. Everything's slow now. I'll go and see him again."

"What tailor did you take it to?" asked Vashvily.

"Over in Westwood."

"What's his name?"

"I don't know. I forget."

"Haven't you a slip, a record, or something?"

"No."

"Why not?"

"Oh, because I take all the suits there."

"And you don't know the name?"

"No, sir."

"All right," screamed Vashvily, "We'll get to the bottom of this. Bring me the phone and the book. There can't be more than one tailor in Westwood—two at the most."

With the book under his arm and looping the phone cord over the Capehart, Walter backed into the dressing room.

"Seems to me his name is Katz," he offered. "I'm pretty sure it's Katz," he repeated, as Vashvily thumbed through the book.

Vashvily got the number. Mr. Katz said he never got the suit to reline.

"You take the receiver and talk to him," said Vashvily, handing the instrument to Walter.

"Why, God damn your soul," Walter began, "you remember that dark blue suit. I said to you, 'Take this suit and put—' "

"Never mind," said the producer, and took the phone out of Walter's hands.

"So you never got the suit, Mr. Katz?"

"No, sir," screamed the tailor, who had an honest voice. "I clean a suit for you, last month. I take out the spots. Once I fixed a cuff. Another time a button is missing on the gray pants. Everything goes in a little book. I have a record of everything I ever did for you. The blue worsted, I never got it to reline. I would know the day it came in and when it goes out. I do all the work myself. The gray was here several times, but the blue—never."

Walter stood by the phone, which was a specially loud instrument for the hard of hearing. He listened, shaking his head and scratching it. As the producer put down the instrument, Walter shouted with sudden inspiration:

"I know where it is. I gave it to the other tailor."

"What other tailor?"

"I don't know his name, but I know where he is."

"Well, get him on the phone."

"He hasn't got a phone."

"Why did you go to that other tailor? What's wrong with Katz?"

"I wanted to try that other tailor on account of Katz takes so long."

"We might as well clear this up once and for all," said Vashvily. "Where's my brown suit—the one with the white stripes—and my new sport coat, and my green topcoat? I haven't seen them for months."

"They're all at that same tailor's."

"The one that's got no phone?"

"Yes, sir."

"But you know where he lives?"

"Yes, sir."

"All right, then, we'll get the car and go there."

"No, you can't do that," said Walter.

"Why not?"

"He's too far away."

"Well, I'm sick and tired of running around trying to get back my clothes," said Vashvily. "Give me the phone. I'll just call the police and let them worry about it."

"Oh, no, boss," said Walter, with sweat breaking out all over him. "Don't do that. I'll have them all here tomorrow."

Vashvily took the towel with which he had covered his nakedness and, waving it at the servant, he said:

"What did you do with my clothes?"

"I didn't want to tell you, boss. I gave the work to a colored tailor in my neighborhood, sir."

"Why didn't you tell me?"

Looking straight at Vashvily, Walter mumbled:

"I didn't think you'd like the idea of a colored tailor doing your work. I thought maybe you'd be prejudiced."

"Whoever told you I'd be prejudiced against anybody?" cried Vashvily. "Haven't I got you working for me, you black son-of-a-bitch?"

Walter just stood there and looked at Vashvily, who had again covered himself up and held the battery of his hearing aid toward the servant.

Barely audible, Walter said:

"You don't have to be black to be a nigger!" He went out, slamming the door.

Vashvily sat down on his tufted hassock, and after a while a slip of paper appeared under the door.

"What's due me you can send to this address," it said. "And mail also."

Vashvily crumpled the note in his hand and went to the closet to get his gray serge. The closet door was locked. At that moment the château rocked as the front door was slammed by the departing Walter. His footsteps echoed on the walk. He carried a hurriedly packed bag, and in the back pocket of a pair of the producer's trousers that he was wearing were the special keys.

Vashvily was on the phone.

"I am sorry," said the superintendent of the Châteaux de Normandie, Inc. "We have a passkey to every door in this place except to yours, Mr. Vashvily. You had all special locks put in."

Nobody answered at the Alert Key Service.

"You don't have to invent a story about having nothing to wear," said Belinda. "If you don't want to come to my wedding, say so. I understand."

SECOND PART

Lust for Gold

In which the scribe Ludlow Mumm delivers himself to Olympia and learns to walk slowly and breathe in warm air.

4. *Fat Canary*

The right hand of Ludlow Mumm, the one he wrote with, was in bandages as the result of a railroad accident some fifty miles out of Los Angeles. The writer leaned forward with a painful move and picked up the phone with his left hand.

"Good morning," said a cheery voice. "This is the Wildgans Chase Agency. You're having lunch with Mr. Wildgans at Romanoff's. Mr. Wildgans wants to discuss the contract with you. We're sending a car for you. It will be there in fifteen minutes. You will find it under the porte-cochere of your hotel."

Ludlow Mumm stepped out on the balcony of his suite and looked down the front of the Beverly Hills Hotel.

"I would have called it a marquee," he said, and went back into the room.

He took a dictionary out of his bag, and, holding it between his legs and opening it with his good hand, he searched under the letter P.

" 'Porte-cochere,' " he read, " 'a large gateway through which a carriage may drive into a court; an extension of a porch; a roof over a driveway.' "

He turned the pages and looked under M.

" 'Marquee,' " he read, " 'a tent; a window awning; an awning raised as a temporary shelter from the curb to the door of a dwelling or a public building.'

"She's absolutely right," said the writer, and put the book away.

He walked back out on the balcony, lifted himself on the toes of his small feet, leaned over the banister enjoying the

35

scene, and scratched his soft brown beard. He had grown it to cover up at least part of a round face that was kind to the point of idiocy.

Ludlow Mumm would have been happiest as a lay brother of a religious order, one not too penitent. He would have fitted ideally into the cloth of that happy group of monks who brew sweet liqueurs to the glory of God in France.

He looked down again, smiling. On a balcony beneath him, stretched on a chaise longue which was covered with an immense bath towel, was all that is real and good in a some-times lazily shifting female form, unclothed, inhaling and exhaling deeply, and occasionally running her fingers through her platinum-blond hair.

Women, in the life of Ludlow Mumm, took the roles of mothers, sweethearts, good wives, sisters, and little girls. Those that disturbed other men were regarded by him as remarkable adornments in that ever-beautiful green valley through whose dewy grass the padre in his sandals wandered with uplifted heart.

"Porte-cochere," repeated the conscientious scribe, looking once more down at the front of the hotel.

Then he went back into his suite again, picked up his hat with the unbandaged left hand, and walked to the elevator.

The happy first impression of the correctness and efficiency of the Wildgans Chase Agency was underlined when, exactly fifteen minutes after the telephone call, a black, polished Buick limousine purred up along the avenue of palm trees and stopped smoothly under the porte-cochere.

The alert, uniformed driver, who had never seen Mumm before this moment, touched his cap and smiled. The doorman opened the door and as Ludlow sat down, the driver said:

"Good morning, Mr. Mumm. Welcome to California."

As the car swung down and halted for the stop sign at the crossing of Sunset and Rodeo, the driver jumped from his seat and made Ludlow Mumm comfortable, suggesting that he move into the left corner of the car. He pulled down the arm rest for the injured member.

"Toni is my name," he said, and was back up front.

"You're in good hands, sir," he said, "when you're with Wildgans Chase. You'll get plenty for that accident. We had you insured from the moment you left New York."

The writer leaned back and smiled. The palm trees swam by and Toni identified the lovely homes of the stars along the route.

"I can get you anything you want in this town," said Toni.

By the time they arrived at Romanoff's, he had arranged for a car and chauffeur; for some color film for the writer's magazine Kodak; and he had promised to smooth out any difficulties and overcome all shortages and needs that would arise during the writer's stay.

Toni stopped the car and ran into the restaurant, announcing Ludlow Mumm to the head waiter, who at once took him to one of the good tables.

"Mr. Wildgans," said Joe, the maître d'hôtel, "is up there now at the first table. He's expecting you. He'll be here in a little while."

Arty Wildgans, a portly, ruddy man, slowly came down the line: like a bucket in the hands of a fire brigade, he was handed on from one person to the next.

"The first thing I always say is 'Hello,'" he said cheerily as he finally arrived and sat down.

Looking over Mumm's head, he waved and smiled at several people in the rear of the room.

"And how are the folks back East?" he asked, picking up the menu.

Without waiting for the answer, he looked up at the waiter and said:

"How's the Vichyssoise today?"

"Well," said the waiter with indignation in his voice, "Joe Schenck just had some!"

"All right, all right," countered Wildgans, equally agitated, "Let's have that to start with—and what else did Joe Schenck have?"

"The bœuf à la mode with gnocchi," said the waiter bitterly.

"All right, we'll take the beef à la mode with the genukki, too," said Wildgans. "Or do you want something different? . . .

Hello, Al," he said, with a wave of the hand to a man who approached the table. He made the introductions: "Al Lein- wand—Ludlow Mumm, the great writer. You heard of him."

"Sure," said Al Leinwand.

Al Leinwand, a fierce man and rival agent, a birdlike creature with the head of a hawk on a sparrow's body, glared into the room over Ludlow Mumm's head, in that peculiar Hollywood restaurant manner in which one is never with the eyes where the ears are.

"Go on," said Wildgans, "about the accident."

Mumm recited the story of the derailment in which he had injured his hand, and Leinwand, who, like everyone here, was able to top any story, listened with an unhappy expression of impatience. Suddenly he cut the report short. Following the swaying rump of a girl in a Vertés print with his eyes, the small man said:

"I read all about your accident, Mumm. I could have been in that wreck too." He looked briefly at Wildgans as if excusing himself for an omission, and added: "In fact, I almost was."

He nodded at a producer three tables away. "I had reserva- tions on that same train. Only, at the last minute, I was held over in New York. Well, so long."

Wildgans salted his Vichyssoise.

"You made him very unhappy," he said to Mumm. "He's heartbroken he wasn't in that wreck. He's got to be in every- thing. Well," he said, stirring the cold soup, "how do you like it out here?"

The writer smiled and was about to say something when Arty Wildgans turned from his plate, looked up and said an indifferent "Hello" to a beautiful and exotic creature, a woman in her best years, who stretched out to him her carmine-gloved arms, pointed her lips, and made the sound of kissing several times as she sat down.

"Arty, mind if I sit down here for a minute?" she asked reproachfully, with a heavy foreign accent.

"Ludlow Mumm, the writer," said Wildgans and introduced the actress.

She talked into the small mirror of her compact, saying "Hello" with a quick glance at Mumm.

"Darling," she said, still reproachfully, "you promised as a favor to get me a test with Vashvily."

"I will," said Wildgans. "I'm crazy about that bit you did in *Jetsam*. I saw it yesterday. It was marvelous. Just a little more of that the next time and then Vanya Vashvily can't throw it in my face that you are nothing but a character woman and I can defeat him."

She purred and put her arm through his. A fourth person joined the group, a sagging individual in a pale blue sports coat, a musician, also with a heavy accent, who took a match from the table and relit his soggy cigar.

"You know Vogelsang," said Wildgans, and explained that the man was a famous composer of background music.

"You are Austrian?" asked the character woman, while Wildgans, whose client Vogelsang was, said to Mumm:

"Great talent. He did the score for *Magdalene*."

"Ja, Ja," said Vogelsang, or rather, "Yoh, Yoh."

"Ah, Austrians," she said with throaty laughter, "such gemütliche people, Austrians. Well, maybe not—nobody is gemütlich any more, except Arty here.

"You know Russians, kind, sing, dance, help everybody, suddenly turn into wild animals, beat innocents. Ach, prrrppzzt —man is terrible. Well, nice to have seen you."

Mr. Vogelsang, with the back of his trousers hanging sadly, stuck his wet cigar deep into his mouth, made a continental bow to the character woman, and left.

"I don't agree with what you said about the Russians at all," said Ludlow Mumm to the character woman. "I can't agree with you at all on that. I think they're a great people."

"I hope you are right," said the actress. "I am one of them." She turned to Wildgans.

"Would you like to have a cheap thrill, Arty? I am going to have a massage and you can come and talk to me."

She was up and without waiting for the answer she sailed off, throwing kisses.

"I always inherit these dogs," said Wildgans, starting to cut the bœuf à la mode.

"Nobody else wants to have anything to do with them . . . just because I have a soft heart and can't say no. Of course, that dame will never be anything but a character woman, but I haven't the heart to tell her that. I could have told her five years ago when she came out here."

They both ate; Wildgans in haste, and Mumm with enjoyment of the sauce, which he mopped up with pieces of bread after he had eaten all the gnocchi.

"We have to get something blight-resisting for this table," remarked Wildgans as a tall, ascetic-looking man came up to the table with his hands in his coat pockets.

The unhappy-looking, pale individual stared at Wildgans, and without any change of expression in his face and tired voice he said:

"I'm still dazed. I fell off my filing cabinet last night when I got your note."

"What did you expect?" said Wildgans.

"I expected a check—money—for the difference between what they said they'd agree to and what I'm getting."

He stared at Wildgans and Wildgans said:

"You know Ludlow Mumm, the writer."

Without taking his eyes off Wildgans, the tall, thin man said, "Hello, Mumm," and continued:

"Listen, Wildgans, I'm just a thin, tired Jew. I don't want anything for nothing. I only ask to be paid for my work, and when I'm not, I get unhappy and the fountain doesn't spurt."

"I'll see Moses Fable tomorrow," said Wildgans.

"Why not today?" said the man.

"Tomorrow is a better day. I'm a little dull today," said Wildgans.

"Did you hear that, Mumm?" asked the thin man. "He said, 'I'm a little dull today!' Why make an exception? Why not just say, 'I'm Arty'?"

Wildgans laughed and handed him a cigar. Jerome Hack rolled it in his long fingers, smelled it, and examined it with his unhappy black eyes.

"What are you staring at the cigar for? It's good. I gave it to you."

"Get busy, Wildgans, and do something," Jerome Hack said as he left.

"Great talent," said Wildgans after the departing writer. "On the same lot as you are—a mechanic, great on construction —turns out rough-and-tumble musicals—cops-and-robbers— anything you want. Very dependable—great sense of humor —a very legitimate guy."

The waiter put the check down and Wildgans signed it. He drove back to the hotel with Mumm.

"Well," he said, "I think we had a very fruitful talk. Good-by, Lud. I'll call you."

"How about the story? When do I start to work?" asked Mumm, leaning forward, ready to get out of the car.

"Oh, about the picture," said Wildgans. "Listen, Mumm, take it easy. Get settled first and don't worry about the picture. These days you can hang a sign outside a theater saying 'No Picture Today' and close up and they'll break down the doors. You don't have to show no picture—just turn out the lights and get a couple of guys to drag wet overcoats through the aisles and step on the feet of the audience.

"You need a rest, Mumm, after that shaking up you got," said Wildgans, and waved to him as he drove off, leaving the conscientious writer standing under the porte-cochere of his hotel.

Mumm scratched his soft beard for a while and looked after the car. He walked to the elevator, past the greetings of the assistant manager, the room clerk, several bellhops, and the elevator operator, who all knew his name and pronounced it correctly. He came to his suite and opened the door.

An immaculately groomed young woman was in his living room. She smiled and went to the telephone.

"Operator," she said with gay inflection and smiling, "Mr. Mumm is back—just stepped in—but please announce everybody before you put them on.

"That will give you some protection," she said, and introduced herself as Miss Princip of the Wildgans Chase Agency.

"You're very popular, Mr. Mumm. You have three invitations for dinner tonight," she said.

"But I don't know anybody here," said Mumm.

"Miss Allbright's secretary was on the phone just now to ask you for dinner tonight. Betsy Allbright, you know, is a famous silent picture star. She's very nice. She has a magnificent home in Malibu and the food is excellent. I think it would make a lovely evening for you."

"Do you think I should go?" said Mumm.

"Well," said Miss Princip, "Miss Allbright is one of the uncrowned queens of Hollywood. It's a kind of command and I think Mr. Wildgans would say emphatically yes.

"Now," she said, opening a brief case, "I'll explain to you about your salary check and how we handle that."

"Ah, yes," said Ludlow Mumm, whose funds were low, and moved toward her on the Modernage divan.

"We pick up your pay check at the studio and deduct our ten per cent commission and then we deposit the rest at the bank. We have opened an account at the bank for you and I brought a checkbook with me."

She pulled a large book from the brief case with six checks to a page and "Ludlow Mumm" printed on each check.

"I can come here and make out checks and keep order in your account, and put things down so that we won't run into a tax situation. Is that all right with you, Mr. Mumm?"

"Oh, yes, yes, yes," said Mumm.

"Well, that's that," she said, and placed the checkbook and some papers on a small bamboo-and-ebony desk.

She reached into the brief case again.

"I brought some cash," she said, "for current expenses. We thought you might find yourself short after the trip and the accident. Here is two thousand," she said and handed him the envelope, "and if you need more, just call me. Toni will bring it right over."

Mumm took the envelope and he said with elaborate, artificial calm:

"Thank you . . . and can you tell me about the studio—I mean, when do I start to work?"

"Your producer, Vanya Vashvily, is in the Cedars of Lebanon. He caught a cold and it turned into an infection of the middle ear—"

"I'm sorry to hear that," said Ludlow Mumm.

"Well, it's too bad," said the girl, "but it's all on Olympia time and he'll be back in the office again in a few weeks. You'll find that time passes very quickly out here, Mr. Mumm. Now, is there anything you want me to take care of? Any letters you want me to answer? Any bills you want me to pay?"

Ludlow Mumm went to his bags and dug up a pack of letters, all of them unopened, and handed them to Miss Princip.

He walked into his bedroom and carefully closed the door while the ambulatory secretary outside uncorked her fountain pen and began to settle his accounts.

Before he sat down on his bed, he made sure once more that the door was closed. Then he took the bills from the envelope and counted them, holding them like a deck of playing cards first and making a fan of them. Then, placing them neatly on the bed, side by side, the fifties, twenties, tens, and fives, he counted them that way again. He put them back into the envelope finally, and through the door that led directly from his bedroom to the corridor he went down to the lobby. He walked up and down for a while and then stopped at the cigar stand.

The fat white index finger of his left hand pointed through the glass of the showcase down to the old friend, the slim Robert Burns Panatela which had been his faithful writing companion for years. But just as the girl was about to lift the box out of the case and bring it within his reach, Ludlow Mumm's finger, like the needle on a seismograph, began to waver and slowly slid across the glass to the opposite side—to the corner which was occupied by the exquisite products of the Republica de Cuba—by the Aroma Selecta; the thick, blunt Romeo and Juliet; the good Punch; the corpulent Upmann Double Claro, nine inches long and in a cedar box all by itself next to its smaller, slim sister.

After some indecision, Mumm pointed to a long Partagas.

"These just came in fresh today," said the girl and showed him an airtight glass jar of fifty Upmanns. She told him the price.

He hesitated for a moment, leaning on the glass case and cupping the bearded chin in his left hand, but then he suddenly shut heavy iron gates on the drab past and he held the bandaged hand over the glass jar as if blessing it.

"I'll take it," he said.

He reached for the envelope with the money but the girl was writing out a slip, spelling his name correctly, and she said:

"I'll just put it on the bill. That's simpler."

He picked up the jar and carried it across the lobby. Ludlow Mumm progressed in the fashion of a ball rolling softly over uneven terrain, taking advantage of depressions in the land. A shy creature, he walked at the sides of corridors, around people and behind potted plants and furniture rather than in front.

He always smiled first when he encountered somebody. He was behind a big plant, on his way to the elevator, when he smiled again as an awkward-moving individual accosted him. A man in black gloves, carrying a cap in his hand, came toward him and in a hoarse voice said:

"I'm George, your driver. I'm down here whenever you want me. Got the car outside, boss."

Ludlow Mumm said, "That's fine," and rolled along the edge of the carpet to the elevator, where he stopped and turned to look back at the individual, who had resumed reading a moving-picture magazine and was leaning against the wall, awaiting his orders.

"I can do this just as well at the office if you want me to," said Miss Princip, looking up from her work as he came in and started opening his glass jar.

"That's all right," said Mumm. "You're not disturbing me in the least. Go right ahead."

"Lady Graveline wants you for dinner tomorrow," she said. "Shall I accept?"

It was remarkable with what speed the writer was accustom-
ing himself to his new habitat. Without a trace of surprise,
delight, or a hint that this was at all otherwise than as it
should be, he took the lid off the jar, picked out a cigar, and
said:

"I think so."

He went to his bedroom and put on a dressing gown and
slippers. Then he walked through the living room, past the
secretary, to his terrace—to a chaise longue upholstered in
bright chintz.

As he placed the weight of his body on it, the intelligent
piece of furniture made automatic adjustments in all its parts.
The back rest sank away to rest his head and shoulders; the
lower part lifted his knees and bedded them comfortably.
Ludlow Mumm lay suspended in the comforts of a feather
bed and as if he were floating in lukewarm water.

He lifted the cigar up over his face and balanced it in his
hand. He looked at it closely and from all angles in the fashion
in which a baby examines a new teething ring suspended over
his crib. He stuck the cigar between his lips and was bothered
for a second by the unpleasant prospect of having to get up
again out of the chaise longue to look for a match.

As he was about to make the effort to rise, the meuble,
whose trade name was the "King of Ease," adjusted itself again
and put him in a sitting position so that he could see, on a
wicker table at his left, a large onyx match stand, filled with
kitchen matches, to which, as a cigar smoker, he was very
partial.

The writer was about to reach for one of the matches when
a voice said:

"Let me do it."

The valet, with a pair of his freshly pressed trousers over
his arm, lighted the match, waited until the sulphur fumes
had blown away, and then moved the flame carefully back
and forth at the end of the cigar without haste, so that Ludlow
got the cigar lit properly and without undue puffing.

The writer rewarded the servant with a raising of his eyebrows and leaned back. The "King of Ease" obliged, and, in great comfort again, Ludlow Mumm resumed drawing on his fine cigar.

The field of his vision was framed by night-blooming jasmine. The crowns of two high palm trees swayed with soft rustling of their dry leaves in the cloudless, dustless blue. He looked through the openwork of the banisters at the immaculate expanse of lawn, spread out like an immense green towel. A tropical garden crowded against the hotel with plants that were like animals rather than vegetation; some embracing one another, others holding large emerald umbrellas in their arms. There was the actuality of grapefruit hanging in trees; the thud of tennis balls; the shouting and splashing of children in the water of the hotel's pool; all mixed and far enough away not to disturb the siesta.

Miss Princip came tiptoeing out on the terrace. She looked anxiously at the writer. When she saw that he was awake, she held up a few bills, all of them stamped "past due," and she said with concern:

"I just wanted to find out from you, Mr. Mumm, whether I should keep up these subscriptions to *PM*, the *Daily Worker*, and the *American-Soviet Review*, or just pay them."

The otherwise mild Ludlow Mumm turned and sat up so abruptly that the "King of Ease" chaise longue for once was behind in its work and squeaked with anguish.

"Of course," said Mumm, and swallowed smoke in the excitement.

"Keep it up?" asked the frightened Miss Princip, with wide, questioning eyes.

Ludlow Mumm nodded violently through a coughing spell. He sat still after that. Under his beard and mustache, his mouth was a bitter line.

"I am sorry," said Miss Princip, as she came out once more with another bill. "The Hotel Wolff in New York—"

"Yes?" said Ludlow Mumm.

"Do we pay them—I mean, do we keep the apartment there?"

"No," he said, "just pay them."

He leaned back again. Now his mouth was clamped together like that of a turtle.

The poor scribe, whose view of the world up to now had always been from third-class accommodations, returned in unhappy memory for a while to the quarters that he had occupied in New York: the cell of a bedroom with the gritty window sill and faded velvet drapes, airless in summer's heat, off the soot-blown airshaft of the Hotel Wolff; the living room whose three pieces of furniture changed forever from red to blue in the reflection of the alternating lights of the hotel's electric sign that hung outside between its windows. He heard the ruthless bombardment of garbage cans and the explosion that awoke him every morning when the cast iron covers of the sidewalk elevator fell shut. And he thought of the big ink spot on the brown carpet, unremoved in all the years of his tenancy there. He had grown resigned to it eventually, and fixed his eyes on it whenever he had to concentrate on the writing of the bittersweet, nostalgic pieces that were his specialty and that had finally released him from his debtor's prison.

He reached for one of the kitchen matches and relit his fine cigar. He blew a smoke ring up at the night-blooming jasmine and looked again at the palms. He was reassured. He regained some comfort from the chair as the "King of Ease" laid him out again, and contentment moved slowly back into his eyes.

There was one moment of concern—he thought he heard a downpour. But the sky was still blue, and his fears disappeared when he saw that the sound came from the hotel's rain machine, which sprayed a soft drizzle on the leaves from hidden nozzles.

"Good-by," said Miss Princip, softly.

"Tell George to take you home," he said, completely repaired and soothed.

He held on to his cigar as a sleeping bird does to the favorite branch of a tree, and then he fell away in the pleasant anesthesia, the dreamless, deathlike sleep, that is one of the many gifts that the glory land extends to the newly arrived.

5. Message Out of a Bottle

"This is Mr. Nightingale, who belongs to the night and whom I call 'Nighty.' He has lit up the garden for us. He's wonderful—I think. Good night, 'Nighty,' and thank you," said the hostess.

Ludlow Mumm, the last guest to arrive, shook the hand of the departing Mr. Nightingale. It was sticky from the black tape with which he had insulated the fixtures that lit up the celebration.

The hostess, the silent picture star Betsy Allbright, her heroic form swathed in a silver lamé-and-chinchilla gown, took Ludlow Mumm by his good hand and pulled him through a tunnel of red, white, and blue flowers, out into the blue garden which was protected against the ocean breezes by high walls and heated with large charcoal braziers that gave the assemblage the air of a camp of very rich gypsies.

Mumm was seated on a folding metal chair and given a program. He was about to turn and speak to his neighbor when a master of ceremonies asked for silence.

A speech was made, and a bulky Wagnerian tenor, who had rushed from the set of a musical comedy, sang the "Marseillaise" under a strong light that showed the inside as well as the outside of his lips still rouged for the color cameras.

The assembled guests stood up and joined the singing. The man next to Mumm sang in the French of the native, drowning out the tenor in his section of the garden. The liberation of Paris having thus been celebrated, parlormaids, dressed as they are in movies of Parisian life—pretty girls with well arranged hair in which elaborate coquette caps nestle and with good legs in abbreviated black skirts—passed trays of champagne.

Mumm took a glass for himself and reached for another,

which he handed to his neighbor. He lifted his glass and said:

"To the liberation of Paris."

"Here," said the Frenchman, "we seem to be celebrating the liberation of the rue Blondel. Have you seen the décor on the outside of the house?"

"I have been in Paris, but I have never been in the rue Blondel," said Mumm.

"Well, you know what it is. They do these things well here. They reproduce anything for you with painstaking detail: for example, the German tourist who just sang the 'Marseillaise,' perfect type-casting."

"It still is," said the tolerant and idealistic Mumm, "the most beautiful anthem in the world."

"Let's go in, monsieur. I am cold and hungry."

They walked to a table in one of the rooms and each took a large crested plate. They stood in line and began to stack the plates with the unchanging food that is offered at buffets: slice of Virginia ham with clove stuck in the rim of white fat; large slice of turkey; pickle; potato salad; cole slaw; spoonful of baked beans; spoonful of macaroni au gratin; stalk of celery; olive; buttered roll; and napkin. They walked to an alcove and sat down on two deep brocade fauteuils, facing each other.

A pretty parlormaid came and bent over to offer Mumm a glass of champagne. Then she turned and served Cassard, presenting the two low-seated men, in turn, with an obscene close-up of garter, strip of white flesh, and brief black lace-fringed underwear.

"I see it all very clearly now," said Mumm.

"I beg your pardon?" said Cassard.

"It will be over soon."

"Oh, you mean the war," said the Frenchman.

"Pssst," he called to the maid, "leave the bottle."

He turned to Mumm.

"And what comes after?" he asked.

"The beginning of the greatest era in the history of the world," said Mumm, steadfastly looking into the other's eyes.

"You think so? Yes? Ah!" said Cassard and stuffed cole slaw into his mouth and drank.

"The new world," said Mumm, who had gained ten pounds since his arrival in Hollywood and was pinched by his double-breasted dinner jacket.

"And how do you envision this new world?" asked Cassard.

"The absence of labels, of nationalities, no more political boundaries, the brotherhood of man, one citizenship—"

"And how will that come about?"

"The plans are all ready in London, Moscow, and Washington."

"I am glad to hear that," said Cassard.

"They will all learn English for one thing—the eight hundred words of Basic English."

"Who will teach them?"

"That's all taken care of. Soldiers. The Army, the Navy. Every soldier will be a teacher."

"And what will all this accomplish?" asked the Frenchman.

"Mutual understanding and trust in one another. Afterward, borders will vanish, roads will be built, commerce will follow. Finns will enjoy oranges from Italy and the Italians will eat sardines."

"Permit me, but the Italians already have sardines, amigo. Sardinia is in Italy," remarked Cassard dryly.

"I am expressing myself badly," said Mumm. "I mean people will have better food, and well-fed people don't go to war."

"But an individual can start trouble again."

"That is what our soldier-teachers will take care of also. They will establish democracy everywhere."

"You believe in democracy?" said Cassard.

"Why, certainly," said Mumm. "Don't you?"

"Alors," said Cassard, and thoughtfully picked a strand of cole slaw from his trousers. "I should like to have it demonstrated to me. I have never seen it." He emptied a new glass of champagne.

"You don't think we have democracy here?"

"A true democracy is unthinkable," said Cassard. "It would never work."

"I beg your pardon?" said Mumm, and sat forward. He spoke with conviction. "We have achieved democracy in many things," he said. "You cannot deny, for example, that the millionaire uses the same car as the bricklayer. A Ford is as good a car as you want to drive. In fact, the President of this country owns one and drives it. And take cigarettes—we all smoke the same cigarettes."

"True," said Cassard, "but allow me to say that your President drives his Ford over the private roads of his estate and blows the smoke of his Camel from an ivory-and-gold holder into the face of a valet, and perhaps also owns stock in the firm that manufactures them, and therefore has every reason to be very happy that so many bricklayers smoke them."

"Well, if you talk that way," said Mumm, "then there's no use continuing this discussion."

Another pretty parlormaid came and took the plates off the pale Aubusson carpet. Cassard asked her to bring some coffee.

From a large new crocodile leather case with golden corners, Mumm offered an Upmann to Cassard, and after the cigars had been lit the two leaned back into the chairs that were almost as comfortable as the "King of Ease" chaise longue at the hotel.

"You, amigo, if I may ask," said Cassard, "what kind of a car do you drive?"

"I don't drive myself," said Mumm.

"Ah, but you must get about," said Cassard.

"Yes," said Mumm. "I have a chauffeur."

"And the car?"

"A Cadillac."

"Ah," said Cassard, "I also drive a Cadillac. I am very happy with it."

The character actress, in a twelve-hundred-dollar Adrian model, placed a sable coat on the arm of Cassard's chair, saying, "Watch it for me, darling," and left.

Cassard looked after her.

"It will amuse you—to talk to her about Russia," said Cassard.

"Now our friends the Russians," said Mumm, coming out of his chair.

"Amigo," said Cassard, stopping him. "Forgive me, but I know what you are going to say. Allow me—"

He filled his own and Mumm's glass.

"I go further than you even in my love of mankind. I will take the Russians; I would subscribe to the British, who make the most excellent rulers; I would welcome the Catholic Church; even Fascism; anything that would unify the world—but my mind refuses to let me. It is not desired now. Not by America. Not by England. Least of all by Russia. I don't think even by nature. The time is not yet. Europe will remain as it is. Small nations are ideal. The ammunition of the French does not fit the guns of the Luxembourgers. The Serbs happily detest the Slovenes and cannot understand what they say. The Roumanians would never trust the Bulgarians with making the engines of a tank for which they make the shells. And all this confusion has its good side."

"And what is that?"

"Oh, a few years of peace—and it gives the others time to get ready again. The little ones are the pawns on the chess board. You move them about at the beginning until you are ready to play."

"You think then that there will always be conflict?"

"I am certain of it. Conflict, amigo, is the first law of life and the theater. It is here in this glass of champagne; in that pitcher of water there. If you will prick your finger and examine the drop of blood that comes out of it, you will find it seething with conflict. Without it, there is no existence and no drama, and the audience runs out of the theater screaming."

"What do you believe in?" said Mumm.

"We French have a peculiar and unhappy talent for seeing ahead and doing nothing about it. But perhaps you will be able to. At the head of the few things in this world in which I have confidence, monsieur, marches the General Staff of the

United States Army. I would put my money on them any time.
They are the only guardian angels.

"You are vulnerable, Monsieur Mumm, from the tip of
Patagonia to Newfoundland. Those are your new borders and
you haven't time for experiments. The ocean is gone."

A butler came with an assistant and a wagon. Cassard
poured himself a brandy and he dropped two pieces of sugar,
which he had placed on the saucer of his demitasse, into the
inhaler. He pressed the sugar with the handle of a fork against
the glass, and when it had dissolved he stirred the awful mixture. Mumm held his champagne glass up to the butler.

"Bring another bottle," said Cassard to the servant.

"Well, all I can say is that I hope you are dead wrong," said
Mumm.

"You live in New York?" asked Cassard.

"Yes," said Mumm.

"I love New York," said Cassard. "I lived there for several
months on Thirty-fourth Street, between Park Avenue and
Lexington."

The glutton Mumm came back to the old subject.

"Everybody is entitled to his opinion," he said. "You don't
see any hope, then, for a United World?—or for peace?"

Cassard made an uncontrolled sweeping gesture. He had
difficulty with his drink.

"Eventually," he said.

"Well, have you a better plan?" said Mumm.

"No, amigo," said Cassard and tried to focus his eyes on
his adversary. "No, but I think I can tell you how it will come
about if you want to hear it."

"Wait until I get myself a drink," said Mumm, holding up
the glass.

The butler came and filled it and left a new bottle.

"I will tell you," said Cassard. "It will happen like this:
Most probably on a lovely day in spring, when the Hudson
river is filled with shad—suddenly, every one of these millions
of fish will be boiled. All of them, as far as Albany. And the
glass in every window in Manhattan will be shattered. The
air pressure will be so great that a car in the underpass which

runs from Thirty-third street to Fortieth, under Park Avenue, will be shot like a pellet from a rifle and crash through the wall of Grand Central Station, decapitating the statue of Cornelius Vanderbilt and also the man in the information booth.

"In the outer harbor there will be heard a cannonade made by the exploding boilers and gasoline storage tanks of Brooklyn and New Jersey, and a rising cloud of steam will disclose an immense plane already cooling itself from nozzles on its hull such as spray the gardens out here, like a giant whale spouting sea water.

"Like the feelers on the head of an insect, two cranes will appear and open doors as big as those on the hangars that house Zeppelins, and out of these doors a ship will float. On the bridge of that ship stands a man from another planet.

"Not a man with one eye in the center of his forehead, not at all like that. A plain type, looking, perhaps a little choleric, someone like La Guardia, with the same kind of black hat. The man will point and the ship will head for the city. And the man with the black hat will go directly to the Stork Club, where he will present his credentials to Mr. Winchell.

"After he has imparted his awful ultimatum to Mr. Winchell, and the President and the rest of us have heard it on the air the next Sunday evening, then, Monsieur Mumm, we on earth will suddenly reach for one another's hands, and there will be a quick recognition.

"But until then, the plan that would work," said Cassard, "would seem so crass that nobody would dare propose it. It would sound so fantastic that not even the bride of a witch doctor would believe it."

Cassard stuck his half-smoked cigar into a mound of left-over potato salad on a plate which a butler was carrying past.

"Why don't you," said Mumm, "tell this to somebody who could write it . . . maybe, make a picture out of it? I think it's wonderful—the car flying through the air out of the underpass; the headless statue of Commodore Vanderbilt; and the Hudson filled with the white bellies of the boiled shad. I can see all that clearly and I think it's very exciting."

"Thank you, amigo," said the Frenchman. "I happen to be a writer, but no one out here is in the least interested in disturbing the world any more than it already is. And the man I work for, Moses Fable, an aesthete, preaches daily that he is in the business of entertaining people."

Cassard lifted himself with great effort from the deep seat.

Ludlow Mumm said, "You know, I'm a writer too."

"Ah, you have sold something, a novel, a play?"

"I also am under contract to Olympia," said Mumm.

"Oh," said Cassard, "and who is your producer?"

"Vashvily," said Mumm, "Vanya Vashvily."

On Cassard's face appeared an awful smile which exposed both his upper and lower teeth. For a second he made a liquid sound as if sopping up cold soup. Then he offered his hand.

"I am Maurice Cassard," he said, singing the end of his name slowly, "Ca—ss—aaard. You will most probably end up by not speaking to me and also hate my wife and children before we are through. Nevertheless, it is my duty to inform you, monsieur, that I am your collaborator, a word which has lately taken on a sinister meaning also."

He laughed fiercely.

"As for the argument, amigo, think nothing of it. I always take the other side. Conflict, as I have said, is the essence of drama. And I fancy myself a playwright."

Sagging more than usual, Cassard began his visits to the four walls of the room. He ran his fingers several times through his heavy black hair. As he came abreast of Mumm he slowed down, and when he was past him a foot he stopped. He tore several paper matches out of a folder, turned his head as if speaking to a person standing in back of him, and asked:

"Have you read the story?"

"No," said Mumm.

Cassard took the last match from the folder and lit a cigarette. He crossed the room again. Touching Mumm's chair, without looking at him he said:

"Well, don't bother reading it. We're not going to use a word of it anyway."

Mumm got up.

"Have you read it?" he said.

"Ah, non!" said Cassard. "You have never before been in Hollywood?" he asked.

"No," said Mumm.

"Have you been to the studio?"

"No," said Mumm again.

"Ah, but then you must go. You will find it very interesting to see how they make pictures."

The character woman approached and Cassard said, happily:

"Ah, here comes my Seeing Eye Dog. I always have trouble finding my way about at this hour."

"Are you still here?" she said.

She had a good clip at the base of the right shoulder strap of her dress. Cassard inspected it and then pulled it away so that the decolletage widened and the start of the two unbrassiered white bosoms was revealed.

"Je ne connais pas la couture, mais—" he began, and then noticed Mumm, who was embarrassed.

"Oh, I beg your pardon," said the intoxicated Cassard. "I said that I knew nothing about dresses, but of what is in them I am a fancier."

He pulled the clip again.

"Look at her," he said to the blushing Mumm. "I have never seen Sex so robust and so pure."

"And so unimportant when you have it," said the character woman.

Cassard tried to embrace her.

"You see," he said to Mumm, "I, too, love the Russians."

"You have water all over yourself, darling," said the actress to Cassard.

"No, it's wine," he said.

She went to the buffet for a napkin.

The Frenchman slid down in his chair and one hand touched the floor. His shirt front bulged and the stud worked loose. He wore no undershirt, and a tuft of black hair stuck out where the white linen bosom parted. He had his eyes closed, and the character woman leaned down over him and dried him off. Then she took a grip on the tuft of hair and pulled it out. He yapped and tried to get up; she sat down on the arm of the chair and took one strand after another out of the bunch and counted, as if she were pulling petals off a daisy:

> "Il m'aime
> Un peu
> Beaucoup
> Passionnellement
> Avec chaleur
> A la folie . . ."

Cassard opened one eye.

"Stop," he said. "You're feeding this to me like opium."

She stopped.

"Come, now," she said. "You have to take me home. When are you ready to leave here?"

"Oh, not for a long, long time."

"I am sorry," said Mumm, looking at his watch, "but I must be on my way."

"Well, then, may I go with you?" asked the woman.

"Beware!" came over the arm rest of the chair. "Beware, Mumm. She has left many cut and bleeding."

They drove home in silence, each sitting in a corner.

6. *The Sun Bath*

Miss Princip had had a large bath towel put on the "King of Ease" chaise longue and Ludlow Mumm regularly sun-bathed there. For the rest, his life remained unchanged, and for a month he rolled comfortably through his harmonious system of living.

He stopped here and there on the paths of the hotel's park

on his morning promenade. Holding the cigar thoughtfully a foot away from his face, he would contemplate the long ash and think about the future of the world in the light of Cassard's revelations. But then he walked on again through mimosa, immortelles, and hibiscus and watched the fat goldfish play in the fountain that is at the entrance of the hotel in front of the porte-cochere.

He experienced a bleak moment when he awoke from his afternoon sun bath and sleep and heard the rippling of the soft, automatic hotel rain, which reminded him of Maurice Cassard's space boat cooling itself in the outer harbor of New York. But he was successful in washing the mood away with a cocktail made from one jigger of fresh grapefruit juice, two jiggers of gin, and one third of a jigger of Cointreau, served very, very cold; a drink known as a "Lady Mendl Special."

On Wednesday, Arty Wildgans, himself, telephoned twice to the hotel to check up on Mumm's dinner date with the producer. The efficient agent got Miss Princip the second time he called.

"He's taking the sun now," she said, "but he knows about it. He'll be there on time."

The "King of Ease" fauteuil out on the balcony, however, basked in the sun unoccupied.

The secretary had lied to protect her charge.

Ludlow Mumm had a very busy day. From luncheon at Romanoff's he had rushed to his shirtmaker, and from there to the tailor who was creating a new wardrobe for him.

George had driven him on from his tailor to a high school and waited with the car around the corner until the conscientious writer had done his stint in a picket line, protesting against the leasing of the auditorium to a subversive group. Mumm, after two hours of walking in circles and shouting a slogan, handed his placard to his relief man and ran around the corner to his car.

He usually rode up front talking with the driver but now he fell exhausted into the back seat of the Cadillac. George covered him with a robe and speeded him back to the hotel.

Miss Princip had a barber waiting, and after Mumm's hair and beard were trimmed he had barely time to shower, put on a new shirt, and change into his tight, somber spare suit.

Without waiting for the elevator he ran down the stairs, and George drove him up to Vanya Vashvily's residence.

Mumm was on time. It was exactly seven. As he approached the heavy iron-bound door it automatically opened. An old-fashioned German of some sixty years with close-cropped hair stood in the hall. Vashvily, who was in a blue velvet house jacket, adjusted his hearing aid, and after greeting Ludlow Mumm, mixed a Martini.

"You better take your drink to the table," he said, "and have it there."

The butler, who stood waiting in the dining room, pushed a heavy Venetian baroque chair under Mumm.

The face of a woman who looked like Hindenburg, only with two buns of yellow hair at the sides of her face, appeared in the door. She was the butler's wife. She handed two plates of home-made noodle soup to her husband.

"Beer or wine?" asked the man.

Mumm asked for beer.

As the butler left the room, Vashvily said in a tone of confidence:

"I had a very nice colored man before they came—was with me for years. I hope to get him back."

The butler came and took the plates away. He put a bottle of beer next to Mumm's plate and also an opener. Mrs. Hindenburg came and handed bread around.

There was absolute silence until they had gone. Then Vashvily whispered:

"You know, I take sun baths; I have a small terrace upstairs where I take sun baths."

The man came in again and put two very large and very hot plates on the table and there was silence again until he went out through the door, back into the kitchen.

"I told you about the terrace where I take my sun baths," said the producer. "Well, next to this terrace are two trees. I'd have them cut down, but the place doesn't belong to me.

They're eucalyptus trees and they are very disorderly, always dropping things. Leaves fall out of them and pods, and even pieces of the bark."

Mrs. Hindenburg and her husband marched in, he with Sauerbraten and potato pancakes, and she with a jardiniere of fresh vegetables, topped by two fried eggs. After they had marched out again, the producer lowered his voice and looked at the door:

"So, my terrace is full of leaves that fall out of those trees, so I tell this son-of-a-bitch to clean it up. They've got nothing to do but to take care of me, no laundry, no cleaning windows, nothing. Well, after a week, I'm up to my ankles in dead leaves up there. So, two more days pass. You know, I'm just out of the hospital and I'm not supposed to exert myself, so I say to him—"

There was absolute silence again as the man came back into the room. He looked sternly at the plates and the producer started eating with fine remarks about the cooking and compliments for Mrs. Hindenburg.

Later, Mumm turned around and looked at the Braque, admiring it, and also at an anonymous still life which Vashvily had picked up in a junk shop downtown and put into a good frame.

(In a telephone conversation, the day after the liberation of Paris celebration, when Cassard had excused himself for his behavior, he had also said about Vashvily:

"A man of taste, not the run of insensible producers. You can talk about anything with him. He is well informed. He has traveled. He knows food and wine and plays the piano beautifully. He has read everything. Only, when he starts talking about pictures he turns into an absolute idiot.")

Mr. and Mrs. Hindenburg passed the platters once more. The sour pot roast was good, the potato pancakes light and small, and both men took more.

"So I say to the son-of-a-bitch," continued Vashvily, as the door swung closed again, "just to shame him into it, I said, 'All right, if you're so busy, I'll clean them up myself—the leaves.'"

Mumm shook his head.

There was another period of silence during the clearing of the plates, after which Mrs. Hindenburg put a large cut-glass bowl of stewed apricots in the center of the table and the butler brushed the crumbs off the table cloth and put down the dessert plates and the silver.

"Coffee," he asked without the inflection of a question.

"Yes, in the other room," answered Vashvily, equally flat.

They were gone again.

"I said, 'All right, I'll clean up myself if you're so busy,'" repeated the producer. "So what do you think he does? He comes up to my terrace and hands me a broom and a dustpan!"

"I don't believe it," said Mumm in astonishment.

"That's nothing," said the producer. "Wait till you hear the rest. So I clean up the leaves myself, and when I'm halfway through, he comes again—I'm just resting. . . . Well, he stands there and he takes the broom out of my hand and I say to myself, 'At last.' But he just takes the broom and turns it around and he says, 'I guess I'd better get you a new broom. This one is just about worn out.'"

The conversation was cut again. The man came in, folded his arms and, standing by the leaded window, stared at the table.

Mrs. Hindenburg carried the tray with the coffee into the living room, past him. Vashvily made haste with his apricots and they both got up.

The candles were snuffed out and the dining room doors shut behind the wife after she had said a grim "Good night."

Vashvily said, "The first thing they asked when they came was, 'How often do you entertain?' He said, 'What time do you eat?' and in the same breath she said, 'Not later than seven-thirty.' And when it's seven and the guests have not arrived, he stands at the window there and glowers through the Venetian blinds. Well," whispered Vashvily, "he won't glower much longer."

"It's very hard these days," said Mumm.

"Hell, they have a sitting room and a bedroom and two bathrooms with dressing room. I pay them four hundred dollars a month. Guests only once or twice a week. Use of a car. What more do they want?"

Vashvily sat down at a black Blüthner concert piano.

"I still get tired easily," he said, rubbing his hands. "You know I spent a month in the Cedars of Lebanon."

He got up again and took a large folder from one of the many bookshelves that covered one wall of the big room.

"I also dabble in art—nothing much, just for myself," he said, and undid the strings of the portfolio.

He brought out a small pen-and-ink drawing:

"This is the view from my room at the hospital," he said. "That bird sitting in its nest in that tree, there, lined that nest with hair from the head of one of our starlets who was having her baby on the floor below while I was there. Every day the nurse who took care of her, when she brushed her hair, rolled up the loose strands and put them on the window sill and that bird came and carried them away over to that tree. Now, nobody would believe a thing like that unless they saw it. You see here, this nest."

He showed Mumm several other drawings he had made. Among them was a pencil study of Belinda.

Mumm felt that he had found a friend. ("Not the run of insensible producers. He has taste. . . .") He felt for the first time since his arrival that he might, under the guidance of this kind, quiet, and appreciative man, adapt himself to film writing and do good work.

The producer poured a glass of brandy for Mumm. He walked back to his bookshelves and came back with a copy of *Will You Marry Me?* He sat down in one of the two sofas that faced each other in front of the fireplace. He pointed to the humidor.

"I don't smoke any more. I've had to give it up for the last two months," he said. "You have one. Go ahead."

"Do you miss it?" asked Mumm.

"Not unless I think about it—like now," said Vashvily. "Or when I see somebody else reach for one and light it."

"Well, then, I won't smoke, either," said Mumm.

"If it makes you feel better, I'll have one myself," said Vashvily, and with the lighting of the two cigars complete accord, a mood rare between producer and writer, was established.

"We've got a great story here," said Vashvily, bending the covers back again. "And *Will You Marry Me?* is a great title for a picture."

He put on his glasses.

"I've had Cassard working on it," he said. "You know Cassard—of course! . . . Now," he said, "my doctor won't let me go back to work yet. I've got to go away for a rest. I'll have a talk with you before I leave, and I'm going to go over this story with you briefly now. After I'm gone, I wish you'd get together with Cassard and kick this thing around and see what you find and then, when I get back, we'll have something to start with."

Mumm nodded enthusiastically.

"You'll make a great team," said Vashvily.

Behind Vashvily hung a large painting of a snow scene with the chrome yellow disk of the sun taking up most of the canvas. From a house on the right side of the painting rose a column of smoke done with bold brush strokes. The snow was done in thick Vlaminck smears of white. A spotlight shone on the painting and intensified the colors.

Mumm looked at the picture.

"I've got a girl in mind," said the producer, and on his face appeared the pained, leaning-into-the-wind expression. "She'll be great for the part of the girl."

Mumm looked into the painted sun and blinked.

"I've marked a few passages here," said the producer, "which I'll talk to you about after I've read them."

("But when he starts talking about pictures, he becomes an absolute idiot.")

Mumm suppressed a yawn by sitting up quickly.

"We begin with the scene in the railroad station," said Vashvily. "That's a great scene."

Mumm fixed his eyes on the Vlaminck sun as he had done on the ink spot on the carpet of the Hotel Wolff when he wanted to concentrate.

"The camera shows a train," said Vashvily, and described

the arrival of the train so well that Mumm began to smell cinders.

The smoke over the house in the picture on the wall floated down over the tracks into the snow and the snow melted into blotches of color.

Mumm was warm and comfortable. He lowered his head. His bandaged hand lay on his chest, and, after he had put the cigar into the ash tray so that it would not fall out of his mouth and burn a hole in the producer's antique velvet couch, he lifted the other hand and supported his face with it. He took a deep breath and was asleep. He looked as if he were relaxed and in his favorite listening pose.

Vanya Vashvily became interested in his story all over again and read it, uninterrupted, to the last page. He slammed his hand down on the cover as he closed it.

"I don't care what anyone says. That's a great story!" he cried.

Mumm sat up straight suddenly, wondering where he was, and searched for words.

"Great," said Vashvily. "What do you think?"

Mumm looked at him. He was speechless.

"I'm glad you like it," said Vashvily, and after a Scotch and soda, he showed him to the door.

Mumm drove back to the hotel. He walked into his bedroom and was undoing his tie when the phone rang.

"What did he say about me?" said Cassard.

"Who?" asked Mumm.

"Vashvily, of course. You just came from there. You had dinner with him."

"But how do you know?" said the astonished Mumm.

"Alors, amigo! You might as well know. Collaboration is like marriage. I know everything, my dear. I know where you had lunch, where you went this afternoon. Don't try to hide anything. Now, come and tell me—what did he say, I mean, about me?"

"He said you were great."

"Ah," said Cassard.

Mumm could see his face and the fierce smile at the other end of the phone.

"That is very gratifying, but, amigo, with Vashvily, everything is 'great.' He buys great novels, hands them to great writers, hires or discovers great stars, and makes great pictures with great directors. It's very simple."

"I find him very nice," said Mumm.

"Allow me to finish. I am speaking as teacher and friend," said Cassard.

"The producer," said Cassard in the voice of authority, "who has bought a story, a book, or a novel, and engaged a writer, or found a girl whom he decides to make into a star, is forever after committed to praising them—for, amigo, he has exercised in his selection the only function that excuses his existence, the reason for his being. You will, therefore, find the word 'great' everywhere. It hangs in all the corridors of studios; in offices, commissaries, and restaurants. You will hear it especially when two producers meet. Clouds of incense form above them as they praise their great stories, great stars, and great talents to each other. By the way, amigo, he told you the story. What do you think of it?"

Mumm was silent for two seconds.

"Good night," said Cassard. "Go to bed now. You must be very tired. I know what it is like to listen to Vashvily tell a story!"

THIRD PART

Life with Moses Fable

*In which we see the last of a slowly
dying race of mammoth men and
learn of his large heart and kindly
hand.*

7. *Folk Music*

After breakfast, Ludlow Mumm walked as usual, trailed by the aromatic thin blue ribbon of his morning cigar.

He was a new man, and rolled over the mimosa path with ease and freedom under the arms, around the waist, and in the crotch. Also, his neck was comfortable. He wore a low-collar batiste shirt made to his measure. On his feet were comfortable tan-and-white moccasin-type shoes. He wore a featherweight Harris-tweed Domenick Punaro jacket and fawn-colored flannels. His new cane of choice Malacca swung lightly on his arm and on his head was a fisherman-type zephyr canvas hat.

He stopped here and there, next to tangerine and orange trees, or mused a while, half hidden by the leaf of an exotic plant. He smiled at children in the pool and at babies in carriages. He drank in the climate with deep drafts and unhindered expansions of his chest measurement.

He was in complete accord with his happy surroundings until Miss Princip appeared on the balcony of his suite and in unmelodious tones called out his name.

He turned his head, looked up, and answered.

"Don't forget, you're having luncheon with Moses Fable," she screamed, "at one. It's eleven-thirty now."

He stood still and looked at the ashes on the end of his cigar for a while, and then pulled himself together and walked to the hotel's porte-cochere.

He arrived at the Olympia Studios ahead of time and was

immediately shown in by the reception clerk. A young woman in bobby socks and sweater took him up to the second floor of the immaculate building.

From the elevator he stepped on a battleship-gray linoleum floor along which are the offices of those writers who earn only one thousand dollars a week and have a common washroom to every six writers.

Passing this region, the girl led the way down a new, deeply carpeted corridor off which were the suites reserved for the three-thousand-a-week writers.

The girl guide's golden mass of hair stopped bobbing up and down at a door on which "Ludlow Mumm" was lettered in bold golden capitals. She opened the door and let him in.

Except for the familiar manuscript of *Will You Marry Me?* which lay on the Sheraton desk in the first room, the suite looked like a roped-off, immaculate sample apartment in an expensive furniture shop.

The secretary came from her office. She was attractive without being disturbing, proper like the hostesses in restaurants frequented by women shoppers. She introduced herself, spoke a few complimentary phrases about the writer's work and her familiarity with it. Then, sliding past him, she showed Ludlow Mumm the various mechanical gadgets of the new office: The button which summoned her; how to get an outside number on the telephone; how to open the window; and how to turn on the air-conditioning apparatus. She took his hat and the cane and hung it on a tree in the small foyer. She asked him whether he wanted anything and when he said no, she departed in that curious disappearing act by which perfect secretaries leave a room. She was so prim there seemed to be no backside to her.

Mumm sat down as if he had just arrived in a strange town and were waiting for somebody in a suite in a new hotel. He washed his hand in the mauve-tiled private bathroom and sat down again.

He tried the leatherette swivel chair that stood at his desk and almost fell over backward. It turned and leaned immediately in all directions without the comfortable, restrained

movements of the "King of Ease." He had to grab for his desk
and kick with his legs to regain balance.

He examined his desk. It was dustless, glass-covered, and
provided with a large writing pad and fresh blotters. The
glass inkstand was filled with ink as clean as if dark green
wine had just been poured into a crystal goblet. There was
a calendar and appointment pad, open at the right date, with
his luncheon appointment entered in a neat hand over the
line that was given to one P.M.

He opened one of the drawers and again found order. No
dust in the corners, containers with paper clips and rubber
bands. In the second drawer, the private telephone directory
of the Olympia Studios and the directory of the extended area
of Los Angeles.

In the large flat drawer, the one in the center, were reserve
penholders, sharpened pencils, erasers, and blank paper in
unlimited quantities and of the very best quality. It was
white paper with a yellowish tint, neatly stacked. There were
also envelopes and message pads with "Interoffice Memo-
randum from Ludlow Mumm to——" printed on them. Mumm
had the impulse to put some of the paper and envelopes in
his pocket. There was no typewriter.

He walked into the washroom again, and afterward took
a cigar and lit it.

He sat for a while on the couch in the bright living room of
the suite, and walked to the window, watching one gardener
clipping a hedge below and another digging up dead blooms,
replacing them with others that were flowering. He was warm.

He walked to the temperature control panel and pushed a
button. There was a soft whirring sound, and presently the
smoke of his cigar began to be drawn slowly upward.

The secretary came back and said:

"Is there anything you wish to dictate before I go to lunch,
Mr. Mumm?"

He thanked her. She left him sitting on the couch, saying,
as she was about to disappear:

"You know about the luncheon, Mr. Mumm?"

He asked where he had to go and she said:

"Don't worry, Mr. Mumm, just wait here. They'll come and get you."

At noon, the electricians on the various stages of the vast lot of Olympia Pictures threw their switches and the large family that worked on the Olympia lot began their leisurely trek toward the cafeterias and the commissary.

At one, the bells of the carillon with which Moses Fable had endowed a Methodist church that stood on a lot adjoining the studio began to ring their changes and the high executives in the administration building started to salivate.

A motherly woman known as Ma Gundel, in white with broad white shoes on her aching feet, would come out of the kitchen then, carrying a large wicker basket which contained various kinds of bread. In the basket were sour-dough bread, sweet rye, Russian rye, matzoth, French bread, pumpernickel, Swedish crisp, potato bread, and Viennese rolls. She covered this with a napkin and put it in the center of the round table at which Moses Fable lunched and walked back through the commissary to get large kosher pickles, almost electric with their sharp, salty tang. She also brought red and green tomatoes, pickled; a dish with chopped chicken liver, Bismarck herring, sliced smoked salmon, sour cream, chives, scallions, immense sticks of Utah celery, radishes, and more pickles; and other good and salty delicatessen according to the day of the week.

Her last trip was for Dr. Brown's Celery Tonic, Pepsi-cola, Coca-Cola, and bottles of milk and buttermilk.

All this done, she sat on a chair outside the executive dining room and looked into the large commissary at the assembled stars, bit actors, and extras, who, in the various costumes of the parts they played, sat there and ate and talked.

Nuns from religious spectacles sat next to gangsters; Gestapo captains ate in peace with the French Underground; and maharajahs were seated below untouchables at another table.

Ma Gundel could have retired years ago under the pension plan which enveloped all regular employees of Olympia. But she loved pictures and could not tear herself away from the forever-exciting scene of their making. She followed every

production with interest. Moses Fable valued her criticism and
had been known to consult with her seriously when casting
important features. She was a person of consequence and
everybody put his arms around her.

Ma Gundel rested her feet and awaited the arrival of Moses
Fable and his guests.

Moses Fable and Olympia were made for each other. No
player in Hollywood could have come near the perfect portrayal that he gave as president of the corporation. If he had
limited his work to impersonating himself, his huge salary
would have been earned.

There was a solid air about him as he walked through the
pandemonium of the plant in his conservative gray suits. The
thin veins on his massive cheeks were like the engraving on
gilt-edged securities.

He moved with weight and deliberation, and when he
wanted to look around he turned with the whole elliptical
body, slowly and steadily, as a statue is moved.

"Here at Olympia," he was fond of saying, "we have both
time and money in unlimited quantities!"

In his solid fashion, he was outstandingly different from his
competitors, who always ran, and always seemed to suspect
that someone was listening behind them.

A beneficiary of mankind in the mass, as he liked to think
of himself, Moses Fable also richly rewarded those around
him he thought worthy. He was interested in the last individual of his large family.

"Anyone can come and see me at any hour of the day and
also the night, if it's important enough" was another of his
favorite sayings.

But, if he was kind and human, he was not gullible, and
while he spoke ordinarily with the rich organ of a psalm-singer
holding himself in, once he was confronted with roguery,
when he found lurking skimmers trying to dip their ladles in
the rich Olympia broth, when his treasures were threatened,
or he caught the competition trying to wander off with one of
his stars, he became dangerously agile and emitted the sounds
of a knife-grinder.

The procession of his virtues is not complete without citing his courage. He was envied and admired for the fortitude with which he regularly threw good money after bad and thereby regularly attained large grosses and fabulous successes with even his worst pictures.

With the same rare mixture of a peasant's cunning and an impresario's play of hunches, he chose people. If he saw talent and good will he was generous with time and money, he forgave the beginner his mistakes, and allowed for occasional failure in old hands.

He read people through his sharp rimless glasses and he filed away what he found. The intricate cabinet in his head never mislaid information. It was a piece of occult furniture that belonged among the paraphernalia of stargazers and spiritualists; it was of paramount importance in his complicated industry, but would have wrecked any other kind of business had it made use of it.

He was given to speeches. His winged words, uncensored, flew out over banquet tables and into the nation's press. He was upswept by his own words and believed everything he said.

The carillon was still ringing from the steeple of the church across the street when Ludlow Mumm followed another girl guide into the inner office of Moses Fable. She left the shy writer standing in the doorway.

The executives who stood in a group in the center of the room slowly moved toward him. They all talked: some to one another in the center of the circle; others shouted over the heads of people who stood between them; and some carried on conversations on the outside.

Vanya Vashvily was talking to a director.

"What did the picture show?" he asked.

"The picture finally revealed," said the director, "that toward the end of the colon there is a small pocket, and in this, food gets stuck and infects the whole system. They'll operate tomorrow and then she'll have to stay on a corrective diet that moves things along easier for a while."

Moses Fable slowly moved his massive form and said to the director who was with Vashvily:

"Who are you talking about, Sandor?"

"That Mexican, Dolores Tarant."

"But I thought she was a nice girl," said Fable.

"Certainly, she *is* a nice girl. She's more beautiful than ever, great talent," said the director, reassuring his employer.

"That's the one we had the teeth straightened, isn't it?" asked Moses Fable.

"Straightened and capped," replied Vashvily.

"Well," said the fatherly Fable with concern, "you had better take care and tell the hospital people to cover them with vaseline if they're going to give her a total anesthetic, because the ether dissolves those plastic teeth."

"Right, Mr. Fable," said the director, and made a note.

"What is this, the emergency ward?" asked Moses Fable, looking past Vashvily at the door, and pointing with slow, deliberate gesture at Ludlow Mumm, who stood there with his bandaged hand.

Vashvily turned around.

"Oh, hello," he said. "That's one of my boys, Mr. Fable. Ludlow Mumm, the great writer."

"I beg your pardon," said Fable, slowly approaching the writer. "It's a great pleasure to have you with us, Mr. Mumm. I want you to meet some of the people here. Wolfgang Liebestod, head of our musical department; Raoul de Bourg-graff, head of the art department; John St. Clair; Sandor Thrilling, the director you've heard about."

Mumm shook hands without surprise. In a town that contains firms like Utter McKinley, the undertakers; a real estate firm of Read and Wright; two Prinzmetals; a LeRoy Prinz; a Jack Skirball; a Jerry Rothschild; a law firm by the name of Dull and Twist; and musicians called Amphitheatrof and Bakaleinakoff, he had become accustomed to unusual and distinctive names.

"Bob Evervess of the story department and Mr. Envelove of the legal end. Come on boys, let's go," said Moses Fable, and taking hold of the writer he advanced with him through the door as the pealing of the carillon faded away.

"Mr. Mumm," said Fable, "you sit over there."

He indicated the chair opposite his own, but before he released him from the strong grip with which he had transported him from the executive suite, over the lawn and through the commissary into the private dining room, he said:

"I hope you're feeling at home here. I hope you'll be with us a long time, Mr. Mumm, and I hope they're treating you right. If they don't, you come and see me. It's not like over at those windbags' "—he nodded in the direction of another studio—"where you have to wade through fourteen secretaries before you can see anybody. Remember, here, you can see me any hour of the day, and, if it's important, any hour of the night."

He gave Mumm a smile and started to tear open a telegram which his secretary had brought to him.

He sat down and the executives followed. Fable looked madder and madder as he read.

"So, what you tukking?" said Mrs. Gundel, and began to recite the day's menu.

Fable looked at her and said, "Just a minute," and then turned to the table and he held up the telegram.

"Gentlemen," he said, "I have to go to Washington next Friday to explain some elemental things down there."

He hit the table and the pince-nez trembled.

"Judas Priest," he cried, "they talk about inflation, and of course I'm right up there next to Louis B. Mayer and maybe this year I'll be ahead of him, right on top of the list. People like me are always the target because we earn the biggest salary in the United States."

"Mebbe, da spacial billa fare you vant?" said Mrs. Gundel, with a trace of impatience.

"Oh, bring me anything," said Fable.

"Da borscht." She looked around and everybody nodded. To the newcomer, Mumm, Ma Gundel said in her best dialect and as if she were in a radio serial:

"Vait till you taste the borscht! You'll going to lick by you de fingehs."

Repeating the order to herself, she walked out of the room.

Moses Fable took a pickle in his hand and continued:

"All right, so what—I pay ninety-two per cent in taxes!! My cars are up on blocks. I eat here the sixty-cent lunch in the commissary. What else do they want me to do? They can back up a truck to my home and take my forty pairs of old shoes away and the rags I have hanging in my closet, they can have those too. It doesn't mean a thing to me."

The pickle crackled as he bit into it.

"But if those idiots in Washington would sit down for a moment and think, they would see that I and the handful of men that earn the kind of money I make don't mean a thing. It's the morons, the millions that never had a God-damn thing. The father used to make thirty bucks, now he works in a defense plant. He brings home $110 a week, with time, over-time, and double pay on Sunday. The mother makes $80. That makes $190, and little Rosie, the riveter, brings in another $60. That makes it $250 a week.

"They never knew that kind of money before, and somehow they manage to buy the last icebox and the last radio. Every dream has come true—the house is painted and they go to the pictures every night, which is all very well and as it should be. But they forget who they owe it to. They owe it to the sixty economic royalists that made it all possible. To the damned and discredited people who built up the industries of this country. The steel men, the oil men, the motor makers, the bankers, and people like you and I who worked overtime and Sundays all our lives, and who carry the responsibility.

"What did they ever do? Those bastards have never given anything to anybody or worked beyond what they had to to keep from starving! They are lazy, mean, and grabbing.

"Now comes that withholding tax and they're asked to give up a measly twenty per cent. And that's what hurts—and in Washington, they scream and blame it on us. 'Look at Fable and his fabulous salary!' they say.

"But that's too easy, gentlemen. They're just trying to get out of that mess in Washington and so that's why they blame people like me. But I'm tired of keeping quiet. I've just re-hearsed, gentlemen, what I'm going to tell them in Washington Friday."

The executives nodded and murmured their approval.

Moses Fable felt for his spoon.

"What a picture! What a documentary I could make about those bums in Washington!" he said bitterly.

"But again, I impress upon you, gentlemen, that we are not in the business of propaganda but in the business of entertainment, and I refuse to use the gigantic resources of this organization to further my personal aims or to influence public opinion. If such pictures are to be made"—he nodded in the direction of the other studio— "let them stick their necks out. I am not pro this or pro that. I just want to be fair and I'll tell them what's on my mind. But those flag-waving phonies, they have to beat the drum. They think they can save the world. I don't want to save the world. I just want to entertain the masses of the people."

Moses Fable had kept his eyes fixed in a hypnotic stare at Mumm during the entire speech. Now he was ready to eat. He stood up and bent forward, reaching into the glass jar for a new pickle. In a slow and deliberate manner he waved the pickle and then pointed with it at each individual at the table.

"I hope I haven't hurt anybody's feelings," he said, and sat down and with a cracking sound bit into the sour delicacy.

"Nu, so drink your cawfee," said Ma Gundel.

"I don't want any coffee, Ma," said Fable.

"No Linzertorte?"

"No Linzertorte."

At the end of the meal he walked over to Mumm and took a grip on his arm again.

"I'll be back in a few days," he said, "and remember, you can come and see me any time. And good luck to you."

He walked, with his hand on Ludlow Mumm's shoulder, through the commissary, and stood outside with him in the sun. Then, as Mumm walked away, he lifted his right arm in farewell greeting and Mumm waved his bandaged arm in return. Moses Fable stepped into the car, the one which was not on blocks, and drove away.

Ludlow Mumm rolled, without a guide, up to his floor and

over the linoleum and turned the corner past the thousand-a-week clatter of typewriters and went on over the carpeted corridor to his door.

His suite was like an icebox now. The sound of the air conditioning was still going and he found that he had turned it down too low. Outside in the midday heat a gardener wiped the sweat from his forehead and went on clipping the hedge. The other gardener had finished replanting a rondelle with fresh red and golden fist-sized flowers.

Ludlow Mumm sat down again on the couch and for a while thought about what Moses Fable had said. He went to wash his hand again and tried the chair once more. This time he succeeded in sitting in it without falling backward.

The secretary came in, but he remembered only after she had gone again that he wanted a typewriter, because he was not used to dictating. It was two-thirty and he had to be on a picket line at four again. Ludlow Mumm sighed deeply.

After a while he walked out into the corridor. The place looked like a combination insane asylum and Pullman car to him. The Pullman car motif came from a Negro in a white jacket who wheeled a chromium wagon along the corridor, a rolling table such as those on which patients are taken to operating rooms. On the wagon were towels and thermos bottles and glasses. The Negro, softly whistling, went into the various rooms and exchanged towels, bottles, and glasses. The smell was that of an institution and the feeling of insane asylum came from a wild-looking individual who was coming down the hall in the tight grip of another. They slowed down in front of Mumm's door and the following dialogue took place:

"He doesn't like the word dog."

"All right, make it hounds," said the other.

"Anyway, they chase him through the woods. He can't run away. We'll find him," said the first.

"In the drugstore," said the other.

"No!" cried the wild-haired one, and sadly shook his head. "Not in the drugstore. I like that drugstore scene, but the drugstore must come out."

The other seemed sympathetic.

"What," he asked, "about the old lady who gives the sleeping pills to the little girl with the crutch?"

"That's out, too," said the wild man in despair.

"I thought that was great," said the other, and, resuming his grip, carted the wild man off down to the linoleum.

Ludlow Mumm walked back into his suite and around his desk.

"If you want me for anything, Mr. Mumm," said the secretary, opening the door of her cubicle again, "I'm right here."

Mumm searched his memory. He had seen the pale wild man in the corridor somewhere before. Finally it came back to him. He had met him in Romanoff's on the first day.

"Hack," he said. "Yes, Jerome Hack. 'Very legitimate, great talent, dependable.'"

The mood of insanity persisted. Without a knock, the door of the suite was suddenly thrown open and Jerome Hack stood there. He disposed his long, thin limbs in the frame of the door as if a piece of scaffolding had been put there to bar entry. Suddenly, with two long strides, he was at the desk. He looked at Mumm with his big, sad eyes enlarged by heavy lenses.

"Hello, Mumm," he said, holding a long pale finger, which seemed to have one joint more than the normal kind, in an accusing hooklike position close to Mumm's face.

He continued. "I thought I saw you a minute or so ago. I also saw you over in the commissary lunching with Moses Fable and the sun gods. You're a lucky man, Mumm. How does it feel to have lunch with Moses Fable? I've been on this lot for twelve years and I never had lunch with Moses Fable. Well, congratulations, Mumm, but don't let it go to your head. Just wait—comes a day when they take that halo and pull it down over your face and make a noose out of it."

With one step he was at the window and looked out.

"Nice view you've got. You know what I look at? I look out on a blank wall. This would be much too distracting for me. I wouldn't be able to turn out a finished shooting script every ten days. That reminds me. The guy who was in here before you—and stayed here two years—from him, I inherited at the end six typewritten pages, of which I can't use one word. Great work if you can get it."

The man who had had hold of Hack before, out in the corridor, came in and reached for him again. He started to pull him out of the room, saying:

"Come on, Jerry, Vashvily wants to see you. He wants to get back to Palm Springs."

While the other pulled, Hack held on to the desk, leaning over toward Mumm. He laughed at the name "Vashvily" as one in hysterics.

"You know what Vashvily is?" he asked in confidential tones. "Vashvily is the asbestos curtain between the audience and entertainment. He always starts out to do something new. He thinks he's going to revolutionize the industry, but in the end he crawls back into his little hole. Vashvily is a coward. He has to take ether when he gets a manicure. . . . So long, Mumm, I hope you'll be with us for a long time. 'We have both time and money here in unlimited quantities.' And remember, 'You can see me any time of the night, and when it's important enough, all night.'" Hack imitated Moses Fable expertly, as the other man yanked him out of the room.

The Negro came in with the new towels and the new thermos bottle and clean glasses, and he hummed and gave Mumm a deep, sonorous railroad porter's greeting.

8. Fresh Paint

The faithful Ludlow Mumm was in his office every day. He sat at the desk and he washed his hand and he thought about his work. The fifth day, he had asked his secretary if he could have a typewriter. He said he was unable to dictate. His calendar was blank. He left the door to the corridor slightly open because he felt more a part of the living that way.

At the ringing of the carillon, he went to the cafeteria and ate. Coming back, he found a large new typewriter beside his desk on a small table. He put a piece of paper in it and typed with the index finger of the left hand.

"Now, we can't make her a Negro afraid of ghosts," he heard outside in the hall.

Going to the door, he saw again the insane hospital scene of the man dragging Hack along the corridor.

"We've struck a snag here. One coincidence too many," said Hack. "Vanya will stand for one coincidence in a picture or maybe two, but the third, that's hard. Otherwise, everything is fine."

"Anyway," said the other, "a song goes in here. You know what will happen if he talks in that scene? The audience will tear the seats out of the theater."

"The only way you can get away with it is with a song. Music soothes the savage breast. We have a scene of romance here," said Hack.

"I'm in total agreement," said the other.

"Right. The love song goes in here. I'll fight for that."

They came to the fountain and Hack stopped to drink. Then the writers went on down the hall.

"Mr. Mumm," said the secretary, coming out of her small cubicle, "Mr. Vashvily's secretary is on the phone. She wants to know if it's convenient for you to come up and see him for a few minutes."

"Now?" asked Mumm, and he felt as he hadn't since he got out of school.

"Yes, now," said the secretary. "Mr. Vashvily is leaving to resume his rest in Palm Springs, and he wants to see you before he goes."

Mumm stopped at the drinking fountain outside, although he had the thermos bottle and glass in his office. Then he went into the producer's office.

Vashvily was in back of a partition where he kept a miniature haberdashery establishment. As he talked, he appeared first with a new soft shirt which he had half put on. Then, with a selection of ties, from which he chose the one that went best with his coat. Between his exits and his entrances, he said he just wanted to know how Ludlow Mumm was feeling. Vashvily's secretary packed for him and put papers, including a copy of *Will You Marry Me?* into his portfolio, and Vashvily spoke a few words about how he pictured the heroine. At the end he came out from his shop, felt in all his pockets, and said: "I think I've got everything."

He walked out of the room with Mumm at his side, and said good-by outside the office. A chauffeur carried his bag and danced attendance, running ahead to open the shining chromium door.

For a while Mumm stood in confusion watching the flashes of silver light that the door shot down the corridor as it swung in and out, activated by the chauffeur's energetic push. Then he rolled to the window and watched Vashvily's departure in a black limousine that was as large as a hearse, and finally he went to the fountain, drank, as all nervous writers do, and then into the washroom of the common crew, where he dabbed water at his face and looked into one of the three mirrors on the wall, as if it could tell him why he was here. He thought of all the things he wanted to be told, and the questions he had had ready for Vashvily. He dragged himself back to his office.

He turned the swivel chair and looked out. The gardener below had finished trimming the trees and was oiling his lawn mower. In the sky above was a passenger plane.

The pilot of the plane let down the wing flaps for a landing and then the wheels. Moses Fable, who was in the plane, looked down at his studio as he adjusted his safety belt. The psychic executive made a note to have a talk with Ludlow Mumm as soon as he came on the lot.

At four, Moses Fable knocked and came into the room. He looked at Ludlow Mumm.

"Stay where you are," he said. "Don't get up. Don't let me disturb you. I just thought you might be lonesome, so I came down to have a little talk with you."

"Thank you, Mr. Fable. I wanted to talk to you too," said Mumm. "I feel awful."

Without asking him to show his tongue or feeling his pulse, Moses Fable looked at Mumm with the searching eye of a great and practiced diagnostician who, standing at the foot of the patient's bed, can tell what's wrong with him by just looking at him.

"How are you getting along? How are they treating you?" he asked.

"Oh, everybody is nice to me," said Mumm. "The only thing that bothers me, Mr. Fable—I've come here almost for a week. now and I haven't done anything."

There was nothing that made Fable happier than a man's throwing himself on his mercy. It warmed him all over. It brought, in some cases, tears to his eyes.

"How is the climate affecting you?"

"Oh, it's not the change of air. I love the climate. I sleep well. That is, I slept well until I tried to start to write."

"Well," said Fable, "it takes a while."

"I can't even read here," confessed Mumm.

"That's strange. What do you think it is?"

"I don't know what it is," answered Mumm.

"You dictate?"

"No, I can't dictate. I have to be alone when I write."

"You write in longhand?"

"No, sir, I type."

"Well, sure, it's the hand," said Fable, relieved. "As soon as you get that bandage off, you'll be able to write."

"That isn't it," said Mumm. "I can't even concentrate."

"Let's see, now," said Fable. "Maybe it's the room."

"Maybe," said Mumm.

"Have you tried to write at home? I mean in your hotel here?"

"I've tried everything," replied the hopeless Mumm.

"It's the room all right," said Fable, and walked to the window looking out on the lovely scene.

"When you write for yourself, Mr. Mumm, where do you write? Or, rather, where did you write?" he asked.

"Oh, I had a couple of rooms in New York. In a small hotel."

"And you were able to write there all right?"

"And I was able to write there all right," echoed Mumm.

"I wrote a lot at night," he added.

"What's the name of that hotel?" continued Fable.

"The Hotel Wolff on West Forty-fourth Street."

"You're homesick," said Fable. "Happens often. We had a writer here—great talent—and he got homesick for New York, so I told him to go a couple of hours a day and sit on Stage Eight.

"We were doing a picture about New York then and we had some sets of New York there. A couple of Fifth Avenue buses, a corner of Fifty-seventh street, and a piece of Central Park. He used to go there every day and walk around and sit on a bench and then he would come back feeling better. But we haven't got that set any more. Maybe that would have helped."

He walked slowly to the empty desk and then said:

"I have every confidence, Mr. Mumm, that you will write a great screen play for us, and I will do all in my power to help you.

"We have two things here at Olympia, Mr. Mumm, essential to the making of good pictures. They are Time and Money, and we don't care how much of each we spend to get the results we are after.

"Now, I tell you what you do. Take your hat, Mr. Mumm, and go to Romanoff's, and don't worry; do anything you want, and don't come back here until you hear from me."

With consideration for Mumm's hurt right hand, the kind president of Olympia held out his left, which the shy writer, who was crushed with gratitude, could shake without embarrassment or fumbling.

Mumm left the building reassured and uplifted. He resumed his walks in the hotel's park and he slept well.

A week later, he was summoned back to Olympia by Moses Fable.

"Now, to do a thing like that!" Mumm said, after entering his office.

"I can't believe my eyes," he stammered, and then looked at

Moses Fable and Raoul de Bourggraff, the head of the scenic department, who had brought about the change, and who were waiting for him.

His old furniture from New York had been flown out to Hollywood. A few minor architectural adjustments had been made to change his office into an exact replica of Numbers 604-605 of the Hotel Wolff.

Mumm got up and walked into the bedroom. There was the old wallpaper, the faded velvet drapes. He touched the window sill and felt the grit. Outside was the sooty airshaft.

"Now, wait. Turn on the lights," said Moses Fable as a father does, instructing a child in how to work a new electric train at Christmas time.

He showed him how to make it dark.

"Remember, you told me you worked a lot at night," he said.

The room was in darkness. A dim light shone over the old typewriter that had replaced the new one, and the bad furniture changed from bluish hues to red in the reflection of the electric sign outside the window. In a drawer of the desk were reams of stationery with the crest of the Hotel Wolff.

"How do you like it?" asked Moses Fable.

"I don't know what to say."

"Everything in place?" asked the president.

"Yes," said Mumm, and then glanced at the carpet. A new carpet had been left on the floor.

"All except the carpet," he said. "My New York carpet had a large ink spot on it—it was in the exact center of the room. I used to look at it when I had to concentrate."

"Well, we want you to be happy," said Moses Fable.

He went to the desk, picked up the dirty brass inkstand and, bending slowly to the floor, he emptied it in the center of the new carpet.

"How's that?" he asked.

"That's fine," said Mumm.

"We had to board up the bathroom," said Fable, "on account of the layout."

"Oh, that's all right," said Mumm.

"Anything else?"

"No, I can't think of anything," said Mumm. "It's perfect."

Fable turned to the building superintendent, who had joined the group.

"Keep the windows open and the fans going. Get that smell of fresh paint out of here so that Mr. Mumm can get to work." He stepped to the door. "Now, I'll leave you," said Fable, "and don't be afraid to call me. Anybody here can see me any time during the day and, if it's important enough, even during the night."

Ludlow Mumm stretched himself on the mangy black tufted leather couch, under the map of the world which was pinned on the dirty gray wall, and folded his hands under his head.

Presently he got up and walked out into the lobby. The Negro came toward his door. He stopped his wagon and took from it a towel.

"I'll take that, if you don't mind," said Mumm, and walked down to the common washroom of the cheap writers.

In this cubicle, which was tiled from floor to ceiling and contained three urinals, three wash basins, and three toilets behind swinging doors, he found Hack, who was washing his hands.

"You know what I think of Moses Fable?" asked Ludlow Mumm.

But Hack put his index finger to his lips, and with frightened eyes he turned and pointed with his long white finger at the center toilet behind them.

The bar-type swinging doors of this compartment were closed and only the tips of the shoes of the occupant were visible beneath them.

"Shhhh!" said Hack, and one of the rare kind words ever said about Moses Fable remained unspoken.

"This place is filled with Fable's spies. You have to learn to keep your mouth shut," said Hack, outside, as he ran to his office.

9. *Shop Talk*

Ludlow Mumm whistled as he got into his car the morning after his new-old office had been unveiled. He carefully moved the four freed fingers of his right hand. Only his thumb and wrist were still swathed in light gauze bandages.

The images that passed through his mind as he was driven to work were luminous. He decided that now the time had come. He would sit down at his desk, at last open the covers of *Will You Marry Me?* and, with a pencil in his right hand, begin to mark the margins and underline the passages that he would later discuss with Cassard.

He got to his office and seated himself at his desk. He sent for the story, which the orderly secretary had put away. And, by happy coincidence, precisely at the moment that she came in and put it on the desk the door opened wide and the collaborator was there.

"Bon jour, amigo!" sang Cassard. "I have read in the columns, over my morning coffee, that you insisted on having your hotel rooms flown out here from New York before you would so much as sharpen a pencil. I said to myself, 'Cass-a-a-a-rd, you have misjudged Ludlow Mumm completely. He is a canaille like yourself. You must go over immediately and apologize.'"

He looked around, running to the four walls. He choked himself by pulling at his muffler, and then stopped to shake hands.

"I must confess," he said, "my first impression of you was not too happy. 'Mumm,' I said to myself, 'is like an iron corset. He will be difficult.' Alors, I was mistaken. You have shown the proper spirit, amigo."

He rubbed his hands together.

"Now we can go to work."

As always, he looked for a match.

On the desk were several empty paper match covers that had been in one of the drawers of the old desk. Cassard quickly picked up one after another, opened them, and, finding them empty, threw them on the desk again.

Mumm pointed to a match stand.

"I have a habit of jotting down things on the inside of paper matches," he said. "Those are just notes."

"Ah, good," said Cassard. "You are like a butterfly coming out of a cocoon, amigo. Everything about you has suddenly turned to beautiful color and delightful surprises. I suspected you of pedantry at first, and of long pages of neatly type-written, labored wordage."

He took off his topcoat and then his bib-muffler, and hat, and, putting one leg up on the couch, he pulled down his sock and scratched his hairy calf. A second later he was looking out of the window at the dirty airshaft, with the fierce smile and the liquid nervous sound that accompanied his good moods.

"I was very touched by all this," said Mumm, with a wave of the hand.

"Brilliant," said Cassard, looking at the ancient typewriter. "Have they taken pictures yet?"

"No," said Mumm.

"They will—for the magazines."

"I think Moses Fable is very kind," said Mumm.

"Shall we say smart?" said Cassard.

He looked at Mumm and continued:

"Let me explain, as teacher and friend. Alors, amigo, he moves a few sticks of furniture, and as a result he gets his own name, the title of his newest picture, the name of the star, the director, the leading man, the author, and even the writer, into every newspaper in the land."

He pulled up his shoulder, and continued:

"You have done him a favor. Nobody here would ever have thought of anything so original.

"Now that it is done, amigo, there is no reason to stay here. I suggest that we meet, say, at a restaurant for lunch, and discuss the story over coffee."

He looked again at Mumm, who was silent.

"Or, if you insist on working here, I can manage it."

"Here," said Mumm.

"Well, then, we shall meet here one day, Romanoff's the next. Alors, then, that is decided. What else?"

Mumm offered him a pack of cigarettes. Cassard took one but did not light it. He put the matches in his pocket and the cigarette in his mouth. He went through his hair and then came over to the couch and extended his hand to Mumm again.

Laughing, he said:

"My sincere admiration, amigo. From now on, we shall get on beautifully."

Then he asked: "Have you seen Vashvily?"

"Yes," Mumm replied. "I talked to him."

"Ah," said Cassard. "And what did he say?"

"He said, 'I have a Serena Blandish in mind. Pure, but—you know—plenty sexy. A young girl with great possibilities.'"

"Ah," said Cassard. "Say what you will about Vashvily, he is original. He knows what he wants. Pure girls are his specialty because he is pure himself. What else did he say?"

"He said that this story was very important to him."

"Ah, yes, he has found a pure girl and he will make her a star."

"And he said," continued Mumm, "to remember that she is simple, unsophisticated. She knows nothing of the world."

Mumm lit a match and offered it to Cassard, whose cigarette was frayed at the wet end. Cassard wiped the pieces of tobacco from his lips.

"Do you mind, amigo," he said, "now that we understand each other, if I give you some advice?"

He looked in his pocket for a match and finally found one, and, with a waving motion and too much flame, relit the cigarette.

"Vanya Vashvily makes a fetish of simplicity," he said. "He

thinks we are blasé. Well, we are not. All right, we have had
the best women. We have eaten the best food. And we have
traveled all over the world. All that makes for an appreciation
of simplicity which is the true value of life.

"I do not say that we are not hungry. But our hunger is the
motivation for our work. We live, we love to live, we know
how to live.

"We know the pleasures of money, the pleasures of the
automobile, the pleasures of love, the pleasures of vanity, and
the pleasures of food, drink, and smoking. We know them all.

"Romanoff's, alors, is not the Colony in New York, and the
Colony is not Fouquet's in Paris, but I love it with my tongue
hanging out.

"In short, our principal aim is not to write belles-lettres,
but to procure the money to live in the fashion that makes
us happy. You agree?

"Now, before we start, amigo, let me explain this business
to you. Let us look at it clearly without deluding ourselves.

"It is fine and good and as it should be. That you ask Moses
Fable to fly the furniture from your hotel out here, it is also
as it should be. That you have that big ink spot put on the
carpet so that you can concentrate on it, is as it should be.
And it is as it should be that from now on we come here for
half an hour a day, and amid raucous laughter discuss a scene,
and eventually tell it to the producer, and that each of us
collect three thousand dollars a week for that."

He paused and walked a while.

"But, let me for a moment be serious and reflect.

"These, amigo, are the fat years. They have so much money
here that this is of no consequence to them and particularly
not as far as you are concerned. You could have done nothing
that would so quickly have established your personality, your
special talent, and your disdain for Olympia, as the fashion
in which you have started here.

"In the meantime, let us examine the situation with a
cold eye.

"Down the corridor, where the thousand-a-week writers
are, you will see lettered on a door in smaller letters than

on your door—you will see lettered the name Valerie Sinnot.

"Mrs. Sinnot is old and ugly and nobody wants to sleep with her, and therefore she has lots of time to write. She writes—because nobody loves her—about love, naturally. All day long of love and sleeping. Of course, in words that pass the Hays office, but every day, amigo, every day, as certain as the arrival of the limousine of Moses Fable at eight-thirty at the front door—even more certain than that, every day, amigo, like a prize hen laying her egg, Mrs. Sinnot delivers from ten to twenty pages of script. In years of work that has mounted and mounted. These scripts are bound and put away in the Olympia files, on a special shelf in the script building, in fireproof vaults. And the volume is impressive, I assure you. I have seen it.

"Alors, amigo, the fat years eventually come to an end. I do not say soon, but they come to an end and then, alors, there is a meeting of the executives and a man comes. This man comes from New York and he has a blue pencil and then things become very uncomfortable.

"'Mumm and Cassard,' he asks, 'what have they done?' 'Ah, a charming team,' says Vashvily. 'Have you seen the office flown out from New York and the spot on the carpet?—and you should listen to the conversation, particularly Ludlow Mumm's. What charm! What wit!'

"But this little man from New York, amigo, is selected for his complete immunity to charm and wit, and he will ask:

"'What have they written?'

"And then there is a collection of paper match covers on which you have made several notes, and the large inkspot—and we are crossed off.

"At that moment, Mrs. Sinnot is almost as happy as if somebody had slept with her. And that moment, my dear Mumm, must be anticipated. The moment when Mrs. Sinnot smiles at us as we walk out of this building. The laughter of Mrs. Sinnot is extraordinarily difficult to listen to. You will find it almost impossible to smile back at her.

"I do not ask you to turn yourself into a Balzac and start writing with a coffeepot at your elbow. I only advise you, as a friend, to help me anticipate that moment, to sense it, and to leave before they throw us out.

"You announce that you must write a novel. You must do a profile for the *New Yorker*. A serial for *Redbook*. Or visit a foreign country. The *Saturday Evening Post* is sending you to Peking. Or you must report the resumption of the passion plays in Oberammergau. But you must leave—suddenly. That is understood."

Mumm lay on his couch and looked at the ceiling. He sighed and then he looked at Cassard.

"It is fatal," continued the Frenchman, "to say to your agent, 'My God, they didn't pick up my option.'

"The stopping of those checks, amigo, is like falling off a building. I have suffered this sensation several times. It is like discovering infidelity in your wife. A windy pain in the pit of your stomach. You must be brave then and not try to get a job with another studio, because, for the moment, you are déclassé. You leave, and later you come back. You can always come back, and on better terms. Alors, now you know the worst. Remember, the moment Mrs. Sinnot smiles, we leave."

Cassard saw the copy of *Will You Marry Me?* on the desk.

"Amigo, you don't mind," he said. "I have mislaid my copy."

He took it and said good-by.

Mumm looked out into the corridor. Hack was swallowing pills at the water cooler and washing them down with the aid of the paper cup.

The air-conditioning apparatus hummed. In the old Hotel Wolff desk which he opened for the first time, he found an old unpaid bill from *Cue*.

Ludlow Mumm sat down on his couch and took a pencil from his pocket. He calculated his earnings, deducted taxes and commissions, his expenses, and the amount of the bills he had paid, and he found that there was surprisingly little left.

Shoulder to the Wheel

In which Belinda returns and is suspended, neither in nor out, until the difficult carpentry that is the writing of a shooting script is done.

10. Belinda in Mourning

A table near the front as you enter Romanoff's was usually reserved for Vashvily. He ate there quietly, violating his diet, drinking and smoking against his doctor's orders. And, with the last fork of food, before the coffee came, he usually fell asleep, sitting with his hands folded over his stomach, looking down. People who passed had the impression that he was in deep thought.

As he did in New York, so he came to the restaurants of Hollywood in the company of lovely creatures who breezed into the elegant rooms ahead of him, chin up, shoulders back, lips drawn over white teeth real or capped, and he trotted behind them, sad-eyed, saying nothing, nodding good evening pointing to the settee, and waiting until the girl had slid in and was seated.

He took the six pink pills prescribed for him before meals and arranged the five green ones that he was to take after near the water glass; and then he sat back and studied the menu. After that, he seemed to be listening to the girls' talk. In rare cases, such as when he was with Belinda, he reached inside his vest and advanced the small dial on his hearing aid so that he could hear what they said.

"We start with the wine today, not with cocktails," he said to the head waiter. Today Belinda was with him. "Open it right away."

The head waiter removed the wine and twisted the cork. Vanya lifted a full glass.

"What's all this for?" said Belinda.

"Now, you will stay around, I hope," said Vashvily, "and do as I say."

"Sure," said Belinda.

"You've got a great future," he said. "Everybody is crazy about your test. Moses Fable is crazy about it. We looked all over hell for you. What happened to you?"

"I told you. I got married," said Belinda. "The night you stood me up—remember? The night you said you couldn't come to my wedding."

"That was four months ago. Still married?"

"No, it's all over."

"Good," said Vashvily. "You're in—and the story is turning out great."

"Thanks, Vanya."

"Well, aren't you glad?" asked the producer.

"I'm getting to be afraid of the bright moments," said Belinda. "You know, when I married Joe, it was like God looking down at me and saying: 'Give her everything.'"

"I know," said Vashvily, "and then it's taken away."

They ate. After the food was cleared away, he looked at her and said: "Need any money?"

"No. That too I got. He left me all his money—I'm rich now."

"Oh, I'm very sorry."

"You should never kid anybody. I used to kid Joe about the wild blue yonder—you know the Air Forces hymn—"

"Where did it happen?"

"Oh, in Boonton—a couple of hours from here. Let me tell you about Boonton. Boonton Field is where he was stationed. We went to Boonton right after we got married.

"First of all, it's a town that before the war was nothing. A seventy-five-cent hotel room was fine. You could have a suite for a dollar and a half. Boonton is a town that has nothing. It's not even a suburb. It had a few oil wells, and the flying field turned it into a boom town.

"Well, Joe said that the day the war was over the boys would get together, burn the town, and hang the proprietor of the Hotel Boonton. But when the war is over it will still be

there. I guess that's what makes us different from other people
—we say it but we don't do it. And now, when I think of
that hotel, it's the most beautiful place in the world!

"That hotel, the Boonton, is the place you stay at, if you're
lucky. There are even worse places. The price of the rooms
that have a bath is five dollars a night for a second lieutenant.
I don't know what it is for a captain.

"The bath is a closet with a cement floor and a shower, and
the shower is fixed so it slants—but it slants the wrong way,
so when you take a shower, the water comes into the room.

"They give you only one towel and you put that on the
floor, next to the bath, to soak up the water. There is no rug,
just a bed and a chair, so after you take a shower, you get in
bed to dry. Also, the toilet is in this closet and the shower
aims at it. The toilet is always wet because even when you
don't use it, the shower drips.

"There's a sink in the corner of the bedroom and over that
sink is a light with no shade and a very dim bulb. Another
one hangs up high, in the middle of the room.

"They're very unco-operative about bedside lamps, so Joe
got fancy and went out to buy an extension cord and a nail
and fixed a light so that we could read in bed.

"The extension hangs down low, so you duck when you go
into the room when it's dark; you have to get to the center of
the room and feel for the string to put the light on.

"Everything is nailed down. Mirrors are nailed to the wall.
The writing pad and blotter are nailed to the desk—that's
true—and if you want writing paper, you go to the office. A
little sign over the desk says so. And when you get there, they
give you two sheets of thin paper and one envelope.

"When the guy is there, it isn't so awful. Only when he isn't
there, it is.

"The Boonton is run by the most righteous man in town,
a very proper, fatherly old man who raises his eyebrows at
everything, but for ten bucks he'll sell you a quart of whisky,
and he was always out of cigarettes—except for a buck he had
a couple of packs—and he was always telling you who the
law should get in that town.

"I've never been in Italy, but the lobby of that hotel looks like what I imagine a cheap Italian whorehouse must look like. It's got a great brass chandelier that hangs from a purple ceiling, and all the lights in it are dim, too.

"When we came there first, I thought that maybe the proprietor was a charitable man on the side. The lobby was always filled at night with service men sleeping on the green overstuffed furniture. I found out that he charged them two bucks to sleep on the couch and one buck for a chair.

"But it's not so bad when you're in Boonton with a guy. When you're in love, you'll sleep anywhere and anything is beautiful. When the lights are out, the first week isn't bad. It's a man's world, you think, and very glamorous. In the morning, when he gets up, it's dark and he leaves you in bed. You smile and remember how warm he was and then you drowse, and then you get up and look around and wake up and you see the spots on the wall and the cracks in the ceiling and then you take a shower and then you go down to breakfast.

"The dining room is full of girls like you, and some have children. You get the morning paper and the waitress is very unpleasant. Here, in the middle of California, they bring you canned orange juice. The eggs are gooey and the toast is wet, and when you complain she says, 'Don't you know there's a war on?'

"So you haven't met anybody yet, and you go out and walk around Boonton, which takes ten minutes. You look in the windows and you can't believe people sell things like you see in the stores. For instance, well, the smart dress store of Boonton has stuff that must come out of the May Company basement—and the dummies resemble the people in the town. You know, when I think about it, the dummies always resemble the people of a town, like at Saks Fifth Avenue. And everywhere, you notice, it's exactly the reverse of what you've heard about 'Help the boys.' If you're a civilian, maybe you get half a break, but the uniform just seems to say, 'This is a sucker.'

"You think about what you can do for the guy. You want to make him a captain overnight, so you want to play your cards right. You figure he's got everything he should have, but he's not smart enough to do anything for himself, and you have to watch out and learn the angles.

"You want the commanding officer to notice him and like him, so you look for a real estate office to rent a house so you can entertain a little for him and do some cooking. Well, so they laugh at you. There are lots of houses, they tell you, only they're not for rent. But they'll be glad to sell you a house. There's a charming place twenty miles from town, an acre and a half. It was a garage, but they put air-conditioning into it and made a two-room-and-a-half-and-plumbing apartment out of it. It's only six thousand dollars—only fifteen hundred down.

"You go out and look at it and the place is all you were afraid it was, and you don't want to give them the satisfaction of buying it.

"But you're not bad-looking and you have style, and you get to meet the guys around the base, and there's one who can do something for you. By the gleam in his eye you know what he's anticipating the first time your husband goes on a ferry trip, so you play along. He's the guy in charge of housing, so you finally get a house.

"Well, it's like your hotel room, only four of them—and you have a bathtub and ants. Millions and millions of ants, so that there is nothing like a sloppy housekeeper in Boonton. They keep you busy. After you're through with dinner, you don't sit back and light a cigarette, or have a drink, or make love— you get up and do the dishes right away or the ants come, millions and millions and millions of ants. They eat incredible things in Boonton: not just sugar, but salt and cleaning powder, and nylons, so you keep everything that is valuable, like nylons, in a glass jar in the icebox. And believe me, the girdle you keep in the icebox, and a hat you care about. You put so many things in the icebox, there's hardly any place for food.

"Anyway, now you're settled and you start to do the best you can. And then you start meeting the wives in the Army. That's a great American institution. You could make a big picture out of that chapter alone.

"Well, the way the whole thing happens is like this. At the club you've said 'How do you do.' By now, you're there three weeks and you go out to a buffet where they have dry macaroni and three per cent beer that tastes like stale beer mixed with water.

"You meet Mrs. Wells. There's always a Mrs. Wells, and Mrs. Wells would be the café society gay girl, if there were any café society. She's about thirty-five, and was very, very attractive when she was younger. Her husband is a captain, not a flying captain, but a Special Service officer taking care of entertainment for the men. He was a Hollywood agent before the war. She's the gossip and she knows everything and she knows you first. She has a good wardrobe and most of the young girls try to copy her. She's the leader of the clique whose conversation always begins with: 'God, was I drunk last night!' And the next sentence is: 'Have you heard what happened to so-and-so?'

"And she's terribly nice to you because she doesn't know anything about you yet. So the day after you meet her she calls you up. She says, 'I'll be up near your house.' So you obviously ask her to come in and have lunch.

"You don't know anything about cooking, but you try to whip up something that will impress her. Oh, you devil some eggs, or maybe you stuff a tomato with a can of tuna, or cottage cheese, and you cut carrots carefully so they look like flowers. By the time you're through, you've made a production out of the whole thing.

"Anyway, you know she's the gossip, and you decide to be very clever and tell her in a cagey way everything you want to spread around that could possibly help the guy. But she starts asking about you. She knows all about him already. So you toss in a careless word here and there about your background and your breeding and you try to make it good—any little thing that's glamorous. And you imply that there's a little money, and you tell her about your husband's place on Long Island, and you throw in a few names and she throws names right back at you.

"Well, after that, you roll bandages twice a week and she

tells you who's pregnant. She is the friend of all the girls in town. She always knows first who's pregnant. She's also the friend of all the husbands, but separately; and, of course, she's playing politics for her husband all the time.

"You're trying so hard to be like everybody else. You'll run with the crowd. A girl told me that before the war, Westchester suburban life was like that; the girls got together and bitched and ragged; and during a dance, you got your leg pinched or danced too close together. All that stuff because life was dull. That's what it was like at Boonton—a cheap country club set.

"There was no bigness. There was no interest in the war. They read the papers and listened to the commercials and talked about promotions, and they went to the movies.

"The Army is full of sleeping. It's never sleeping as it should be slept, but indiscriminately, all over the place.

"There are two attitudes about Army wives. Either you love your husband and you worry about his flying because of the danger and you worry about him being sent away without you because of the other women. Or, if you don't love your husband, you know damn well you can have as good a time as he has when he is gone.

"In Boonton, they don't even wait until he's gone. The women usually go into the bars in twos. Well, this is a woman's war at home. You know that. Officers' wives become very rank-conscious and when they chippy, it's usually with a higher grade. The men aren't so particular.

"So he's sent away on temporary duty and you decide to stay true. You don't remember anything like reading or music. Obviously, there is nothing like that in Boonton. If you brought a library, you wouldn't read a book. So, you cook for yourself. . . . And the butchers! They're very war-conscious, too. They don't even slice your bacon. They, too, tell you there's a war on. What that means, nobody here knows. You read about it in *Time* and in the newspaper, but it's as impersonal as it is for civilians. If an Army man has a brother who is over there, so he's over there and maybe it's different, but they say only four out of a hundred actually fight the enemy—so you got that much of war.

"And you turn off the radio and right after dinner you do the dishes on account of the ants I told you about. The rest of the day passes and then you have a choice of three things: You can go to a movie; you can go to bed; or you can get drunk. And you almost always get drunk. Day after day this goes on. The day is monotonous, the night is monotonous.

"No matter what you try to do, it's a messy business; and you get lonesome and somebody calls you and you go out again with the guy that got you the house. But you hate the cheap guys. You hate the cheap chicken. You hate the nasty jokes. You hate the snide suggestions. And so, you go home. . . . And then I got a telegram and it said he was coming back, and everything was all right.

"I was cooking home that night when I came back from the club. They had been talking about a crash, very casually, and it frightened me. They said that the fire was so big you could have roasted wienies at it. That shocked me, but then I thought, they can't go home and cry every time somebody crashes. I never saw a guy cry or even look blue. They just get drunk.

"I was baking potatoes and making a meat loaf and whipping up a chocolate pudding and it was seven-thirty when the doorbell rang. And what you do then, when you run to the door and open it and the chaplain is outside, I don't know. I never got any further. I still feel I'm standing at that door with the chaplain outside. . . ."

Belinda turned to Vashvily. She had never talked about this to anyone. He sat there with hands folded.

The story had been told to the glasses and the table. Vashvily had fallen asleep during the description of the shower stall and the ants.

If anyone else here had heard it, he would have listened and let his eyes range over the room and the faces of the clients and would have occasionally come back to the table with his mind to see if it was ending. Or he would have stood by, the way Moses Fable always listened, leaning forward as if into the wind, with eyes half-closed and an automatic suggestion of melancholy and sympathy in his voice. And here and there, one would have said to himself: "That's a swell ending . . . the little woman at the oven—she runs to the door—the door opens—there's the chaplain . . ." And he would have seen it on the screen with Pat O'Brien with a cross on his collar. But what happens to the one who lived it, the sad tale itself—nobody wants to hear that. The story of Belinda and Joe remained untold as far as Hollywood was concerned.

"Anything else?" asked the waiter.

"No, thank you," said Belinda on Vashvily's behalf. "Here," she said to Vashvily, "take your pills, sweetie."

Vashvily opened his mouth automatically and searched for the glass of water.

The head waiter signed the check, added the tip, and said that the car was outside.

"Come on, Vanya," said Belinda, pulling his sleeve. "Let's go."

The head waiter held open the inner door and the coatroom girl held the outer.

Outside, in a chauffeur's cap, Nightwine, the latest and most perfect of Vashvily's servants, stood by the limousine waiting with the lap robe neatly laid over his left arm. He saluted and opened the door.

Vashvily, as always, proceeded with the muscular stiffness of the sleepwalker from his seat at the table to the seat in the car.

At the château, Belinda held the door open and Vanya wandered through the hall and sank into his cataleptic state in the right-hand corner of the huge sofa.

"Look behind you, Belinda," he said, and pointed with his thumb. "See anything new?"

"Oh, an Utrillo."

"Very good," said Vashvily.

"You're getting a new frame for it—I hope."

"Now, you'll stay around, I hope, and do as I say," said Vashvily. "You've got a great future ahead of you."

She took his hand.

"Sure," she said.

Nightwine lit the fire and brought a tray with glasses, brandy, and a box of cigars.

"You can go to bed now, Nightwine," said the producer, as the servant lit the cigar.

Vashvily stared into the fire. He drank brandy and his face became blue.

"A great future," he repeated. "They're all crazy about your test, and we looked all over hell for you."

The cigar wobbled uncertainly. Presently she took it out of his mouth. He was asleep again.

"I'll put you to bed now," she said, and, as she had done at the hotel in New York, she got him to stand up and steered him to his room.

He sat on his bed, half asleep again, and she pulled his clothes off and helped him into his pajama top. His eyes still closed, he stuck his nude legs under the covers, and she folded his hands over the satin coverlet and kissed him as if he were a child.

She walked out on the terrace and looked up at the small clouds that moved past the moon.

"You up there," she said. "I and six other people I know could run this world a whole lot better."

She walked past Vashvily, who lay in his bed like a dead man. She closed the door carefully, and passing the astonished butler, who stood in the hall and offered an obligatory good night, she walked to the guest room and went to bed.

11. *Will You Marry Me?*

"It is remarkable testimony to the gullibility and regimentation of man," Cassard observed to himself as he was driving along Wilshire Boulevard, "that in this place, which is gutted with flowers, in which the rarest of them grow like weeds, a florist can make a living and that flowers are sold at outrageous prices on virtually every street corner."

He stopped the car at the flower shop that he regularly patronized. He wandered about among various kinds of roses, looked into the icebox at the assorted orchids, and read the price tags, which are higher than in Paris, London, or New York.

Mr. Nircassio, the florist, smiled at him. He was busy with the order of Jerome Hack.

"And a small corsage," said Hack.

"Something with orchids—say twenty dollars?" asked the florist, as he wrote down the order.

"No—anything—five is enough."

"Excuse me, but I'm ashamed to send out an order like that with your card on it, Mr. Hack."

"It's all right," said the writer of Olympia, "it's for my mother."

"Well," said the florist, "let me make up something nice myself."

"Don't put yourself out," said the writer. "I particularly want you to send something very simple, you understand."

The confused florist stood looking after him as he left the shop.

A young man with long white fingers, who sat on a stool among half-finished wreaths and heaps of wired flowers which he was preparing for a bridal bouquet, tossed his head and said, "I always knew Hack was a jerk. He had a standing order for a bunch of lilies every day to the star of *Mary Magdalene* while they shot that picture—he was in love with her—and sends five dollars worth of flowers to his own mother!"

"Mr. Cassard?" asked the florist, turning to Maurice.

"Three dozen of these roses," said Maurice, and waved a small card at plain red roses. He handed the card to the florist and gave him Belinda's address.

The florist read the card and looked up and seemed even more confused than by Hack's order.

"Anything wrong?" said Mr. Nircassio. "Not like your kind of card at all, Monsieur Cassard."

Cassard had written: "Welcome back to Hollywood" on the card.

"Are you sure you want to send that?" said the florist with concern—the way one tries to keep someone from mailing a letter written in haste and anger.

"Since it seems to bother you so much, Mr. Nircassio," said Cassard, "I shall explain to you why I wrote this. I am sending it because when she gets it, and reads it, she will know that I could have thought up something a good deal more original to say, if I cared a good God damn whether or not she was back. Good-by!"

"Why do people want to be mean like that?" said Mr. Nircassio to his assistant, as he took the plain red roses out of the tub.

It was late afternoon. Cassard pulled on his gloves as he waited for the light at Sunset, preparing to turn right. Just then he saw Belinda in her car, driving past on Sunset in the opposite direction. He changed his plans, turned left after the light changed, and followed her. It was Thursday. He followed her down to the road which he called the "pretty" way—the old road he had driven on the first day he had met her, out of Beverly Hills, past the Bel Air estates, past the Botanical Garden Park sign, down to the ocean. There she turned left and drove along Malibu Road.

"Ah, alors," he said to himself, "in memory of our first meeting, she is driving to the old place."

The golden moment in which a hopeless, lonesome man discovers himself truly loved was Maurice Cassard's. Belinda's car turned under the arch of the Santa Monica pier and went down the ramp. He was sorry he had sent the small roses and written the limp message.

He did not altogether trust his fortune. "Perhaps she is meeting someone else," he said, and put on the brakes.

He waited. She turned and took her car into the parking place. He waited again until she had entered the small café, and then he parked his car next to hers, and walked around for some minutes. He looked in through the windows of the restaurant, and finally entered. He stood at the bar next to one of the chained stools for a few seconds.

Belinda was sitting under the red paper lamp, at the same small table where they had talked—and the waitress was removing the second place. She was alone. The bartender was mixing one of the bad Martinis.

On the way to the washroom, he went past her and then turned around, as if he had come by strange coincidence.

"Belinda," he said, stopping suddenly. "Do you mind?" And he sat down at the edge of the bench opposite hers. She was sad, and the light of sincerity came forward in his eyes. He took her hands, and with reproach in his voice, he said:

"I must hear from people who have seen you in restaurants that you are back. I have to read about you in the papers. I am told at the studio that you are going to start working. I have to run into you by accident—you do not call me, you do not write—I must think that you have forgotten me—and then, I find you here."

"Sit down," she said.

He began the struggle with his muffler. He tore off his coat and dragged it to a hanger, without taking his eyes off her.

"It's meaningful and fate," he said, "that, of all places, we meet here. I will slap your face now, and then I will go out the door, and come in again and embrace you. Now I have to go and wash my hands." He was gone.

"Ah," he said as he came back, "it is the same as it was before—everything is the same—only so much better."

The waitress served a fried abalone steak to Belinda, and Cassard ordered the same.

"Now I can go to work," he said, rubbing his hands. "I have been thinking every day of you, but I could accomplish nothing. Now it will be easy. I shall write the story in a day. I shall tailor it for you. It will be the greatest love story ever done out here."

He moved his silverware to the other side of the table and sat next to her. "Eat, before it gets cold," he said.

Belinda cut a piece of the breaded cutlet and speared two French fries on her fork.

"We can dispense with words—now," said Cassard, "and speak like adults. The fact that you came here tonight, Belinda, is my cue. I must declare myself now. Now that you are back, I will never let you go again."

The breaded abalone steak was tough. Belinda looked at him and swallowed, and looked at him again. She wanted to say something. He placed his hand over hers and said, "Don't speak. We shall have between us the perfect relationship possible between a man and woman of intellect, the historic pattern of greatest love."

She said, "Look, Maurice—"

"Let me finish, darling. Let me say what I must say," begged Cassard. "I know exactly what you are going to tell me. You are going to say: 'But you are married.'"

"That's one of the reasons," said Belinda.

"Yes," said Cassard, "but I have an understanding with my wife, and if you want it, Adrienne will give me permission in writing."

"I would never have anything to do with a married man. I never have," said Belinda.

"But that's very old-fashioned," said Cassard, "and anyway, it's different out here. We are people of talent."

"I don't care. It's a code with me. I live by a code. If I had a man and I was his woman and somebody came around, I'd go out and cut her throat. Seriously, I don't want anybody to do it to me, and I don't want to do it to anybody else."

"Even if your happiness depended on it and you knew the other woman wouldn't care?"

"There is no such thing. It's just convenient for you to think that she doesn't care."

"I can guarantee you—"

"Well, then, you must be very unhappily married, Maurice, and I feel sorry for you," said Belinda.

"Ah, that, at least, is something," said Cassard. He pushed away his own plate, which the waitress had just put down.

"Go on and eat," said Belinda.

"I am not hungry. Until this is settled one way or the other—" said Cassard. He ordered another Martini. "You are wrong, Belinda. I beg of you to consider . . . It would work out perfectly. I have a good home life. We are the best of friends. We love our children. I am a very lucky man."

"I shouldn't say so, Maurice. I don't think anybody who talks like that is happy."

"But how do you know?"

"I've been happily married."

"Ah . . . forgive me, Belinda—I know—but allow me to say that you were married a few months and under most unusual circumstances, in the presence of danger and uncertainty, and in a romantic setting. I believe you when you say you were happy. It is easy to be happy that way. But, if it had gone on . . . once the war ended, it would have been a different story. Wait for the seventh year, then you'll find out . . . then you will know how it is in marriage. And never mind how you, yourself, feel about it. The important thing is how it is with the man."

"You mean about infidelity?"

"Well, that is one of those horrible and arbitrary American terms. If you want to call it that, yes, about infidelity."

"Well, whatever you call it, if it happened to me, I'd know the moment it happened, and I'd walk out."

"Ah, but perhaps you wouldn't know."

"Yes. With a guy like you I'd expect it to happen the first day, and that's why I'd never marry you."

"The Americans, of course, are all saints—they never cheat!"

"I didn't say they were all saints. But I'm psychic. I wouldn't be taken for a fool, or lied to. I could tell when it happened. I'd know the moment he came into the house that he'd been with somebody else. No matter how well he lied."

"Very interesting. What would you resent more, Belinda, that he had done it, or that he lied to you?"

"I wouldn't bother asking myself that. I'd just walk out. That's all."

"No you wouldn't, Belinda. Let us suppose he gets home, he's in time for dinner, he's sinned in the afternoon and he's been careful about the smell of her perfume, and the lipstick, and he comes in and says, 'Good evening, darling,' and then you look at him and say, 'I'm psychic, Joe. You have been infidel to me.' You say that and pack your bag and go?"

Belinda shrugged her shoulders.

"Especially if you loved him?"

"If I were sure he'd been with another woman, I'd go."

"Ah, but you would tell yourself that you are mistaken."

"I would never deceive myself."

"Now, let's look at the other side," said Maurice, and ordered more drinks. "Let us assume that you married a man, not an actor, not a producer, but a writer. And you have two children—one is a boy, and the other is a girl—and everything is fine until you are thirty. You're still very attractive and now, suddenly, you meet a man and you know that it would be wonderful and new and exciting and also, you have, with that fine instinct of yours, suspected that your husband cheats on you occasionally, but you have not done anything about it. Now, you admit to yourself for the first time that he has cheated, because that gives you license to do the same. *Will* you do the same?"

"No," said Belinda sharply.

"And why not?" asked Cassard.

"I'll tell you why not: because if he was nice, that new man you arc talking about, and it went on for a while, I would become involved, and then what would happen to the children and my life and the home? Because, if I did it, I'd go all the way—and that would be disastrous."

"You see," said Cassard, "how unfair the whole thing is. I just wanted to show you how fortunate it is for us that I am the one who is married and has the children, because I can handle the situation—a man always can. A woman can't.

"My wife is contemplating going to Paris as soon as possible. She asks me every day, 'Do you think it soon will be possible for me to go to Paris?'" He picked up his knife and fork and began cutting his lukewarm food. He ate in haste and wiped his mouth with the paper napkin after he had cleared the plate. He held the paper napkin, which was soggy from the mopping, for a while, and then, rolling it into a ball, threw it under the table. Belinda looked out of the window, watching the lights along the pier.

"Belinda," he said, "will you marry me—would you marry me, if I were free?"

"No," she said, without looking at him. "Never."

"Well," he said, "that's simple enough."

"They played that the last time we were here," said Belinda, as the juke box started a tune. "It's something Vanya wrote," she added.

"I didn't know he wrote music," said Cassard.

"Yes, he does—under another name."

"That is very interesting."

"He writes his own lyrics," said Belinda. "Listen!"

"I'd like to hear that melody once more," said Cassard, and stretched to get at his trouser pocket.

He brought forth a nickel, but in his jerky, nervous movements the coin escaped and rolled off the table and fell to the floor. Cassard got another coin and ran to the machine. He punched the button and played the song once more.

"Not bad," he said, "for juke box music. Perhaps, with an orchestra, it would be very nice."

He seemed uneasy.

"Why don't you pick up that nickel?" asked Belinda. "I know it's bothering you."

"Ah," he said, "leave it where it is. The cleaning woman will find it." But he looked under the table.

"Go ahead, pick it up," said Belinda.

Cassard got down on the floor. The nickel had rolled to the wall, behind the post that supported the bench on which Belinda sat.

"A knife, please," said Cassard, and finally dislodged the coin. He combed his hair with his fingers. After he got up, he said, "What were we talking about?"

"Vashvily," said Belinda.

"Ah, yes, Vashvily. He writes songs under another name. That's very interesting. Under what name does he write?"

"Under the name of Danny Spellbinder."

"Extraordinary man!" said Cassard. "Would you marry him?"

"I like Vanya a lot—but, anyway, he doesn't want to marry anybody."

"What kind of a man would you marry at this stage, Belinda? Who would you fall in love with? Maybe I can play the part."

"You know what I would fall in love with if I could, Maurice?"

"No, tell me."

"A doctor. Yes, I would fall in love with a doctor, I think."

"You've gone Hollywood," said Cassard. "I have always wanted to know why every actress sooner or later wants to marry a doctor. Please explain that to me if you can."

"I can tell you. Because when I am acting and I come home with my troubles and I am tired and talk about my script and the fights with the producer and the director and I feel that all that is terribly important, he would say to me, 'All right, I've listened to you. Now, you just shut up and listen to me. Tomorrow I have to do three major operations and I will most probably be called out during the night to see that little girl that has some terrible disease.'"

"Spinal meningitis," offered Cassard.

"All right," said Belinda. "Be funny—spinal meningitis. And that would be so much more important than my small worries that it would be wonderful."

"How unimaginative women are!" said Cassard. "Because he works in a hospital, because he wears rubber gloves and smells of ether, no matter how dull he is—and God knows doctors can be dull—still he is wonderful. And do you mean because a man is a doctor he is different from other men? And as far as cheating goes, I can tell you some stories. Have you ever listened to doctors talk?"

Cassard paused and looked at her. "Oh, how stupid of me," he said, "I should have known."

"What are you talking about?"

"You are going to a doctor."

"Yes—what about it?"

"I suppose he is a very good-looking doctor."

"Yes," said Belinda. "Very nice."

"He examines you regularly, I suppose."

"Yes," said Belinda. "Every Thursday at three."

"And the first thing he asks you is to take your clothes off."

"Unfortunately he is only for the nose and throat."

"Shall we go?" asked Cassard, and asked for the bill, making a gesture, as if signing his name in air, to the waitress.

"You better leave your car here," said Belinda. "I'll take you. You can't drive."

"The similarity between that last time we were here and now is astonishing," said Cassard, staggering out into the dark.

A plane flew overhead and she looked up. He studied her face. She followed the plane until it was out of sight, and in that time it dawned on Cassard that she had come on account of the flying lieutenant.

"I forgot that you met him here," he said. "Forgive me—I am sorry. I thought it was because of me that you came, Belinda. I have forced myself on you. I promise you that this will not happen again."

He held his arms away from himself and the open coat flapped in the wind around his thin legs. "I will give you advice, Belinda. I will give you my time. I shall widen your horizon. Like the doctor, I shall come any time you call me. I will do everything I can for you, and I ask in return only that you give me your friendship."

"That you will always have," said Belinda.

"Of the other," he said, "we shall never talk again."

He sat bundled in his corner and Belinda started her car.

"Have you ever known anybody who was completely happy?" she asked, along San Vicente Boulevard.

"I once knew a Catholic priest who believed in God and who was happy. And an Englishwoman who was the governess of my children and who had never grown up herself. She was sixty and thin and ugly and she hopped around playing ball and kept a pet turtle. I think, to be happy, you must be able to forget yourself completely. You must be without self. I haven't got it. You haven't got it. Do you know an actor who has it, or an actress? I can't think of a single actress. As for actors, I think, perhaps, Red Skelton has it. He must be a good man."

"Why did you pick him?"

"I was listening to him on the radio before, while I was following you. And a man who plays the fool as he does and makes the noises he makes—the way he says, 'Bless his little heart' when he imitates that little boy—must be pure in heart; and it jumps 'over into the audience like a spark. They know it's real. And that is also why you will be a great actress. They know immediately who is real, out in the audience."

"Who else? Is Vashvily happy?"

"Yes, I think he's happy. I think he's a good man."

"Talk to me more about that," said Belinda. "I like you when you talk that way. What about married people?"

"Oh, I have known a family of idiots once . . . I am not being funny. . . . They were very happy. Otherwise, I don't know of any."

They came near the night clubs and the name Mocambo shone in magenta letters on the side of the large white building in which it is housed.

"The last time, you left me in the car and I almost froze to death," said Cassard. "This time I want to go in. I'll just sit with you and you can think about Joe," he said. "I'll listen to the music. Emil Coleman is playing."

A boy took the car away and they went into the flamingo-covered lobby. It was early. The room was empty and the tropical birds that are in a huge glass cage along the ceiling sat on the branches, their heads buried in plumage, waiting for the music to start.

Belinda and Cassard sat down on one of the small banquettes along the wall. Belinda looked straight ahead and patted his hand. Cassard ordered a bottle of champagne, knowing it was thirty-five dollars, and he felt almost as good as the priest who believed in God.

Three people came into the night club.

"In this village of glass houses," said Cassard to himself, "you can't get away from anybody."

He told Belinda about Jerome Hack, the writer at Olympia,

who had ordered the cheap corsage of one orchid that morning at the flower shop.

Hack stood at the door and spoke to the head waiter, who snapped his fingers and then indicated a table in front of the one at which Cassard and Belinda were sitting.

With Hack were an old man and an old woman. The woman had refused to leave her fur coat in the checkroom. The old man looked back with bewilderment at the sofa in the lobby, which was upholstered in artificial grass.

"Bon soir, Monsieur Hack," said the captain, and steered the group to their table.

Cassard saw that the cheap corsage was pinned to the woman's fur coat. The table was decorated with a small vase of flowers, and a bottle of champagne stood in a cooler at the side.

One of the waiters handed a menu to the woman, but the head waiter took it away from her again and said:

"Everything is already ordered."

"You didn't have to go to all that trouble, Jerry," said the old man, unfolding his napkin.

"Oh, it's all right, Pop," said Hack. "Look at the birds. Ever seen anything like that?"

The woman had just finished surveying the room with a mixture of curiosity and disdain. She now turned and looked at the birds.

"What is the name of this place?" she asked in a flat, hard voice.

"Mocambo," said Hack. "It's the leading night club here."

She turned and stared through her pince-nez at Belinda and Cassard, and then, with suspicion, at the column painted like a candy stick that stands in the center of the room.

The orchestra tuned up.

"My God," said the woman. "I left the room key in the door." She clasped and unclasped her hands again, and looked in her bag and then at the old man.

"That's all right, Ma," he said.

She turned to look once more at Belinda and Cassard. The lighting fixtures were reflected again in her rimless pince-nez.

The soft putty chin and cheeks, the crepy throat, all shone rosy in the dim light.

The waiter put a large silver dish down before her.

She asked shrilly, and again with suspicion, "What's that?"

"Cracked crab," answered the young man. "Try it. You'll like it."

She looked at the food for a while and then picked up the very small fork.

"There's Gary Cooper and his wife," said Hack, as the music began. "Hello, Coop," he said, as the star passed.

The woman turned her head too late. The soft bulges all swayed. She used her arm as a wedge against the table to turn her body and stopped eating to wait until Cooper came by again. Then she bestowed a smile on him.

The old man at the table smiled too. He had a kind face, honest and good, deeply lined, loose skin draped over a strong, good frame, and large ears. He smiled shyly. He looked for the kind of fork that his wife was using, and then he looked at Hack and smiled again gratefully, and ate. He looked up whenever the writer pointed out celebrities to him.

The waiter opened Cassard's wine and poured it. The orchestra played and the birds had come to life. The smaller fluttered in group flights from one end of the room to the other; the larger stretched their wings and hopped about, or hung upside down from limbs, looking into the room and screeching; and some beat out the rhythm of the music with extended, furiously colored wings.

"Look at Emil Coleman," said Cassard to Belinda. "You know what he reminds me of? When I was a child my father brought me home a toy from a Paris exhibition—a Russian Easter egg, made of wood, and on the outside of it a man was painted, and when you twisted it, it came apart; but inside it was another egg, just like the one on the outside— and then another and another. That's what Coleman reminds me of—the man painted on the outside and the inside of that wooden Russian Easter egg. I can listen to his music forever."

"I like it, too. I just love to sit here quietly."

"We like everybody tonight," said Cassard.

Belinda lifted her glass.

"To friendship!" he said.

"To our friendship," she said. "Let me buy the next bottle."

The waiter filled the glasses again and Belinda asked him for paper and pencil. She sent the name of Vanya Vashvily's song to Coleman, who nodded and started it as soon as he was through with the conga he had been playing.

Cassard looked again at the three people in front of him.

The head waiter came and bent down. "How was the chicken, madame?" he asked the old woman.

She was taken by surprise. Her mouth hardened into a small, bitter line, and she placed her round arms away from herself, with all fingers separated, as if she had eaten with her hands and the fingers were covered with fat, and she looked at him and said something, and then looked away, embarrassed, out over the dance floor. After the head waiter was gone, she looked after him and then folded her hands.

Hack sat at the side of the table, his chair turned toward the floor and his legs crossed, and he drummed with his fork on the table. The old man looked at the people that passed by and smiled at everybody.

After the Danny Spellbinder melody, the dancing stopped and a waiter wound his way past the tables, holding a silver platter high above his head. As he brought it down, a small birthday cake appeared on it, and as he came to Hack's table, the orchestra played "Happy Birthday to You."

The maître d'hôtel handed a knife to the woman. "Will madame cut the cake?" he said.

Everyone in the room looked at her. She raised the knife and cut the cake. People smiled and applauded, and now the old man was embarrassed, but he looked up and when he saw the people smile, he smiled and bowed, and somebody handed him a cigar.

The old man had not touched the champagne; the woman had slowly sipped it all evening long. He bent over to Hack, who called the waiter and ordered a rye and ginger ale for him.

The music started again and the birds flew. Cassard watched the table and Belinda was far away.

So it went on until the crowd thinned and the music stopped. Hack had ordered more drinks for the old man and now he sat close to him. He held the man's hand in his and he looked at him.

"Do you love me?" he asked. "Have you loved me as much as if I'd been your own son?"

"Sure, Jerry," said the old man.

"You know I loved you, Pop, a hundred times more than if you'd been my own father."

"We loved you as much as if you'd been our own," said the woman.

Then none of them said anything. The young man looked at the man he called Pop and the old man looked sadly at the birds.

"Well," said Hack, "I just wanted to ask you—you know, like man to man, across the table— You loved me? That's the truth, isn't it?"

"Sure, it's the truth," said the old man.

The woman pulled the new gray fur coat up over her shoulders and she looked at her wrist watch.

"Hey—pssst, garçon, l'addition," said Hack.

The bill came. Hack turned it upside down without looking at it. On the back, the total for food and drink was added with a red pencil. Hack took a golden pencil and signed the bill and reached into his coat for his wallet.

The woman watched all this sharply and with petulance, and her hand moved, opening and closing into a fist and tapping on the table.

Hack put a five-dollar bill on the plate for the waiter. He took another five-dollar bill from a packet of money and then picked out a twenty-dollar bill and folded it small.

The captain bowed and called the head waiter. The waiter said, "Merci, Monsieur Hack," and the head waiter said, "Merci, Monsieur Hack."

The woman's mouth was compressed and her eyes hard with enmity.

"Remember, Pop," said Hack, "when we had the stationery and candy up in Fordham? Remember how glad we were when somebody came in and bought a stick of chewing gum?"

The old man looked down sadly and nodded.

"Try and get some now," said the woman.

"I'll get you all you want. I can get anything," said Hack sharply, for the first time looking at her and turning his chair to face her. "What was it you used to say to me?"

"I used to say you were a show-off," said the woman.

"And what else did you used to say to me?" He leaned toward her. She had a new wrist watch that was on a black elastic cord. He pulled it away from her arm, half an inch or so, and let it snap back into her soft flesh.

"Jerry," said the old man, and he lifted the empty split bottle of ginger ale, holding it upside down and waving it like a miniature club, threateningly, and with a sad smile.

"Jerry, don't talk to your Mom that way."

They got up.

"You shouldn't spend so much money on us," said the old man. "The hotel room, and the flowers, and the coat for Mom, and this dinner—"

"Forget it," said Hack as he straightened out the smart double-breasted jacket of his gray suit. "Forget it, Pop. I'll charge it up to entertaining."

They filed out.

"This is the saddest, most heartbreaking, and lonesomest place in the whole wide world," said Cassard.

"I know," said Belinda, who had been silently crying.

12. Story Conference

During the ten days he waited for the return of the script of *Will You Marry Me?* that Cassard had taken along on his last visit, Ludlow Mumm occupied himself with strategy. The map on the wall over his couch was marked with variously colored flags. Cassard came in as Mumm stood before his map, rearranging the Eastern Front.

"I hate to predict things," said Mumm, "but I am ready to write what I am about to say on a piece of paper and stick it in an envelope with the date and write on the outside 'To be opened in June' and bet a hundred dollars that I am right."

"I'll take it," said Cassard. "Write it down, amigo."

Mumm sat down at his desk and put a piece of paper in the typewriter.

Moses Fable, who was passing in the corridor outside, was about to knock and open the door to see how the boys were getting along; but, hearing their voices and the typewriter going, he only stopped with a quiet smile and then went on down the hall, where he saw Hack and another man laughing hysterically. Fable walked very quietly and his face darkened.

Hack was in high good humor. He tossed his head and laughed in staccato outbursts, and the corridor was filled with resounding shrill echoes as if someone were bowling with tumblers and throwing glasses against the walls. Moses Fable was about to say something when he heard Hack say:

"So, at that same story conference yesterday, Fable says: 'Gentlemen,' he said, 'I had a dream last night. I was at a banquet in Berlin and Goering was seated at my left and Hitler at my right—and, strangely enough, they did not seem as bad as I expected them to be. Hitler didn't scream. Also, the food was excellent, and the wines very good. And toward the end of the dinner, Hitler leaned toward me and said in perfect English: "I'd give anything to know what they really think about me out there in Hollywood." Well, I was about to tell him—when I awoke—'

"Can you beat that?" said Hack. "The son-of-a-bitch, he wouldn't dream that he was a little Jew boy kicked around by the Gestapo. No, it's got to be a banquet!"

"I suppose Fable dreams in technicolor," said the other.

"Of course, and his dreams all gross several million. They're holding the last one over at the Olympia Palace in New York. Sometimes, you know, I feel like setting fire to this God-damn joint, only it's Fable that owns the match. . . . What was that?" asked Hack suddenly, looking around with frightened eyes. It was the soft, pneumatic thud with which the doors of the private elevator into which Moses Fable had stepped closed in back of them.

"One hundred dollars, alors," said Cassard, "on the ending of the war by June." He shook hands with Mumm, and the envelope was given to the secretary to put in the safe downstairs.

"Will we still be here in June?" asked Mumm.

Cassard engaged again in his liquid smile. "Alors, amigo, I hope you predict the war correctly. I will make another bet: I predict that we shall still be here after Hitler and Mussolini are dead."

"I'll take that," said Mumm.

"Oh—the script!" said Cassard. "I forgot to bring the story. It is in a drawer of my night table."

"This came yesterday from the front office," said Mumm, and handed a folder to Cassard. On the folder was written *Will You Marry Me?*

"Aha!" said Cassard, and opened it. He looked at the first sheet. "You see the initials, amigo. This is a treatment that Mrs. Sinnot has written, alors—the lady with the fatal smile at the end of the corridor. This is one day's work." He dropped the script as if it were a filthy bandage. "I have often come to the conclusion that I don't like anything done by women in the way of art or literature," said Cassard, and he stretched out on the couch.

"Well," said Mumm, "that is hardly fair. You assign them to the kitchen, to children—yes, and to church."

"I think in that department the Germans were right," said Cassard. "Women have no talent for anything else."

"You know, of course," said Mumm, "that most of Utrillo's pictures were painted by his mother."

"I grant you exceptions, of course," said Cassard. "What I mean is—we have been sent this treatment of the story that has been written by Mrs. Sinnot, down the hall. Now, what I meant is—" Cassard got up and went to the desk. He sat down and pulled up his trousers. He moved the chair forward to the typewriter and put a sheet of yellow paper in the machine.

"Now, when a man writes, he sits like that—that's all right—you can write that way. But when a woman writes—" He showed how a woman sits at a typewriter. "She has her legs spread, and what does she do with that?" He indicated a large bosom. "She has to make a detour around them. How can anybody write like that—write at all, with that in the way?"

"You told me," said Mumm, "that she writes twenty pages a day. . . ."

Cassard picked up the *Saturday Review of Literature.* "Look," he said. "All right: most of the books are written by women. Now, why should I read *Forever Is Now?* What does she know about eternity? All right, you'll say *Gone with the Wind.* All right . . . good luck. Or, you say Pearl Buck. Good luck again. You can have them. I never read a word written by a woman. I have no intention of reading this. You can, if you want to—I don't even want to talk about it." He picked the manuscript from the desk, where he had dropped it, and threw it on the floor.

He began an agitated run to the four walls. "Alors," he said bitterly, "from now on, amigo, it is going to be gruesome. It's like one of the experiments that vivisectionists make with animals when they nail dogs on boards, and let the blood of one run through the other. And we, amigo, are the dogs.

"Vanya Vashvily did not send you this to read. He is beginning to stir now, and to prod. You do not understand the strange way in which producers behave. Vanya handed you this script to indicate that he would like to see what we had written. After all, we are here now how long?"

"Three months," said Mumm.

"And he expects something. Ah," said Cassard, lifting a hand, and picking up the phone with the other, "allow me, amigo. Here is where I take over." He asked for Vanya Vashvily's secretary, and putting his hand over the mouthpiece of the telephone he said, "It is high time that we see the Idiot at the end of the corridor and tell him a story.

"Could you set up a conference—a story conference—for tomorrow, Alice darling?" he asked the secretary.

"I had an idea," said Mumm, who was still lying on the couch. "Now, you can throw it out if you don't like it. But you know that refugee that is on the same train when they get to Paris?"

"What train?" asked Cassard.

"The train on which they come back to Paris at the beginning . . ."

"Alors," said Cassard, "forgive me if I seem confused. I must make a confession, amigo, and I count upon your strictest confidence. In my spare time, I have been working on a play, a play that I intend to produce in New York with the help of a good friend . . . you have met her—Betsy Allbright . . . and this has kept me busy. I shall, I am afraid, have to put that aside now. Tell me about the train."

"Well, on that train on which they arrive at the gare Saint-Lazare in Paris is a refugee, and he appears to be poor, but he's rich, and that is not very clear, so I thought that his fortune could consist of a priceless set of stamps which he carries under his toupee—"

"Very good," said Cassard. "Where did you read about that refugee?"

"In this treatment that Mrs. Sinnot made—"

"Ah, but, amigo," said Cassard, "we are not going to use any of that."

"Tomorrow at eleven," said Vashvily's secretary on the phone.

"Very well, darling," sang Cassard. "Tell him that we shall be there."

"You see how easy it is," he said to Mumm. "We shall see the Idiot tomorrow at eleven. Now I have to make a few calls, and I shall meet you here tomorrow at nine-thirty sharp, and we shall go over what we will tell him. I shall have read the story by then, at home, and I promise you, he will be very happy. Leave everything to me." He pulled out a piece of paper on which he had written several telephone numbers, and called them.

Mumm was hot, but Cassard, who had taken off neither topcoat nor muffler, was cool and smiling into the telephone. He was talking to the lawyer who, he said, "makes the best divorces in Hollywood."

13. *At the Gare Saint-Lazare*

As he brushed his teeth the next morning at seven, Ludlow Mumm stopped the brush inside his cheeks several times and looked into the mirror. What he saw there was terrifying.

At nine he was sitting in his office, and at nine-thirty he was facing the corridor. He finally opened the door to Hack's office. Hack sat bent over his typewriter. It seemed as if he had half-digested it. It had sunk away into his chest and stomach, and his arms and legs, like the tentacles of a sea animal, were wrapped around the metal table. He sat that way when he thought.

"Hello, Hack," said Mumm. He talked for a while about the difficulties of writing.

"Listen, kid," said Hack. "Don't let it get you. We're only making pictures here. No matter what you say about Fable, you must admit he has no pretensions about art. He manufactures entertainment, like hats or shoes.

"Now, from a writing standpoint, when it gets up on the screen it will either be good or it will be bad, and the chances are that it will make more money if it's bad. So what have you got to worry about? Let me tell you. In the beginning, I tried to write—you know—write nice words. That was awful. Then, one night, I had a revelation: 'Write—just write!' I said to myself. And since then, I have no trouble. The thing is to get it over with."

Mumm went back to his office. He walked the corridor and looked out the front of the building and watched the cars and the people coming in. It was eleven.

Ten minutes past eleven, Cassard, with his muffler trailing behind him, came running down the corridor. He came into the office to the sound of the telephone ringing and jumped to pick it up.

"We are ready," he said, and, putting his hat away and unwrapping himself, he disappeared to wash his hands.

He came back, and, as if they were going for a walk in the park, he hooked his arm into Mumm's and said quietly, "Alors, amigo. Come. We are going to see the Idiot at the end of the corridor now and tell him a story." He stopped at the fountain for a drink and wiped his mouth.

Mumm hoped to hear a quick résumé of what they were going to tell Vanya Vashvily, but Cassard spoke of other things.

"I would have been here sooner," he said, "but I had to take my wife and the children to the train. Adrienne is taking up residence in Reno. She has never been happy here. She detests California. She is going back to France as soon as possible. It is all amiable. Only, the traffic signals in this town are abominable. Some are hidden in palms, others are only one foot off the ground. I went through a red light and I received

a ticket. Alors, and because I did not have my driver's license
with me, there was a lot of explaining to do, and that is the
cause of the delay, amigo."

They came to the end of the corridor. At the door of the
producer's reception room, Cassard stopped. "Alors," he said,
"we are going to see Vashvily now and tell him a story. You
don't mind, amigo, if I do the talking?"

"Oh, no," said Mumm, with the look of the drowning going
out of his eyes.

"Alors," said Cassard, pulling down his coat. "Let's go in."

Vanya Vashvily sat in his beautifully furnished inner office
at a desk covered with knickknacks and souvenirs. The walls
of his office were cluttered with the photographs of actresses
and actors. He was on the telephone.

"Try it six degrees darker," he said. "And let those clouds
move faster—and fix those leaves. They have to blow. You've
got to know that a storm is coming up. I want a Brontë mood
in that . . ."

Belinda walked into the room in a traveling costume. Vashvily hung up the phone and looked at her with the pained
expression and the half-closed eyes. He was very critical. He
looked at her a while and then asked her to turn around.

"Which was the hat that we liked yesterday?" he asked.

"That's the one she's wearing," said the young man who
had come in with her. "That's the one you liked yesterday."

"Well," said Vashvily, "it's the hair then. Christ! look at
those bangs in front. Now do something about that. Do you
think they'd let a girl like her have a hairdress with bangs on
like that, for God's sake?"

"Well," said the young man, "you're not going in for realism,
I hope!"

"Alice," said Vashvily to the small box on his desk, "get
me make-up."

"You liked the curls and the bangs fine the last time,"
pouted the young man. "We took all of yesterday's shots with
the bangs."

"The bangs are out," said Vashvily, angrily, to the box. "I

want her hair pulled straight back—and look at the back of her head while you're at it. Those God-damn Hollywood hairdos! Get rid of that too—"

"But, Vanya," said the young man, "we'll have to shoot that other scene too, if you do that."

"All right, so we shoot that other scene again too, and if it isn't right the second time, we'll shoot it again, and again, until I get what I want. I want this test to be right."

He got up and turned in another direction, leaning into the wind again with the pained expression.

"Is that all?" asked the young man.

Vashvily was away in thought, and the young man said, "Come on," and took Belinda out of the room.

Vashvily sat down at the wide desk and put some papers in order. The box made its buzzing sound. "Show them in," he said to the instrument, "and see that nobody disturbs us for the next half hour. Call me only if it's very important—or Mr. Fable. And Alice, bring me a new battery."

The girl came in and handed a new battery to Vashvily, which he put into his hearing aid, and then Mumm came in and stopped. Cassard walked to the desk and greeted the producer and he began the search for the cigarette, which ended when Vashvily pushed a large crystal cigarette-box in his direction and opened it. In it were all the well-known brands, and Cassard stuck one in his mouth and then began looking for the match.

"Ah," said Cassard, stopping in the center of his pacing area.

"Just a minute," said Vashvily.

He got up and adjusted the Venetian blinds so that the disturbing light which fell in strips on the desk and the carpet changed to a mellow, all-over color. The producer went back to his leather chair, lit himself a cigar, and sank back. The pained expression left his face.

"Now," he said.

"Who is going to tell the story?" said Cassard to Mumm, who had made himself comfortable in the corner of a leather couch.

"You," answered Mumm frantically.

"Very well," said Cassard.

"Alors," he said, destroying the first cigarette in the producer's ash tray. "One evening, Vanya, a few days ago, I went to a restaurant with an exquisite creature—"

"I thought you were going to tell me a story," said the producer.

"One moment, Vanya, I am coming to that," said Cassard.

"Go on," said the producer, and folded his hands again and sat back. "I'm listening."

"As I was saying, on that evening that I went to a restaurant with this exquisite creature, and the orchestra was playing, I said to her: Listen to what they are playing. What a superb melody!—It was a ballad, good music, yet easy for the ear. To be brief, I asked the waiter to go to the chef d'orchestre and find out what the tune was, which he did, and he came back and said that it was a piece by Danny Spellbinder. Alors, I said, that is the kind of music we want for our picture. Well, this girl says to me: Don't you know who Danny Spellbinder is? And I did not know, and she tells me that it is you who write music and lyrics under that name."

"What was the name of the piece they played?" asked Vashvily.

"It went something like this," said Cassard, and sang, "La la tralalala—"

"That was 'Love Is Lost,' " said Vashvily.

"Well, the name does not matter," said Cassard. "But there and then, I said to myself that no one but you should write the score for *Will You Marry Me?*"

"Well," said Vashvily. He pointed his lips slowly as if he were starting to whistle softly, or preparing to kiss his sister. He looked for a moment like a bear cub drinking out of a bottle, and then he put on a chaste look, and cast his eyes down, and said with a quiet smile of satisfaction, "This is kind of funny, boys, you saying that—to tell you the honest truth, I've been thinking about that myself."

He pulled a sheet of yellow foolscap from under other papers on his desk. "I've put something down here called 'Au Revoir at the Gare Saint-Lazare.' Have you got a little time?" he asked. "Come into my other office, boys."

They all went into another room and Vashvily sat down at the Steinway in the adjoining office and ran over the keys. "I bet that's what they played," he said.

"Ah, yes," said Cassard, "that is it."

"I know that piece," said Mumm.

"He wrote it," said Cassard proudly, pointing to Vashvily.

"This is one of my tunes," said Vashvily, and played another popular song. "And this." He struck the martial cords of a patriotic melody and from then on lost himself in musical memories, playing the entire repertoire of Danny Spellbinder.

"Coming back to the picture," he said, getting up and shuffling the sheet music on the piano, "I'll play our theme song now that runs through the whole show. That's a number you'll like. It's the song called 'Au Revoir at the Gare Saint-Lazare.'"

He looked through the many compositions on top of the piano. "Sets the mood, the mood of utter lonesomeness, that I'm after in this scene," he said, looking for the melody. "It's going to help you visualize this scene as you listen to it.

"We're in a railroad station, you know, Maurice—the gare Saint-Lazare—and we hear the whistle of the incoming train, a French train whistle. We have a recording of it and also a real French locomotive with a whistle. The whistle sounds like a small dog being stepped on somewhere down the street, and then we hear the choo-choo sound. We use all these sounds in the orchestration.

"Now, out of the train comes a former music hall star—looks like a bum—he's been in a concentration camp . . . this is after the war is over, of course. . . . He's back from internment, but nobody knows him until he leans up against a clock and begins to sing 'Au Revoir at the Gare Saint-Lazare.'" Vashvily sang the words and played the music.

"The moment he sings they recognize him. Then comes a chorus of French redcaps that gather around him. Well, I'm working on that now. It's not finished yet, but I've got the railroad station. Come in here, boys." They went to the third room of Vashvily's offices and there was the model of the gare Saint-Lazare.

"They're building it over on Stage Eight," he said. "Go look at it. It'll make you homesick, Maurice. . . . Well, boys," said the producer, and put one of his arms on a shoulder of each, "you're doing a great job. Keep on going just the way you are. Let's set up another conference soon."

He walked part way down the corridor with them, and said, "So long, boys."

They went to Stage Eight. Mumm craned his neck and looked up at the smoky glass ceiling. The station was copied exactly, to the inches of the telephone pay station slots and the miles of tracks that ran into the distance. And two locomotives, not paste, but steel, with French railroad cars, stood beside the platforms.

Painters high up lettered advertising signs for Chocolat Meunier, Fernet Branca, and the Galeries Lafayette. Others sprayed coal dust and the brown dirt of engine smoke on those that were finished. And the clock with the four faces that stands at the entrance to the trains was being installed.

The perfect detail went to the German signs that were left, on which appropriate comments were written in French.

Raoul de Bourggraff stood in the waiting room with his architects.

There was a French taxi at the door.

The realism of the scene had hit Mumm so powerfully that his hand had suddenly begun to ache again from the forgotten train accident, and he was surprised that the taxi they had taken stopped at Romanoff's rather than Prunier's.

After they had ordered lunch, Mumm said: "Vashvily is in love with that railroad station. We must be sure to get that into the script."

"Amigo," said Cassard to Mumm, "the trains from Germany arrive at the gare de l'Est—not the gare Saint-Lazare. But keep your mouth shut, it'll throw all of Vashvily's rhymes out of focus if we tell him."

14. *Nightwine*

A week later Cassard and Mumm sat again in Vanya Vashvily's reception room.

"I don't know what can be the matter," said the producer's secretary. "This has never happened before. He's always been on time every day or called—and he told me especially to make sure that you'd be here for this conference."

The secretary tried Vashvily's house again. "Nightwine, his butler, usually answers the phone, but the butler isn't there either."

"Everybody has trouble with servants these days. My wife took the maid with her when she left," said Cassard. "The house is a mess. It is almost impossible to find anyone to work for you."

"Well," said the secretary, "I guess we'll have to call the conference off."

"Mr. Vashvily's house is on my way. I shall stop in and see if anything is wrong," said Cassard, and left.

Cassard drove to the producer's home and rang the bell. After waiting a while for someone to open the door, he walked around the house and went in through the servants' entrance.

As Vashvily felt himself tapped on the shoulder, he turned and looked at Cassard. "Oh," he said, "I just called, but it was too late. You had already left. I overslept and then I couldn't find anything.

"Something awful has happened. Nightwine's left me. I couldn't find my pants this morning—the whole house is upset. He was the best man I ever had. I'll never get anybody like that again: didn't drink, never asked for a raise, never com-

plained, never took a day off—and when I told him there'd
be ten for dinner instead of four, he just smiled—"

"But why did he leave?"

"On account of Belinda," said Vashvily sadly. "He doesn't
like women in the house." Vashvily put a pot of coffee on the
stove.

"What did Belinda do to him?"

"Oh, nothing. He just got the wrong ideas about her—you
know, about the relationship between her and me. He was a
very proper man.

"This is a big house . . . I have two guest rooms and bath.
She lives in the farthest down the hall. She had to get a place
to stay—they throw you out of every hotel after five days.
Christ, everybody in town knows I'm like a father to her. So
yesterday, he pushed her elbow off the table as he was serving breakfast. 'I thought you just came here to eat, miss, and
not to sleep,' he said. 'It's either me or she,' he said to me, so
I tried to explain things to him, but he left."

"With servants as hard to get as they are now, you should
have known better," said Cassard. "Where is he?"

"He's gone to a hotel," said Vashvily sadly. "He gave me
his number. I've got it somewhere." He reached in the pockets
of his dressing gown and brought forth a crumpled pink
slip. "Here's the number," he said.

"I wish you'd call him. You're a man of easy words,
Maurice. Tell him that it's not the way he thinks it is. Explain
things to him. I'm sure the old fool is sitting in his hotel
room and that he'd be glad to come back. Now, do that for
me, will you?"

"I'll see what I can do," said Cassard. Without touching the
coffee, he ran out of the house and drove to the nearest public
telephone, where he dialed the number.

"How would you like to come and work for me?" said
Cassard. "I know why you left Mr. Vashvily's house. You don't
have to be afraid of anything like that happening in my home,
Nightwine."

"I'm awfully glad, sir, to hear that, sir," said Nightwine.

He arrived at the Cassard ménage on Chrysanthemum

Drive early the next day. He took his baggage from the taxi only after a thorough inspection of the premises and after having interviewed his new employer at length.

Of the house he said, "It's been neglected, sir," and of Cassard he said, "You've been neglected, sir—badly neglected, sir."

Cassard rubbed his hands as the perfect servant carried his luggage into the house.

Nightwine was a model of controlled efficiency. He ordered over the phone. He kept records. He directed a cleaning woman that had come to scrub, while he himself warmed the house with a thousand new comforts. He never passed without a smile. He asked Cassard brief questions about the temperature at which he liked his bath, the amount of vermouth in his Martini, his preferences in whisky, tea, and coffee.

The windows began to shine and the carpets were straightened. While all that was done under his direction, he himself lit the fire with one hand while he straightened a lamp shade with the other. He left the room briefly to return with a small cabinet in which he kept his recipes.

"What would you like for dinner, sir?" he asked.

"I leave that entirely to you."

"Do you expect anyone tonight, sir? How many will there be for dinner?"

"I don't entertain much," said Cassard.

"What a pity, sir," said the butler. "I just love to see a well-set table and a lot of people around it."

"Later, perhaps," said Cassard. He went out into his garden, where he walked, in moments of content and good fortune, on a path made of large slabs of blue stone, shaded by eucalyptus trees.

Nightwine, dressed now in a striped waistcoat with black satin sleeves and a valet's apron, came out of the house carrying a broom, with which he removed the leaves from the walk. He announced that a Martini awaited the master in the living room.

Dressed in a new change of clothes, by candlelight, the butler served dinner off newly polished silver. Cassard felt sorry for Vashvily and he gloated in anticipation of many happy evenings at home. He said a few words of praise to Nightwine, but the butler stopped him short.

"Allow me to get started properly, sir," he pleaded. "When everything has the proper Nightwine touch, sir—then, sir, I hope to be complimented."

Later that night, Cassard, contented as Vashvily once had been, sat with hands folded, looking into his fire. Nightwine placed a tray with Scotch and soda at his side. He poured a finger and a half of liquor into the glass and filled it to the brim, exactly the way Cassard liked it.

"I've had a look at your car, sir," said the servant. "The hood is covered with fine scratches, sir."

"That's the cat," said Cassard.

"We'll fix that," answered Nightwine. "We had that problem, sir, when I was in the service of the late Maharajah of Kashgar, sir. Mind if I tell you about that, sir?"

"Not at all," said the writer, who always felt melancholy and in need of companionship at that hour. He folded his arms and leaned back in the wing chair. The perfect butler lit a new cigarette for him and, standing so as not to obstruct the view of the cheery fire, he began:

"The Maharajah of Kashgar, my late master, preferred American butlers to English. He thoroughly disliked the idea of the British, sir, but he realized, sir, that the British were necessary. The Maharajah often said to me in his vivid words, which I remember clearly to this day—he said: 'Nightwine, things would not be so good for us were it not for the English being here. The warlike northern tribes would come down, and there would not be a virgin or a rupee left from Peshawar to Bombay, for they would go through the soft, non-fighting Hindus, the followers of Gandhi, like a red-hot knife through butter.'"

"Very interesting," said Cassard. "But you started to say something about the cats."

"Ah, yes, sir," said Nightwine. "I got off the track, sir. The cats—I took care of them. Cats, sir, are highly esteemed in India. We had three of them, named Kitty Cat, Pussy Cat, and Mike, and what pets they were . . . and all over the place, leaving their hair on furniture—everywhere.

"Now the evenings in India, sir, are quite as cool as they are here, and the cats loved to sleep on the warm hood of the Maharajah's car when he got back to the palace, and they left scratches all over the hood of that fine car. Well, sir, I got some hot India pepper and put it in a pepper shaker, and, tying a napkin around my face, covering my nose, I went out to the garage and sprinkled the hood of the Daimler with pepper, doing a very thorough job of it. Kept them away, sir—for good."

"That was very clever," said Cassard.

"Not altogether clever," observed Nightwine. "You see, sir, during the day, India is hot as blazes, and the next day the Maharajah went out driving and he opened the vent in front of the car and some of the pepper had got in there and the current blew it into the car and into the face of the Maharajah. He lost control and ran smack into one of his white elephants."

"I always wondered," said Cassard drowsily, "whether there really was such a thing as a white elephant."

"Oh, yes, sir. Certainly, sir. Everybody who is anybody has them in India."

"What for?" asked the writer.

"Oh, just to show that you can afford them."

"What are they good for?"

"Oh, you just have them stand in front of your house—one on each side, or as many as you can afford."

"Well," said Cassard, with a great deal of effort, "that was very interesting." He made a move to get out of his chair.

"Allow me to help you," said Nightwine, and pulled him up. He walked a foot and a half behind the writer on the way up to the master bedroom.

"Of course, sir," he said, "I wouldn't use that pepper on the cats again without first making sure that the vent was closed air-tight, you know."

"I hope so," said Cassard, and walked into his bedroom. The butler stayed outside and, raising his voice, he said:

"Things happen like that with cars. All kinds of things can

happen with cars, but cars are not so bad. The real trouble starts when you go in for boats. What can happen to you with boats is nobody's business. Now, cars, sir, even the costliest, come in one size, and there's a limit to what you have to pay for a car. But you take boats—you start out with a sixty-foot cruiser, sir, and you end up with a seagoing yacht.

"I traveled a good deal with the Maharajah. Now, sir, once we were halfway up the Kiel Canal on a vessel of fourteen thousand gross tons, Diesel-powered, when the Maharanee discovered that a string of her favorite pearls was missing. That was, sir, before I had reformed, sir."

Cassard staggered out of his bathroom. He went to his bed and climbed into it. The butler picked up his clothes and continued without further encouragement:

"I worked for the Maharajah and the favorite wife he had taken along. We were staying in London. The lady had more jewelry than I ever hoped to lay hands on. I could have amassed a fortune there, but one has principles after all. The job was more of a cover-up, sir. You see, my position was most convenient, sir. I was the head of a gang of thieves, and I got the layout of the houses to which my master was invited and so on . . .

"Ah, sir, how surprised they were—the men from Scotland Yard—when they came one day to pick me up and found, sir, that my hairbrushes were of solid gold and much better than those of the Maharajah. The inspector, sir, was beside himself when he went through my wardrobe—my suits, my overcoats, my silken dressing gowns. But he was most surprised and speechless when he discovered that I had a 'gentleman's gentleman's gentleman.' A man of my own, mind you, who came through the servant's entrance to valet me; who pressed my things and kept everything shipshape—'You'll have a hard time in lock-up,' joked the inspector."

Cassard tossed in his bed. He began to envy Vanya Vashvily the gadget with which he could detach himself and escape the world of sound. "Did you go to jail?" he asked, hoping that the announcement of the sentence would end the ordeal.

"Two years I got, sir," answered Nightwine. "Two years and eighteen strokes of the cat."

"You don't have to tell me the whole story now," said Cassard.

"Two years and eighteen strokes of the cat!" cried the butler. "You asked, sir, whether I had been in jail, but the important thing is—Was I reformed? Ask me that!"

The writer turned his face to the wall and mumbled, "All right, Nightwine, were you reformed?"

"Certainly, sir, I am thoroughly reformed, sir. The lashes of the cat did it. That is what reforms, sir. You see, sir, you are never told when you will get them. That's the awful part of it. The two years, sir, that's nothing; but the cat, sir—Has anyone told you about the cat, sir?"

"No," groaned Cassard.

"Well, then, I'll give you a good description of that cat. I'll never forget it. The cat has eight thongs and they are of leather, and into each, three knots are tied. Three times eight is twenty-four. That's twenty-four knots, sir. And when she's tied up in knots like that, sir, she's soaked. They soak her in oil, sir, and then she gets tight and hard, sir, like wire, sir, like barbed wire."

"Sounds terrible," said Cassard. "Good night, Nightwine."

"Well, sir," continued Nightwine, "they came for me on the second day and took me out. They make you remove your blouse and then they tie you to the post. The arms are drawn upward and then the man with the lash, a brute big enough to swing it, measures the distance and first swishes it at your back gently to see that he lays all the strands across it, with the knots so that they hit the muscles on your back, right and left and at the center near the spine, and then the doctor listens to your heart. No, excuse me, sir, he does that before, and the brute, who is proud of his work, steps back, takes a good, strong stance and raises himself on his toes, and you have the first crack. Then he swishes again, and it comes once more—and then the third one. The doctor then fixes up the cuts and you're free to go.

"Well, after that, and it's bloody awful, sir, I laid down and cried and I said, 'If they'd let you out now, Nightwine, you would never do anything like it again—never, not if you lived a hundred years.' I was completely reformed, sir, but that was after the first three lashes and I had two years less two days to go, and I had fifteen more of the cat coming. The awful thing is that only while you heal can you be sure that they're not taking you out again. In fact, the two years passed so quickly because day and night I was afraid they'd come for me again—and it comes with awful rapidity. It was the middle of October when they came the second time to lash me. It was early morning. I remember it as if it happened yesterday."

Cassard lay helpless on his bed with his hands folded behind his head, his mouth and eyes open like a fish on land. The butler continued until at last he came to the last lashing and to the day of his discharge from the institution. The writer again said good night to him.

The untiring servant said: "But, sir, I have not told you why I was lashed. Sir, that is the most important part of the whole story. It was on account of the 'gentleman's gentleman's gentleman.' The men who arrested me, sir, didn't look like police at all. My man mistook them for my accomplices. He came into the room, sir, and said, 'Your gun, sir, I forgot to put it in your pocket, sir,' and he hands me the bloody gun on a tray, if you please. And that made the whole thing so dreadful because, in England, only armed robbery gets the lash. Without the gun, sir, I should have got off with two years and no pain, sir."

"Well, good night," said Cassard. "You've certainly got a story there."

Nightwine was electrified by these words. "You really think so, sir?" he said. "Allow me to get it for you—it's all properly typed, the story of my life—it's a great story, a finished script." Before the writer could say anything, he was out of the room.

Cassard stared at the ceiling. His predicament became clear to him. "How do I get rid of him?" he said to himself.

"Here it is," said Nightwine as he came breathlessly into the room, handing Cassard a script on which, neatly pasted, was a label that read: *The Cat—Screen Play by Arthur Nightwine.*

"I like the title," said the writer.

"I like the way you open a script, sir," commented Nightwine. "Some people, you know, sir, break open a script. They bend back the covers like this and like that, and they break the back of it. The same with books. They break the back of a book. People who break the back of a book will do anything."

The butler went and turned out two lamps that stood on a dressing table. The room was in darkness. He came close to Cassard and reached over his head to adjust the miniature spotlight by which Cassard worked at night.

Fear added itself to the clammy feelings of the writer. He was glad that he had opened the script carefully.

"How stupid of me," he said to himself. "It's the oldest plot device in the world—the perfect butler who turns out to be a murderer. And what a perfect name—'Nightwine.'"

"I can read only when I am alone," said Cassard.

Nightwine walked backward to the door. He kept looking at Cassard. He reached for the door knob and opened the door. He looked at Cassard as long as he was able to, while slowly closing the door from the outside. He released the crystal door knob from outside, gradually, so that it turned a while after the door was closed and so that the metal click of the latch was never heard.

Cassard pulled out the drawer of the night table and looked for his gun. The gun had been under the script of *Will You Marry Me?*. He pulled out the script and everything else that was in the drawer and put it all on the top of his night table—but the gun was gone. Just as he was going to move to the other side of the bed, where the telephone stood on the other night table, he looked up and saw with a sickening sensation that Nightwine was standing a few feet away from him.

"I came back, sir, to tell you how glad I am about the upset, sir, at the house of Mr. Vashvily," said the butler. "If it hadn't been for that, sir, I wouldn't have come here."

Cassard licked his dry lips.

"Working for Mr. Vashvily, sir, was like working for a ghost—one never could talk to him."

"What did you do with my gun?" asked Cassard.

"The gun?" said Nightwine. "I put it in a safe place, sir."

"Where did you put it?"

"You see, sir, if you found yourself in sudden danger in the presence of an assassin, sir, naturally the first thing you would do, sir, is to reach into the drawer of that night table there, and the moment you did that, sir, you'd be done for—you'd be shot before you ever had a chance to use the gun, sir."

"What did you do with my gun?" asked Cassard.

"I put it where it is safe, sir. I have it in my pocket, sir." He came close and said: "You don't think I am without talent, sir, do you?" He pointed to the script.

"I am sure you have talent," said Cassard.

"Then, read," said Nightwine, and he sat down on a chair in the dark part of the room.

Cassard, damp with sweat and now wide awake, kept his eyes on him.

"I won't let anybody disturb you until you're through, sir," said the butler. "Read."

The helpless writer reached toward his night table, but in the confusion he picked up the wrong manuscript. And that is how Maurice Cassard, at long last, read the story of *Will You Marry Me?* in one sitting and with rapt attention.

15. *The Rich Uncle*

"Most of what is written about this place is not true," said Ludlow Mumm. He lay on the couch reading a Chicago paper which he had picked up in the commissary. "Look. Here is an article that states that every week three hundred young girls disappear in Hollywood. I wonder what happens to them?"

"I know what happens to them. They are lured here by the false promises of men like Vashvily who are the procurers for people like Moses Fable," Cassard said, looking out of the window.

Below, Moses Fable walked out of the building toward the stages that stand like huge cement warehouses in a row. Out of one of the stages poured an army of young girls, all in white graduation costumes. They advanced like the foam of breaking waves toward the somber hulk of Moses Fable and then parted, smiling at him and saying sweetly, "Oh, hello, Mr. Fable," "How do you do, Mr. Fable," "Good afternoon, Mr. Fable." He nodded back with dignity and smiled benevolently and walked on through the chorus of the religious picture. The mother superior nodded to Moses Fable, the priest nodded respectfully, the sacristan and the bell-ringer nodded.

"Which one of those little ones will report to him this afternoon?" asked Cassard. "Come, Mumm, get up and watch that horror. Look at that lewd form. Poor little girls! None of you are safe from his advances. Look at him. There the foul lecher walks through the flowers in white graduation dresses—especially nervous-making with their black stockings and chaste panties. And all the others on the various stages with braided hair and titian hair and long hair and waved hair—in dresses of silk, satin, velvet, and homespun. Oh, what a field for a dog like him to bury his bones! All of them whores, waiting for a nod from him. In bare shoulders, without the need of brassieres or girdles, smelling of every perfume and also stinking, if he wants them that way. And trotting to him, jumping, running, diving for him—in tanks, in bathtubs, with only bubbles to cover them, lying on couches, in bed, on the grass, on the sand, astride horses, in all shades of skin and eyes—all of them combed and brushed with meticulous care—all of them obedient and grateful, nodding, bowing, and smiling at anybody from an assistant director on up—and all these blossoms in the Olympia garden are forever opening their lovely petals and leaning toward the sun—that is, Moses Fable."

"What has Moses Fable done to you?" asked Mumm.

"Nothing," said Cassard. "But it is a civic duty to show up a dolt, an old goat and libertine.

"This unhappy man whose idea of joy is to be Moses Fable . . . Ah, now he's stopping to talk to Mrs. Sinnot. He's complimenting her on the twenty pages she has written this morning. Now he's walking past Stage Eight and looking at the gare Saint-Lazare, and he's talking to Raoul de Bourggraff. He's most probably telling him that the cesspool in the new house he built himself in Palm Springs is not big enough. Now a brace of hounds from the Baskerville set. The hound and his stand-in hound are barking at him. Alors, don't you know any better? 'Bad dog,' says the man, and slaps them, and now they smell Moses Fable's pants—ah, *now* they know who it is! Now, alors, comes the elephant from the set of *Carnival in Bombay*—Very nice! The mahout leans down and makes several deep bows. He'd like to use his rusty elephant hook instead, Monsieur Fable, and push it you know where. And the elephant lifts his trunk. He's got some confetti in his nose and blows it into the air, and he nods, now, to Moses Fable. He nods deeply. He has a long memory, that elephant. He remembers that this same story he's in was once before sold to Moses Fable under the title of *Week End in Calcutta*, and before that it was known as *A Tale of Two Cities*. Now the elephant is waltzing off and Moses Fable exchanges a false smile with one of his executives who picks confetti off his boss's shoulder—'Thank you'—and now he disappears into the gymnasium to have a steam bath, a massage, an alcohol rub-down —all on Olympia time. . . . Good-by, Mr. Fable. I wish I were that masseur for just ten minutes!"

"What time do we see Vashvily?" asked Mumm.

Cassard turned from the window. "We have a conference at four."

"What are we going to tell him?" asked Mumm.

"We are going to tell him that tomorrow is Saturday," said Cassard.

Moses Fable was undressed and resting in a darkened room after his steam bath and massage. Here he had lain a month ago after the masseur had slapped and pounded him, tossed his baggy figure about, and made him groan. At that time he had been disturbed in mind as in body. It had been time for love again in Moses Fable's life. He fell in love about once a year and it always ended disastrously.

The masseur had pulled his toes and covered him up in a dark room, and there Moses Fable had busied himself with the words in which he would manifest his feelings.

He had got up and dressed and then walked to Stage Nine and straight into the cone of powerful light in which Belinda sat, on a trunk, in a traveling costume, and in the new hair-do and hat that Vashvily had decreed for her.

The director of the test had stepped aside respectfully and Moses Fable had advanced to the small platform on which Belinda was being photographed. He had held out his hand to her, and with all the light shining on him he looked like a monstrous half-wit standing in a dank cellar as he mumbled:

"I hope they treat you right here, miss. I want you to know that I'm behind you all the time. Now, I'm up there"—he pointed to his office—"ten hours every day, and any time you want to see me, you know where you can find me."

It was a Japanese ceremony. After he had spoken, he turned and left.

That was how it always started. It was followed by an invitation to dinner, issued by his private secretary—a painful dinner that usually took place at an obscure Italian restaurant. Then came elaborate gifts of flowers and a week end at his place in the country, where the girl was properly chaperoned. And about then he was in love, and entertained the idea of asking the girl to marry him. He always wanted to marry them. He frowned at other arrangements. At this stage he allowed himself to be seen with the girl of his desire in the popular places, and was photographed with her, and the pictures and the story got into the papers. Then the sons and daughters of Moses Fable got together and called the one man who had power over him, and who, up to now, had always been able to put a sudden stop to his nephew's romances, his Uncle Adam in New York. Adam Fable then deserted his department store and came flying to the rescue. Now he had been summoned again.

Adam Fable was an upright citizen, a good man. He was bigger, heavier, and rounder than his nephew Moses. Ordinarily his face shone with benevolence. He was the high-blood-pressure type of executive. His opinions were positive on all subjects. When he talked, he jabbed with both fists as if boxing, handing out short uppercuts and keeping his elbows close to his sides. With the tough gestures went a hoarse voice. He was a married man with a large family and great deference for respectable womanhood, and he was the sworn enemy of irregularities in business, in private life, and particularly in relations with women. In the presence of a woman he found it difficult to talk, for the language of this moral man was interlaced with obscenities.

When he was in Hollywood, he lived at the house of Moses Fable. He appeared at the pool early in the morning, wrapped in a huge Turkish bath towel which was draped about his middle. His heavy white arms hung out over the top of this toga. Out from under it stuck his feet, which he kept in high laced black shoes. He also wore black socks held up with garters. This mixture of Roman senator and half-dressed man was given the executive accent by sharp pince-nez and a bunch of papers and telegrams which he carried in his hand, and by the same purple veins and exploded capillaries that covered the cheeks and nose of Moses Fable.

He never went into the water, enjoying only its reflection, sitting at the side of the pool on a modern metal chair in the shade of a large umbrella. There, he lectured to the lovelorn nephew.

Moses Fable had sat with him quietly, dressed in a bathing suit, for several hours while Adam had lectured to him, and then he had slowly and thoughtfully walked along the side of the pool back to his house.

"Now you think that over—what I told you," Adam shouted after him.

Moses Fable slammed the door of his house, and went on from there to the studio and then to the masseur. Meanwhile Vashvily came down the garden path.

"Hello," said Vashvily to Adam Fable. "When did you get here?"

"Well, hell, I just got off the plane yesterday," Adam Fable began. He brought both fists up and the color rose to his face. "And, Christ, where do I go? I go right away to see Moses. It's eleven A.M. and you know when he lets me go? Two the next morning! So I say to him: 'You know why I'm here?' 'Yes,' he says, 'I know.'—The poor bastard! He has nobody to confide in. He's full of bad news, all of which I have read and seen in the God-damn papers. So he pours out his heart and he tells me he wants to marry the dame and I say, 'Well, what do you want to do that for?' So he keeps on talking. You wouldn't believe what that poor son-of-a-bitch has been through. Well, I argue with him but I see his mind is made up, so I talk to him for a while—the way he wants me to talk—about family—about his family. I told him what he had done for the bastards. 'Look where they are today, all on account of you. Why, they wouldn't have got anywhere by their own efforts—Irma, she'd be slicing salami at a schtickel-for-a-nickel joint on the East Side of New York, if it hadn't been for you.' So he agreed. 'You shouldn't do anything for anybody,' he said.

"So he said that he was going to dinner with them. They had all ganged up on him again. He looked as if he was going to cry. 'Here I am!' he said. 'Look at me! Every day at the office before anybody else. I close the joint six days a week— and now, because I want to live like everybody else, and get a little happiness out of life, they all jump on me. On Sunday I lock myself in and play pinochle. Now is that a life? I ask you?' The tears were in his eyes. 'Now,' he said, 'I'm getting old, and I'm going to live my life from now on. I don't care what they say. I don't tell them how to lead their lives. But

I've got to go to Irma's. I'll hear plenty.' He's got the courage of eight lions, that guy, to go to Irma's when they're all together. So there is that poor son-of-a-bitch that everybody envies!

" 'I'd like to live like Wildgans,' he said, 'just a couple of years!' Can you imagine anybody envying an agent? But the poor sucker, he's taking the worst rooking anybody ever had. That dame is no good. I hear she runs around with a lot of the boys. You know, when a dame has a fish like that on the hook, she can write a hell of a ticket.

"Assuming for a moment that he goes through with it and divorces the old woman. All right, say the dame waits a year. For Christ's sake, you know he can't marry her for a year after the divorce is granted. Okay, she waits for a year and they are married. You know about community property out here . . . well, there won't be much else that's going to interest her. He's an old man, she's a young and beautiful woman. So that's a terrible thing . . .

"Now if she changes her mind after he has divorced the old woman—a year is a long time, anything can happen—well, he'll cut a fine figure then. And if everything is the way he wants it, he's in a worse mess, because six months after, he'll see something else he wants. What the hell are you going to do with a dame like that after you have had her a couple of weeks? What are you going to talk about? What can you tell her? What can she tell you? Where can you go with her? Catastrophe! That's what it is. I told him that, just like I am telling it to you now. He agreed after I read him the riot act.

"Now," said Adam Fable, "listen, Vashvily, I got him to lay off, but we have to let the poor guy down easy now. I hear that floozy is being seen with—what's his name, that actor, what's his name?"

"You mean Buddy van der Lynn, the star in her show?"

"Yes. Now, you know as well as I do that we can't let a lousy actor take her away from the head of the studio, for Christ's sake!"

"Mr. Fable," said Vashvily, "I came here to talk to you about this same thing. The girl doesn't want to marry Moses Fable. She's a nice kid. She doesn't even want to go out with him. She's bored to death. I know she'll be glad to settle it. She chucks Buddy van der Lynn, and in return Moses Fable won't ask her to go out with him any more. That's settled." Vashvily got up.

"There they are again," said Adam Fable, looking toward the garden gate. A deputation of rabbis with black felt hats, long beards, and black coats had entered the garden.

"They come every year to tell Moses and a couple of others that they shouldn't allow themselves to be paid the biggest salaries in the country. They say it's bad for the Jews. Hell, it's bad for the Jews anyway. Well, let them come. I tell them every year that if they'll cut off those beards and throw away those hats, Moses is going to cut down his salary. But they won't meet him half way. Listen, Vanya, before you go: about the girl. Now she can't just disappear from the scene. That would make it worse for everybody concerned."

"Don't worry," said Vashvily, "everything is under control. I take her out myself. Besides, I've got a guy, a writer on my unit—quiet and a nice guy—she likes him and he can be seen with her occasionally. And besides, as soon as I get my shooting script, which is due any day now, we'll start the picture, and then she'll be legitimately busy."

Adam Fable said good-by to Vashvily. The dark men had advanced to the pool. They mumbled a patriarchal greeting in Hebrew. Adam Fable turned his bulk and adjusted the toga and faced them.

Cassard and Mumm were waiting in Vashvily's suite at four o'clock when Belinda came in.

"Excuse us one moment," said Cassard, and pulled Belinda into the office with the piano.

"Good Lord!" said Cassard. "I saw you at Romanoff's yesterday, and it was a disgusting exhibition. I watched you rubbing against Moses Fable and touching his leg—or feeling it, at any rate—all evening."

"I hardly sat next to him," said Belinda.

"That is strangely feminine reasoning. How can you 'hardly sit next to him'?"

"Well, I sat next to him only after the coffee when the others joined us. And anyway, I had that Adrian gown on with the six layers of gauze—And I *didn't touch his leg!* Your mind is in the gutter again, Monsieur Cassard."

Cassard started to apologize and told Belinda again how much he loved her. And then he said: "Chère amie, tomorrow night is Saturday. Tomorrow a good friend who is very important for you to know has invited me to dinner; and in the afternoon I am looking at a ranch in the Valley that a writer wants to sell. I could call for you at noon. We have a lovely drive through the beautiful San Fernando Valley and then we have dinner with Betsy Allbright, who is a lovely woman and wants to meet you . . ."

Vashvily, who had just returned from the conference at the pool, entered the room. "I'm sorry I kept you waiting, boys. I had an important meeting," he said, looking at the clock. "We'll have to put our huddle off until Monday."

Cassard turned to Belinda. "Are you coming with me?"

"Well, I'll come," said Belinda. "That is, if I don't have to go to Mr. Fable's for the week end."

"No, you won't have to go," said Vashvily. "You're having dinner with me tonight and you can go with Cassard tomorrow, that is, if you want to—"

"Well, thanks," said Belinda.

"Have you found anything?" Vashvily asked Cassard.

"Yes," said Cassard. "Yes, we have found something, but I prefer to tell it to you on Monday. On Monday, then, amigo, be so kind and call a general conference and I shall run through the whole thing."

"Great!" said Vashvily.

Mumm and Cassard left. In the corridor they met a deputation of bearded rabbis with black hats who asked them the way to Moses Fable's office.

In the Beautiful
San Fernando Valley

In which we find that Cassard hates
flowers but is very kind to animals,
and learn of a stepchild pig and the
sanatorium of Dr. Crippenwald.

16. Dirty Eddie

In the beautiful San Fernando Valley, on a small farm, in great comfort and plenty, lived a mama pig and a papa pig with twelve children, eleven of whom were rosy, round piglets who led orderly lives and were allowed regularly at the family table. The twelfth was regarded with suspicion. He was refused his mother's breast, and whenever he showed himself he was chased away with hard stares and angry grunting. He was different from his brothers and sisters. He was black, and his mother called him Dirty Eddie.

At mealtime the members of the vulgar family poked one another in all the parts of their bodies and, shouldering one another out of the way, crashed into their trough, sliding into the swill with smacking sounds of delight. Unrestrained by concerns of delicacy, some of them were of such wolfish rapacity that they ate standing on their heads, supported by the pressure of the others, and looking like obscene candles with twisted tails for wicks.

The papa and mamma pig alone fed themselves with any degree of comfort in the places of honor at the ends of the table, where they worked with the sound of bilge pumps.

When all appetites were stilled, the group left the trough as suddenly as they had come and ran to the great foul nest which they had uprooted in the center of their pen. Using one another's bodies for pillows, while the sun dried their swill-smeared mouths, they nodded away into the deep sleep of the just

The wind occasionally swept the aroma of plenty across the barnyard and under the farmer's house. Each pungent whiff was a reminder to the cold soul who waited there in the shadows that he was forever separated from the good things of life.

Dirty Eddie pressed his nose against the dry, cracked board of his mean and drafty lodging and squinted through a crack in the wood. He listened to the pleasant sounds of mealtime and to the wheezes of contentment that came from his rich relatives. He took deep draughts of the airy broth, as if he could subsist on it, and then went back, fearful lest he make a sound and betray his presence. The unhappy creature folded his thin haunches and carefully placed them on the dry, razor-edged eucalyptus leaves that were his bed.

Farmer Weatherbeat, stoop-shouldered from carrying buckets full of the best slop to them, was one with the good pigs in their dislike of Dirty Eddie, whose young life was almost ended in the early days of his exile. Driven by hunger, he had left his hiding place and run out into the light to lick the bottom of the cat's dish. With his head buried deep inside the pot, he pushed it loudly over the concrete slabs into the farmer's angry sight. By fast thinking and quick turns, he had escaped the ax that time and had taken profit from the lesson. The slothful feeding habits of the stabled animal had fallen from him fast right after that.

Now wary, sliding like a mink in shaded places, he went abroad in search of food and he subsisted in the garden and the fields on turnip greens, on uprooted daffodil and tulip bulbs, and on half-ripe potatoes, until the farmer found him out and made Dirty Eddie his sport, blasting with his squirrel gun at anything that moved, at swaying ferns, at tilting grass, and at every flower that nodded.

But the farmer wasted ammunition. The black target sat again shivering under the house with a new chapter added to the manual of surviving. He waited for the dark. With birds of prey that swooped down on him and coyotes that howled, the night declared herself his enemy.

As his senses became sharpened to his many dangers, Dirty

Eddie found that his good hour was the one when Farmer Weatherbeat slouched to the dinner table overhead.

The clatter of the soup spoon in the plate became his signal of safety and the starting bell that sent him galloping through the barnyard over the summit of a dungheap to the end of a wall of cacti, where he stopped and turned to cross the dirt road.

He ran from there to an abandoned plot whose trees were growing wild as he. Half in bloom, half bearing fruit, the bittersweet, scented grove provided him with a citrous diet. He sat beneath the trees and munched the limes that had fallen to the ground. Afterward he stilled his thirst with rusty water that collected in a basin formed by the lower half of a crankcase that lay among broken bottles in a corner of the grove.

In this free and wondrous hour the light underwent a change. The dry hills, the texture of camel's-hair, sharpened in outline and the valley seemed smaller. The land darkened and the small white clouds, hanging above in the blue like the plumes of smoke over volcanoes, functioned like huge barber shop lamps with their white glare. And, as they were fading together with the blue of the sky, the horizon changed to the colors which the California sunset shares with picture postal cards and blast furnaces. Dirty Eddie trotted home the road he had come, trailing with him the perfume of the waxen, bridal-bouquet blossoms of his garden, and he checked in long before the wearied farmer wiped his mouth with his unwashed hand, lit his pipe, and turned on the light.

This furtive, danger-fraught existence had left poor Dirty Eddie, in the second month of his life, little bigger than he was on the day of his birth. While his brothers and sisters swelled to their proper pattern, like so many balloons into which air is blown, Dirty Eddie stayed the same—a creature apart.

If small, he was clean-cut, resourceful, and forever thinking. If thin, he was fleet enough to run from his enemies. His black coat was well cut, smooth, and clean. Down his back ran a small mane that rose to bristly defiance when he was angered.

But it was his countenance that most set him apart from his tribe. The ample exercise of the emotions with which his life provided him gave his sharp face a mobility for which an actor might have envied him.

He portrayed, in effortless, quick sequence, utter despair and hopelessness, hauteur, fury, and blind hatred. His eye was deep, his ears forever alert, and around his mouth there played, in the moments in which he allowed himself to relax, a slow, sardonic smile.

One windy cool late afternoon when the signal had sounded and the farmer was bent over his soup, Dirty Eddie set out again for the abandoned citrus grove. He quenched his thirst and turned back toward the eucalyptus trees. When he was half across the dirt road, a fast-moving car approached.

For a moment the small mane bristled. For a second he hesitated at the new menace. He offered hopeless defiance as he took a fighting stance. And then he was knocked down, he screamed, and his senses left him as he lay there in the dirt.

Cassard had just waved his hand over a field of tall flowers that were grown for the Christmas market.

"Poinsettias they are," said Belinda.

"Don't tell me the name," said Cassard. "I detest them—they look like handkerchiefs in which people have had a nose-bleed."

At that moment there was heard a shrill scream, and Belinda said, "Oh, God—now you've run over somebody!"

He stopped the car.

"I'll back her up and see what it was," he said.

But unfortunately he shifted wrong and the heavy vehicle jumped forward. The left mudguard and headlight crashed into an already broken fence.

Belinda got out of the car and ran back down the road. After stopping the motor, Cassard went to the front to examine and estimate the damage done to his vehicle and the property.

The farmer, chewing, came out of his house.

"Oh, you poor, poor baby," said Belinda, as she bent down to Dirty Eddie, who lay silent, limp, and covered with dust.

Little more than a syllable, like the air that escapes from an accordion when it is picked up—a sad, weak squeak—came out of him at first, but as she touched him, one of his eyes blinked. As he came to consciousness and looked up at her, he opened his small mouth and sent forth a heart-piercing scream.

Belinda spread her coat on the road and bedded his small form into the soft, snowy fleece of its lining, on which he lay, silently bleeding, his eyes half closed, his lips trembling.

She knelt in the dust beside him, her hands folded on her breast, her lovely hair falling along her face, and she wept like a child.

"Isn't anybody going to do anything?" cried Belinda, looking up to the two men who approached.

"Allow me, ma-am," the farmer bleated as he reached, with huge, dirty hands, for the hurt animal.

"Let our good friend here end his misery, chérie," said Cassard. "Look at your lovely coat. It's all bloody."

Bending over him, Belinda shielded Dirty Eddie.

"Leave him alone," she sobbed.

Picking up the coat, she lifted Dirty Eddie as if he were lying in a hammock and brought him with infinite care to rest on her shoulder.

"I want," she said, with tear-choked voice, "the address of the nearest veterinary."

"Certainement, immediately, my dear," said Cassard in a warm, reassuring voice.

He stood behind her and, as articulate in sign language as he was with the spoken word, he instructed the farmer to be quiet, to leave the idiot woman alone, and to go back to his house, where he would follow him.

Loudly, and with resolution, he said to the farmer:

"We better go in and call up a veterinary."

The farmer opened his mouth and started to say, "I have—" but Cassard took him by the arm and, propelling him in the direction of the house, added his missing words: "—no telephone."

"I know that you have no telephone," continued Cassard. "All the better."

Inside the house he said:

"What do I owe you for the pig?"

"You don't owe me anything for the pig," said the honest Farmer Weatherbeat.

"Nevertheless," said Cassard, who knew the benefits of on-the-spot settlement for damages incurred, "I insist on paying you."

He lifted his topcoat, and, reaching to the back pocket of his trousers, contorted his body as he undid the button with which the flap on that pocket was held in place. He pulled out his wallet and removed from it a stout rubber band, opened the leather case, and, drawing back a zipper, reached in to bring forth a crisp new five-dollar bill. He zipped up the zipper, put the band around the wallet, stuck it in his pocket, and buttoned the pocket. Before handing it to the farmer he snapped the bill to make sure that it was not stuck to another. The farmer looked at the bill.

"For the pig," said Cassard.

The farmer didn't reach for the money.

"That varmint! He's been digging up my garden. I've been wanting to do away with him for a month. He's no good," he said. "You don't owe me anything for that pig. It's yours."

"The point is, alas, I don't want the pig, amigo," said the writer. "As soon as we are gone, do as you like with the pig. Kill him."

"I could take it for the fence you broke," said the farmer. "That would be all right, I guess."

"As you like," said Maurice Cassard, "but now we must go back. You don't mind, amigo, if I do the talking? It will be like pulling teeth to get that pig away from her."

Followed by the farmer, Cassard went back to Belinda and bent down to talk to her.

"This good man," said Cassard, "who knows everything about animals and loves them, is going to take excellent care of this pig. He will carry him into his house and bind his leg, yes, and succor him, and then put him back with his mother where he belongs and where he will thrive, and in a little while he will be fat and well again."

"So that he can go to the butcher," said Belinda. The farmer had his hands outstretched again and was trying to mold his stony features into a look of concern and humanity.

Belinda looked at the farmer and held on to Dirty Eddie.

"I want," she repeated stubbornly, "the address of the nearest vet."

Cassard made a gesture of impatience and reached into his hair. He changed his voice, placing it somewhat lower, and put his hand on her shoulder.

"Belinda," he said and paused. "Please listen to reason, just for once. Alors, you are right. The farmer is not interested in the pig. It is not much of a pig, as you can see. Besides, he has no telephone. As for the pig, it is fated to die eventually anyway. Now, the easiest fashion in which we can settle this is to do what the farmer says. It will be quick and painless and the pig will never know."

Belinda looked down at Dirty Eddie, who, looking from face to face, had followed every word of the conversation. He wore an expression of such immeasurable sadness that even Cassard had to turn away as he said:

"Now, let the farmer have the pig and let's be off!"

"Look, he's crying," said Belinda, herself in tears again. "Mama's not going to leave you," she said to Dirty Eddie.

"Alors," said Cassard to the farmer, shrugging his head and shoulders, "there is nothing we can do."

Belinda got up with relief, holding Dirty Eddie tightly, and said:

"Now we must hurry, Maurice. I'm afraid he's going to die before we get to a doctor."

Snapping the clean five-dollar-bill between his hands, the farmer leaned over his fence and watched the car start.

Cassard, being an expert at unlocking his fenders from those of other vehicles, backing out of ditches, and disengaging himself from municipal encumbrances and objects of nature, performed admirably. Waving at the farmer with one hand and steering with the other, he wrenched his car away from the tree. Dragging a small piece of the bark, he disappeared into the dusk.

"It is strange, darling," he observed, after they had driven a while on Ventura Boulevard and had come close to running down a man walking, in violation of the California rules, with the traffic instead of against it, "and unbelievable that in this place, which is normally littered with the establishments of veterinarians, with dog and cat hospitals, and pet shops, and has almost as many of them as there are undertakers—that you do not come across a single one when you need it."

"I was just about to say that, darling," answered Belinda.

"You watch on your side and I'll watch on mine," he said, and touched her hand, driving with the other.

He looked at her in the mirror.

"You are exquisitely beautiful as you are now, with this bundle in your arms—like an old Italian painting," he said—and missed the intersection where he should have turned off, to cross over the hills into Hollywood.

He smiled and continued:

"Vashvily is right. If you will do for the camera what you did back there when you were kneeling in the dirt; if you can cry like that for the screen, you will make the rest of them look sick."

"Thank you, you are sweet," said Belinda. She was looking out of the window.

"I haven't seen one yet."

"You haven't seen what yet?" asked Maurice.

"A veterinary," she said and withdrew her hand.

Maurice thought, If this goes on long enough, and we don't find one, maybe the pig will die. . . . "How is he?" he asked.

"He's breathing. He's asleep," said Belinda.

"It's seven-thirty now," said Cassard, and turned on the radio.

"HellotoallofyououttherefromHollywood," said the motherly voice of the famous columnist and oracle. Next she slurred: "Now listen to my first exclusive!"

Cassard leaned forward.

"Remember when I told you some months ago on this program that when her decree from Sean McMahon became final, Betsy Allbright would marry Lieutenant Casey McMahon?

Well, Casey has just returned from overseas. He is the brother
of Betsy's former third husband, the father of her son Bren-
dan. This makes Sean his own son's uncle. The happy couple
have just returned from Las Vegas and are entertaining their
most intimate friends at a surprise dinner party at their beautiful Malibu Beach home tonight. Congratulations, Betsy and
Casey!"

"My God," said Cassard. "Betsy's dinner—!"

He suddenly stepped on the brake and a bus almost crashed
into them.

"We must telephone her immediately." He drove to the curb.

"I asked the station attendant for the nearest veterinary,"
Cassard lied as he came back from the telephone, "and he
said to try in Beverly Hills."

When they came to Coldwater Canyon, he swung the car
to the right and drove up the mountain, negotiating the
tortuous turns slowly and creeping down the other side in
gear into Beverly Hills.

"There's one," said Belinda.

She pointed at a huge cement dog, a statue of a Saint
Bernard, who carried a sign in his mouth on which was lettered
"Dr. Grippenwald." Behind the dog was a chalet with "Cat
and Dog Hospital" on it and all its windows lighted up.

"I hope they take him in. It's awfully hard to get into a
hospital these days—for people, even," said Cassard.

The bearded, kindly Dr. Grippenwald, whose practice
extended, besides pet dogs, to turtles, deodorized skunks,
coati-mondi, and to all the vast menagerie that are employed
in pictures, disappeared with Belinda and the patient through
a white door.

Cassard unwrapped his muffler and smiled at an immaculately uniformed nurse who was not without allure and had
extremely good legs. He was about to say something amusing,
his mouth was already open, when the nurse smiled at him,
motioned to a small desk and chair and handed him a pen
and a blank form. She waited a moment and then asked him
to fill out the paper.

She also asked for twenty dollars.

Cassard, who was already seated and had studied the paper, let her repeat the sum. Then he got up and went through the business of button, rubber band, and zipper. Extracting two ten-dollar bills, he handed them to the nurse.

"Poor darling," said Belinda, coming out of the white door. "The doctor thinks he'll pull through, but he'll have to stay here for a while."

"I am very glad—for you," said Cassard, as they drove away.

For the rest of the evening he spoke in short phrases and sat thinking and looking at his hands.

He was so absent-minded that he ordered ham with Madeira sauce at Mrs. Weiss's Hungarian Restaurant and when Belinda, studying the menu, had said, "I'll never eat meat again," he asked why and let her explanation float away without hearing it. He was very tired.

"You are kind, Maurice," said Belinda as he drove her home. "I appreciate what you did for me."

He sat in bed later, dressed in his nightshirt and a silken muffler. And as he always did before retiring, so tonight he pulled out a drawer of his night table and took from it a small black ledger in which he wrote down the day's expenditures in a script so small that he could have written the Lord's Prayer on the heads of pins with it.

He searched his mind for the various items and put them down one by one.

"Alors," he said, looking bitterly at the addition. "It is a nuisance, this pig."

He turned out the light. His forehead was in pleats and he folded his hands in back of his head. Then he stretched and sighed.

The quality of his thinking in the dark and in this position was surpassed only by that which he did when running up and down and from one of the four walls to the others.

Suddenly, that night, a wild, small cry escaped him.

"Ha!" he screeched in a high falsetto voice. He jumped out of bed. "Ha!" again, as he began his trek from wall to wall.

Then he smiled like one who comes unexpectedly on lovely surprises and great treasure.

He picked up the phone and called the hospital.

The neat night nurse answered.

"Yes," she said, "Dirty Eddie is all right."

"Ah, I am relieved," he said. He dialed Belinda's number.

"Mon beau," he said, "I hope I have not awakened you. I could not sleep myself—I was thinking of the little creature at Doctor Grippenwald's sanatorium—"

"Oh, you are sweet!" said Belinda.

"I have just called the hospital," said Cassard.

"You dear!" said Belinda.

"He is resting comfortably. . . . Belinda," said Cassard, and made a large pause.

"Hello, hello—" said Belinda, afraid they were cut off.

"Belinda, my darling," he said with sincerity in his voice, "I must ask you not to mention the affair of the pig to anyone."

"But why not?"

"I cannot tell you over the phone," he said. "It is of the greatest importance, chérie—I go so far as to say that fate drove the car and not I. Belinda—Are you listening, my love?—Will you trust me, mon beau? Will you believe me for once?"

"Of course, darling," she said, and he could feel her eyes melt.

"You must forgive me, my love. This afternoon it must have seemed that I acted awfully matter-of-fact, but you know I am not the demonstrative type. I was merely concerned with ending the animal's suffering. But now that he will survive, I shall provide him with a home and a future such as none of his kind has ever dared to dream of . . ."

"Thank you, and bless you, dearest," said Belinda.

After once more impressing upon her the need of absolute secrecy, Cassard hung up, and almost set himself on fire with smoking for the next three hours. He got up early the next morning, and drove out to see Farmer Weatherbeat. . . .

Belinda was awakened by the delivery of an immense box, in which she found, this time, a major effort of the florist's skill. Half of Mr. Nircassio's icebox was there, all of it in white—lilies, roses, and gardenias, with orchids strewn through the lesser blooms. To a solitary red poinsettia was tied an envelope with a small pig drawn on the outside by Cassard, and inside was a song of love.

Cyrano de Bergerac and all the sorrows of Werther shone through it. But Cassard had crossed out all the words he had written and put under them: "Will you marry me?"

17. *And Then, and Then, and Then, and Then*

Vanya Vashvily's office was humming with conversation on Monday morning and everybody there wore an air of great expectancy. By Maurice Cassard's request on Saturday, the important conference had been arranged and there were, in the room, besides the producer, Sandor Thrilling, the director; Raoul de Bourggraff; Evervess of the story department; Jerome Hack; and Moses Fable.

At the approach of the writers, conversation stopped. The audience sought their places and the moment was like that exciting part of a circus performance when the acrobat drops his cape into the sawdust and, in shimmering tights, climbs upward to his trapeze for the roll of the drums and does his sure-handed, death-defying act in minutes so filled with thrills that time stands still.

Cassard shook hands and dropped his bib and topcoat on a chair in the hall.

"Alors," he said and walked with firm step toward Ludlow Mumm, who had pressed himself in the protective arms of an easy chair that stood in a corner. "Alors, which one of us is going to tell this story, amigo?" he said.

Ludlow Mumm gave him the signal with a wide sweep of his arm and a nod of the head.

Cassard warmed up by running in circles for a while, eventually running so fast that, like a skater, he had to stop short at the edges of the desk and in front of the sofa on which Moses Fable sat. He stopped to think. He found things to look at and then, suddenly, he turned. He bit the nail of his right thumb and seemed to be on the verge of going into a cataleptic state. He ran to the door and opened it and walked out, trotting up and down in the hall. Then he came into the room again and finally opened his mouth.

He spoke with vehemence, over the heads of his audience, as if he were at one time the judge, the lawyer for the defense, and the prosecuting attorney at a great trial. He addressed the jury:

"Gentlemen, I shall not begin at the beginning." He tore through his black hair with his widespread fingers. "I shall not bore you with a dreary recital of our findings and how we both have developed this story. I shall instead begin exposing its cardinal faults and tell you how we have remedied them.

"For the writer of screen plays, there are decisions to make that involve time and money. . . . No one knows that better than I. I must, therefore, say to you that the decision we have made is the result of thorough examination and months of fatiguing argument and labor. We have not always agreed on some things, but in this one instance we have always come back to the same discovery. Am I right, Mumm?"

Mumm nodded.

"All right, what is it?" asked Fable anxiously, while Vashvily moved forward in his seat. "Let's have it."

"We have come to the conclusion: A—that the locale of the story is wrong," said Cassard, sharply. "B—that Belinda is miscast."

Vashvily changed color. "What do you mean?" he asked.

"The story is wrong from the very beginning," said Cassard.

"You mean the gare Saint-Lazare?" screamed Vashvily.

"Yes, I mean the gare Saint-Lazare. That's out," said Cassard.

"My God!" said Vashvily to Moses Fable. "You're not going to let him do that!"

"Let him talk," said Fable.

"The gare Saint-Lazare," said Cassard, playing with the sound of the words and saying them once more, "The gare Saint-Lazare, gentlemen, is a railroad station in Paris at which a train arrives. This train arrives from Germany. Out of this train comes a tattered and hungry man whom nobody recognizes until he sings a sad song. Alors, you succeed in bringing into the theater, in one scene alone, the memory of the war, the stench of the concentration camp, the unhappiness of a refugee. On top of that, another studio is just about to make a picture with that very same mise en scène."

Moses Fable leaped up and patted Cassard on the shoulder. "Right," he said. "Absolutely. Now, if pictures like that have to be made, let those—" He did not finish the sentence. He nodded in the direction of the other studio and asked: "But what are we going to do with that station? That God-damn station cost a lot of money. We spent a fortune on the gare Saint-Lazare."

Cassard changed his track. He had been walking between the sofa of Moses Fable and the chair on which Mumm was sitting. Now he walked to Vashvily's desk. The producer sat with arms folded, his anger rising, ready to argue for his French railroad station and to fight for Serena Blandish.

Cassard picked up a paper clip and straightened it out and then touched Vashvily with the end of it. "As for the station," he said, "nothing will be lost. Not even the lyrics. You simply change it from Lazare to La Salle. And, since the Chicago station is at least as dirty and grimy as Saint-Lazare in Paris, there is no need for repainting. The alterations are all minor. All you have to do is change the text on the advertisements and the names of the cities at the gates." And turning to Moses Fable, he said: "My friend Mumm and I are not without concern for the production costs of a feature such as this, Mr. Fable."

Moses Fable looked around among the faces of his executives and said, "Gee, for a moment, I got scared there . . ."

They all smiled and loosened up.

"How long will it take?" Fable asked the head of the art department.

"Give me two days," said Raoul de Bourggraff.

"Great!" said Fable. "Go ahead."

Cassard took a drink of water and wiped his forehead and then went back again.

"The story, as you can see, gentlemen, now moves to a happier background—to the New World—to this country—"

"What was the original story about?" asked Moses Fable.

"The original story, Mr. Fable, was briefly as follows:

"A Russian who does not believe in communism falls in love with a Clare Luce type American woman who is an ardent leftist. But, in the end, love is triumphant over all ideology."

"A very original plot," said Vanya Vashvily.

"Highly controversial," said Moses Fable.

"We've fixed that, too," said Cassard.

"Tell us," said Fable.

"The Russian is a communist at the beginning, but the girl isn't and she reforms him."

"I like that," said Moses Fable and then, suddenly, had a doubt.

"Yes?" said Cassard, looking at him sharply.

"How does this Russian get to Chicago?"

"Ah, but we're not making him a Russian. He was a Russian in the original version."

"What is he now?" asked Moses Fable.

Cassard walked out into the corridor, where he paced up and down for a while. When he came in, he said:

"The boy, who originally was the grandson of a Russian Grand Duke and active in the French Underground, is now the scion of a Philadelphia family, but he works for a living, as a photographer for a *Life* type of magazine. He is on an assignment in Chicago where he meets the girl."

"That's all right," said Moses Fable.

"What's happened to the girl?" asked Vashvily, who seemed near collapse. "To the lonesome girl?"

Cassard took refuge again in his corridor and paced, and

Moses Fable turned around to where Mumm was sitting. "What happens to the girl?" he asked. And just at the beginning of the dangerous moment that would have compelled Mumm to shrug his shoulders, Cassard came back into the room.

"The girl," he said, "the girl—" and walked. "The girl, who was the daughter of a rich collaborationist and ex-Vichyite in the original, is now the daughter of the biggest pork-packer in Chicago."

Cassard sat down for a second.

"The father is against the marriage?" asked Moses Fable.

"No," said Cassard, who had found his feet again. "Not in the beginning. Believing the boy poor and hard-working, he encourages the marriage."

"I like that," said Moses Fable.

"He is only against it," said Cassard, "when the boy's Main Line identity is disclosed, and when she is about to elope with him to take up a life of ease among the East's upper crust."

"How are you going to bring them back to Chicago?" said Moses Fable.

"Ah," said Cassard with the liquid smile, "that is where the railroad station comes in." He left for the corridor again for a short run. He came back suddenly gay. "You will like this very much, Mr. Fable," he said. "We have other good things, but this is one of the key scenes in the picture, about which my colleague and I are extremely happy."

"I'm listening," said Fable.

"The following happens just as they are about to leave— from the La Salle Street Station—for New York. They are at the train, when there is delivered to them—"

Cassard made a pause and shaped with his hands a small package which he held to his chest with great tenderness.

"There is delivered to them a little black pig—"

"What for?" asked Fable.

"Which the father has sent to the daughter to remind her of her humble background. He's a packer, you remember."

"Great!" said Fable. "But will they like it in Chicago?"

"Alors, perhaps the Armours will not like it," said Cassard. "But imagine, Mr. Fable, a little bit of a black pig, intelligent and sweet, with a large bow made of pink silk at the side of its face, and carried to the train by a liveried chauffeur, delivered like candy, in a hatbox, sitting on a bed of four-leaf clovers. It will be wonderful and new. I prophesy that this small black pig will become the national omen of good fortune."

"I like that idea," said Moses Fable, who made a fetish of animals appearing in films.

"What did you do to the character of the girl?" asked Vashvily, with a murderous look at Cassard.

Cassard pointed the end of the clip at him again and said:

"The role of the girl was •not for Belinda. It was a crass example of miscasting. Dear Vanya, believe me, Belinda as a girl from a polyglot background, out of a Swiss finishing school, is a joke. You may send her to the charm school for a hundred years—she will still be Belinda. Now, let us face that fact. I have taken it into consideration that the girl has no talent—that you have spent a good deal of money on her. I have made the necessary repairs in the story with that in mind. You will not lose the Serena Blandish, dear Vanya. Belinda is still a pure girl, but . . . while she was impossible as a pure girl from Paris, she is believable as a pure girl from Chicago."

"He is right," said Moses Fable. "That's great. I like the whole thing."

"Basically, dear Vanya, nothing is changed. Everything is the same. We have left all the elements, the effects, you are after. The music goes into the same spots. That song has much more meaning now, as the train leaves . . ."

"As the train arrives," weakly protested Vashvily, whose mind was cluttered with the debris of his beloved statue and her temple, collapsed and shattered anew.

"No," said Cassard, stabbing him again with the paper clip. "I am sorry, Vanya. That is changed. The train sequence is now at the end, instead of at the beginning."

"You say you'll have that set dressed in two days?" Cassard asked de Bourggraff once more.

"Well, then, we can start shooting on Thursday. We'll shoot

the end of the picture first," said Fable, "so we don't lose any time."

    With this signal, the Vashvily unit of Olympia pictures went into high gear.

    Raoul de Bourggraff and his crew worked all night, changing the advertisements in the railroad station and painting out the color of the Paris sky. The locomotives were exchanged, and the station personnel and citizens drew new costumes. Vashvily adapted his lyrics, and only the casting office was nervous. They seemed to have trouble finding a small black pig on such short notice.

    "I pride myself on doing things the hard way," said Cassard to Vashvily the next day, as he sat in the producer's office and turned down candidates for the role of the pig. "And you must grant me that I have accomplished the impossible."

    "And what is that?" asked the producer.

    "That a girl from Chicago plays a girl from Chicago. That, alors, is a miracle!"

18. *Trouble with an Actor*

After great efforts on the part of the casting office, after herds of pigs had reported at the Olympia studios and not one single talent had been discovered among them, when everybody had given up and there was talk of dropping the entire project, at the last moment there presented himself a man from the near-by San Fernando Valley, a farmer, who had a pig that was a candidate for the job. The part seemed to be written for him. Farmer Weatherbeat, who owned him and had brought him to the casting office, was immediately rushed to

the producer. The pig answered exactly the specifications laid
down by the studio. Maurice Cassard, who happened to be
in the producer's office at the time, was introduced to the
owner of the animal and congratulated him.

"I do not have to tell you, Vanya," said the writer, "that we
are extraordinarily fortunate in finding—what's his name?"
he asked.

"Dirty Eddie," replied the farmer.

"—in finding Dirty Eddie," said Cassard.

The personality pig sat on the leather couch, but when
Moses Fable came in, Dirty Eddie jumped off the couch,
which was Fable's favorite seat, and ran to a small chair on
which he jumped with grace. He politely refused a drink when
the secretary brought in a paper cup with water, by shaking
his head and smiling that engaging, sardonic smile that was
to endear him to the millions.

"Nice pig," said Moses Fable, who usually paid no attention
to bit players and extras.

As Belinda came in, Dirty Eddie made sounds of affection.
His small eyes shone. He smiled again and bowed, and his
tail twisted itself into a tight spiral. Belinda had difficulty in
disguising her emotions and limiting herself to being surprised
at finding a pig in the producer's office.

"How do you think he will photograph?" asked Cassard.

Vanya Vashvily looked at Dirty Eddie with his camera eyes
—the way he had once taken Belinda's measure. He studied the
structure of his face. "I should think he'd photograph all
right," said Vashvily. He pushed a button on his box and
arranged for a color test that afternoon.

"Then we can start tomorrow with the gare Saint-Lazare—I
mean La Salle," said Sandor Thrilling.

"Right," said Fable. "We'll look at the test first thing in the
morning. . . ."

"Who made this test?" asked Fable early the next morning
as he walked into his private projection room.

"Oh, one of the boys," answered Vashvily.

"Why didn't you get Thrilling to do it?" asked Fable.

"Mr. Fable," said Vashvily, "when you see this test, you will

see that the worst director can't harm him. His left profile is
as good as his right. He photographs perfectly from every
angle. I tell you, if any of the actors on the lot—with the
economy of motion and the sincerity of that small—"

"Well, let's see," said Fable. "You don't have to sell him to
me, for Christ's sake. I saw the Possibilities!"

He pressed the button on the desk that was built around
his easy chair and the lights went down. Dirty Eddie appeared
in colors. In the few minutes that the test ran, Fable laughed
loudly, a thing he very rarely did. He said at the end:
"Great—great—great! What a ham! He's set for the scene at
the station all right."

Dirty Eddie was on the lot at five-thirty on the first day of
shooting. He held absolutely still while the make-up crew
rouged his mouth and while his coat was brushed. He delivered
himself, later, of his small part with such perfection that no
film had to be wasted on retakes.

The next morning, when Moses Fable saw the rushes of
the scene taken the day before, he hit the arm of his leather
chair again and he called a conference.

"I want," he said, "that pig's part vastly enlarged. Write
him into every scene, or at least into every possible scene.
Put Hack on this picture. Get Hack to write some stuff especially for the pig. Get the publicity people busy . . ."

A three-column picture of Dirty Eddie smiling—a three-
quarter profile—was released to the nation's press the next
day. The promotion specialists worked overtime preparing
film books and tie-ins, and even considered a personal appearance tour.

On the set, Dirty Eddie endeared himself to everyone. He
was patient. He posed endlessly. When shooting started, he
looked at the director and immediately understood what was
wanted of him and simply did it, and always did it right the
first time.

He became the symbol of good fortune. When he was on
stage, everything went well, and everything went wrong on
the days he was absent.

Moses Fable visited the set every day. Frequently he assembled the cast and said: "I thank you all for a great performance"; and as he said that, he always looked fondly at Dirty Eddie.

When he was not acting or rehearsing, Dirty Eddie sat at the foot of Belinda's day bed in her dressing room, where she studied her lines, rested, and fed him candy.

When the carillon rang, Farmer Weatherbeat came for him and they went together over to the commissary where they ate.

At the same table with Weatherbeat and Dirty Eddie, in costume, were the mother superior of the religious spectacle, a crook who played in *Two-Gun Lucy,* and the banker whom he had to slug in that picture. In armor, next to the crook, sat Prince Hal and the seductive woman who played Lola Montez in *The Mountain King*. There was also a singing cowboy with long legs and pearl-handled pistols.

The cowboy always sat down next to Dirty Eddie. He threw his ten-gallon hat a distance of fifteen feet and hung it in this fashion on a peg on the wall of the commissary. Turning to Weatherbeat one day, he said:

"I reckon you're sittin' purty with this here critter."

"Cain't complain none," said the farmer.

"Bet he's a-makin' more than the rest of us sittin' here put together," said the Westerner.

"Oh, we're doin' good all right," said the farmer with a satisfied smile, and petting Dirty Eddie. "Ain't never seen so much money in one bunch," he added.

"If you don't mind me asking," said the banker, who had to wear a blood-soaked bandage on that day, "how much do you draw for Dirty Eddie?"

"Forty bucks a week," answered Weatherbeat with pride.

"What?" screamed the lot of them.

"You're kidding!" said the mother superior.

"Well," said the farmer, "that includes me bringing him to work and taking him home, and tendin' him."

"I say—! Forty dollars a week! The swine!" said Prince Hal,

and hit the table. He was about to fold his arms in a civilian gesture of disgust, but was prevented by his armor from doing so. He shook his head.

"You mean you're satisfied with that?" asked Lola Montez.

"Sure," said Weatherbeat. "He's just a pig. The whole pig wasn't worth more'n five bucks a coupla weeks ago."

"Are you crazy?" said the mother superior.

"Do you know what this pig is worth?" asked the banker.

"A fortune—his weight in gold," said the mother superior.

"He can't do nothing—he's signed up," said the crook.

"We didn't sign nothin'," said the farmer.

"Oh!" shouted the mother superior. "That's good!" And with glee she added, "Then you're all right."

"You just withdraw Dirty Eddie," said the banker.

"And make them pay through the nose!" shouted the mother superior.

"They'll get another one and then I'll have nothin'," said Weatherbeat, who, up to now, had considered himself a very lucky man.

"Another pig like that?" said the mother superior, lighting a cigarette. "Never!"

"There isn't another like it in the whole world. Besides, by now, they've shot half the picture. They've got to pay you what you ask," said the banker.

"To protect their initial investment," said the crook.

"How much should I ask?"

"Anything that comes into your head. They've got to pay," said Prince Hal.

"Take my advice—you're no match for these bastards. Get yourself an agent," said the mother superior, and reached over to pet Dirty Eddie, who had followed the whole conversation, as usual, looking from face to face—hopefully, then doubting, and finally convinced that he should get more money. He looked very darkly at the end when they mentioned Moses Fable's name.

"How's a hundred a week?" asked the farmer.

"You'll never get anyplace," said the crook. "Get yourself an agent. Get Al Leinwand or Wildgans Chase to handle him."

"Waal, I got a silent pardner in this," said the farmer. "Reckon I'll talk it out with him before I do anything."

"Don't take less than five thousand," said the banker.

"Right," said the mother superior, and even the cowboy agreed as he picked up his hat and tightened his gun belt.

On his way out of the commissary, Ma Gundel always came to talk to Dirty Eddie and give him a tidbit—a stick of celery, a carrot, or some left-over piece of Linzertorte, the favorite dessert of Moses Fable. Today she fed him and talked to him and petted him as usual, and Farmer Weatherbeat asked her to watch Dirty Eddie for a moment while he went to the writers' table, where Cassard and Mumm were sitting close together, listening to the plot of *Er Riecht Nach Knoblauch,* an old European film that Cassard had seen which had a pig in its cast.

The farmer stopped and Cassard turned and was about to remind him sotto voce that he was not to be too friendly to him in public when the farmer, talking out of the side of his mouth, said that he had to see him—urgently.

"All right. On Stage Twenty-one, in half an hour," said Cassard, in the low voice of intrigue and conspiracy. . . .

Cassard, Weatherbeat, and Dirty Eddie were in a deep forest on Stage Twenty-one. The golden sleigh of the Wittelsbach prince with two outriders that carried torches and six Lippizianers in saffron leather harness waited for Lola Montez at the door of the mountain castle.

The wind and snow machines were started, and somebody shouted, "Quiet!"

"Alors, amigo, let's get out of here before he catches pneumonia," said Cassard.

The farmer picked up Dirty Eddie.

"Let's try the next set," said Cassard. They opened the heavy inner and outer door of Stage Seventeen and found themselves in the tropics. A shot-down B-29 was lying among jungle plants, the waters of a lagoon lapped lazily against the shore of a South Pacific atoll, a group of natives sat on one end of the set and rehearsed native music and drum beats, and a scenic crew sandpapered the sides of outrigger canoes, giving them the proper degree of wear and tear, as specified in the script.

The farmer and Cassard sat on a log down under the wing of the crippled bomber, and Dirty Eddie ran along the shore of the lagoon and through the tall sea grass.

Cassard brushed the white cornflakes that had been used as snow on the Lola Montez set out of his trouser cuffs as he listened to the farmer, who told him what the group at the table had advised him to do.

"Now, I think these people here, Mr. Vashvily and the others, have been mighty nice to me and to Dirty Eddie," Weatherbeat continued, while Cassard chewed furiously on a leaf of elephant grass. "Anyway, I didn't want to do anything without first talking to you, since you are a half-part owner of this here pig."

"I have been working very hard," said Cassard, "or else how could it have escaped me!"

The realism of the set was so profound that dirty oil dripped down from an engine nacelle on Cassard.

"Let's go inside," he said, and the farmer followed him into a thatched hut, where Cassard began his trek to the four bamboo walls.

"Alors," he said to the farmer, who watched him intently. Cassard left his mouth open during two crossings and a finger extended as a signal that something of greatest importance would be forthcoming.

"I don't like for people to be grabbing," said the farmer, referring to the round table of hungry actors.

"Alors, you do not know how right you are, Mr. Weatherbeat. When you think of the money they are making and going to make out of this—these penurious bloodsuckers!" He was thinking about the front office.

"I have been too busy writing," said Cassard, suddenly stopping. "And I have neglected this completely. It is not too late, however—if we act immediately."

He pointed the finger at the farmer. "The first thing you do," he said, "is, you go now, from here, to the accounting department—that is, immediately. You go to the old red wooden building at the back of the writers' building, and you ask for Mr. Envelove. When you get to him, you tell him that you want a raise for Dirty Eddie. If he asks how much, then you say that you want five thousand a week."

"Five thousand a week?" asked the confused farmer.

"Yes, five thousand a week. You also want other things, but about that, you must first consult with your agent. However," said Cassard with his liquid sound of happiness, cruising back and forth with a new speed over the soft mud floor of the native hut—"however, in order to assure Dirty Eddie's appearance on the lot tomorrow, you must have a written guarantee, signed by an officer of the corporation, that his salary is going to be five thousand a week from Monday on, for the rest of the picture. Can you remember that?"

The farmer dutifully and correctly repeated the demands. "But will Mr. Envelove give it to me?"

"Mr. Envelove, amigo, will laugh at you, or scream at you. He will tell you that you should have your head examined or that you are a crook. But one thing he will not do, he will not throw you out. He will send you to Vanya Vashvily, who will try to send you back to Mr. Envelove. Envelove is a nobody. You will, therefore, state your demands to Vashvily, and if he does not meet them, which he can't, you turn on your heel and walk out of the studio and take Dirty Eddie with you. And you will wait until you hear from me before you bring him back. Is that clear?"

The farmer went over the whole procedure carefully, and then they walked down to the water, where they found Dirty Eddie waiting patiently. He had kept his eyes on them and listened while his hindquarters soaked in the warm lagoon.

"We must be careful. I will leave first by that other door," said Cassard. While the farmer dried Dirty Eddie, Cassard ran along the beach, stepping over a row of outriggers, and walked back to the office of Ludlow Mumm, who was busy with his map. He joined him in looking at the world as if nothing had happened.

Vanya Vashvily had a late conference and after that a dinner date with Belinda. He did not want to lose time by going home to change, and while he talked to an author whose novel he had bought for Belinda's next picture he had shaved and then disappeared behind the screen into his haberdashery store and picked out a shirt. He had tied the knot in his bright cravat when the author shook his hand and said:

"I agree. We'll make her a Serena Blandish with plenty of sex." And after that he left.

Vashvily had slipped into his coat and was about to go out of his office when his secretary came in and said that Mr. Weatherbeat had been out in the reception room for a considerable time waiting to see him.

Weatherbeat was shown in with Dirty Eddie under his arm.

"Oh, hello," said Vashvily.

"How do you like my pig?" asked the farmer.

"I'm very glad you came," said Vashvily. "I meant to talk to you before and tell you that Dirty Eddie is doing a very good job. Incidentally—I'm sorry, I have a dinner date, or I'd talk to you more about that. Anyway, we're very happy about him." Vashvily reached for his hat.

"He's great!" said the farmer.

"All right," said Vashvily, trying to get past him, "he's a hell of a pig!"

"He's sensational," said the farmer, blocking the way.

"I agree with everything you say," said Vashvily, "but I must ask you to let me go now. I'm late already."

"You got to listen to what I have to say. I came to tell you that Dirty Eddie wants more money," persisted the farmer.

"What does he get now?" asked Vashvily.

"He gets forty a week."

"Well," said Vashvily, putting his hand on the farmer's shoulder, "I don't think we'll have any trouble getting him a raise. He deserves a raise!"

The astonished farmer let Vashvily pass out into the reception room.

"We'll make it sixty," said Vashvily pleasantly.

The farmer shook his head. "No," he said, "Dirty Eddie wants more dough!"

"Well, I'm in a hurry now. Tell you what to do. Tomorrow you go over to the accounting department and ask for Mr. Envelove and explain your situation, and I'm sure the whole thing will be cleared up."

"I was there. I already saw Mr. Envelove," said Weatherbeat.

"What did he say?"

"He sent me to you."

"Listen, Mr. Farmer, I've got to leave now. You come and see me first thing in the morning—tomorrow . . ."

"Dirty Eddie won't be here tomorrow. He won't come to work unless he gets his raise," said the farmer with finality.

"Well, why don't you tell me, then, what Dirty Eddie expects," said Vashvily.

"Dirty Eddie wants five thousand a week," said the farmer.

"You can't do that to me in the middle of a picture!" cried Vashvily. "You're out of your mind! That isn't business, Mr. Farmer, that's a holdup! Listen! If you pull anything like that, I shall see to it that neither you nor your pig will ever work in any other picture."

The farmer, who had been conditioned by the outbursts of Mr. Envelove, stood his ground.

"We don't give a damn about that," he said. "Dirty Eddie doesn't like pictures anyway. Besides, he can sign a contract with any other studio if he wants to. I just wanted to be fair."

"Fair!" cried Vashvily, bitterly, and watched the farmer leave.

Weatherbeat went out of the building. He put Dirty Eddie into the car, sat down next to him, and drove off over the hills to his San Fernando Valley home.

As Vashvily was leaving, he encountered Cassard in the lobby.

"Ah, amigo," said Cassard, smiling, and then suddenly changing to solicitous inquiry— "But what is the matter with you, Vanya? You look upset."

"Oh, nothing," said Vashvily. "Just trouble with an actor. I'll straighten it out in the morning."

19. Research

The color camera stood abandoned in a corner, the stage was deserted, and light shone only from the galleries above, where electricians worked, and in the dressing rooms of the stars.

"I welcome this costly disturbance," said Cassard to Belinda. "It may be of some benefit. I come from the projection booth —I saw the latest rushes and, as your friend, Belinda, I must say that I was made very unhappy by what I saw."

"What did you see?"

"The love scene at the train gate."

"Oh, the kiss," said Belinda.

"It is hard to be outstandingly common and obscene in America," said Cassard, "but Mr. van der Lynn has achieved even that. I have advised Vanya to cut out the whole scene."

"Everybody thinks it's great. What's wrong with it?" asked Belinda.

"The way Buddy van der Lynn kisses you."

"I didn't see anything wrong in that."

"Have you ever watched the attendant at a filling station trying to get a wet inner tube into a tire? Well, that is exactly the way he kisses you."

"Buddy is a nice boy—and the director wanted it that way."

"In this village of glass houses, Belinda, one cannot lie, because everything comes back immediately. . . . You said you were at Vanya's last night when you were out with Buddy van der Lynn, and people saw you both dancing at Mocambo."

"We were dining together at Vanya's and afterward he asked me to go to Mocambo. Besides, he dances divinely."

"What did he talk about?"

"Oh, nothing . . ."

"Well, dance with him all you want—and be sure to stop there, or you'll be very disappointed."

"What do you mean, Maurice?"

"He can't be any good. You know Americans: they're good only in a kind of football-playing fashion—they run for the goal and then it's over. The problem is what you do after they fall asleep."

"He didn't mention anything like that at all," said Belinda. "He talked to me about his home and his people. Buddy is a nice boy."

"Well, then, most probably he's a fairy."

"I'm wearing low heels for this hat," said Belinda. "Do you think I can walk into Romanoff's without bending?"

"Who are you going to Romanoff's with?"

"Oh, I'm only kidding, Maurice, and you fall for it every time. I'm going out with you. Where are we going?"

"I've arranged a beach party," said Cassard.

"I've been to a beach party," said Belinda.

"What's wrong with a beach party?"

"Oh, everything. Kids chasing dogs through wienies—sand gets in the sandwiches and on the butter and the corn—you're cold when it's hot and hot when it gets cold—and your eyes ache from the smoke. And I'm not supposed to get sunburned."

"It's not that kind of a beach party at all," said Cassard. "I have a friend who has a lovely house on the beach. He let me have it."

"Oh, the old refrain again," she said.

"It's a little house right on the beach, with windows from which we can see the ocean, an open fireplace. I have made a plan that shows you how to get there. I go ahead in the meantime and prepare everything. Bring your overnight things."

"Sounds wonderful," said Belinda, combing her hair. "What time?"

"Oh, say around two, so we can get some sun and take a little walk along the beach."

"Do you want me to bring anything—some potato salad, a pie?"

"No," said Maurice, "everything is taken care of. I've ordered everything."

"You're not having a lot of people?"

"The house is very small," said Cassard thoughtfully.

He left her the directions, and drove to Beverly Hills, where he loaded the provisions into the car. A man backed out of a driveway and almost ran into Cassard's car, but although Cassard, for once, was in the right, he did not stop to argue, but smiled and drove on.

He had the top down and it was Thursday. Along the road down to the ocean, like statues of doom, stood servants on their day off waiting for buses. In their faces were traces of enmity, the remnants of a week of domestic strife. The women in their mistresses' discarded hats, the butlers—among them Vashvily's Walter with a stolen cigar in his face—all of them glowered at Cassard. The sky was also overcast, but Cassard smiled and whistled.

"Tonight or never," he crowed, and arranged in his mind the details and the progress of events for the romantic evening which he had plotted with care from beginning to end.

The little shack stood among others of its kind on a road that runs from the Roosevelt Highway down to the beach, an hour out of Hollywood.

Cassard unlocked the door of the house and carried the provisions inside. He connected the icebox, turned on the water heater, and displayed further domestic talents by piling logs on the fireplace, arranging furniture, finding linen, and making up a double bed. He knew where everything was. He swept the porch, and after an hour's work was exhausted and hot. He fell on a couch and listened to the waves for a while and then got up to take off the hat, the overcoat, and the muffler, which he had worn throughout his chores. He ran out to his car for his bag.

He busied himself with the food next, placing meats and champagne, butter, and a large can of caviar on ice. The pie he put on a shelf over the oven, and he unpacked a fruit salad that looked as if the remains of a lot of Old Fashioneds had been spilled into a wooden bowl. The coffee was in two thermos bottles. Sugar he put in a larder that was already stocked with canned goods.

Finally, Maurice took his jacket off and began to fill with caviar small pastry molds in the shape of boats. The caviar was not the slimy gray kind but was salty and there was a lot of it. Belinda loved it. He filled a tray with these caviar boats and sliced a lemon. He also got out a knife and chopped hard-boiled eggs.

The sun came out and the sea turned green. From his bag Maurice took a pair of faded linen trousers and a red-and-white-striped sailor shirt with short sleeves. He pulled a beret on his head and put on canvas shoes with rattan soles. To make himself especially rakish, he tied a thin colored kerchief around his throat.

He ate two of the caviar boats and walked down the front stairs of the beach house with nautical swing. He took deep drafts of sea air, and, in expectation of things to come, stretched himself in the sun and slapped himself hard on his chest. He smiled at passing children.

Restless, he got up again and left the rattan footprints in the wet part of the sand. He became interested in the various souvenirs that the ocean washes ashore here—purple crab's claws on which the towers and bastions of crustae are imbedded, starfish, and bits of wood, polished, ground, and sand-rubbed into variegated shapes. He listened to the cry of the sea birds overhead and watched the small sandpipers running busily back and forth as they followed the receding waves. He came, at last, to a large bunch of seaweed peculiar to this coast, an endless amount of rubberlike tubing, obscene with gelatinous green leaves and bulbous floaters.

Maurice Cassard returned to the beach house and inspected the bathroom with the thoroughness and efficiency of a gynecologist's nurse. He also unwrapped an extra cake of soap, hung up additional towels on the glass rack, broke open a box of hard-to-get tissues, and then tossed his black hair out of his face and combed it with a wet comb.

His color was heightened from the exposure to wind, sea, and sun. He went back into the small living room and sat down at the piano in swashbuckling fashion, legs apart. He struck a chord, but every string was rusty and loose.

"Don't worry, little piano," he said, giving it a pat, "tonight we shall play on other instruments."

He smiled at the sea and waved at people in a fishing boat. Then he looked at his watch. It was two; then ten past two; and half past two. He went out to the road and he saw no car. He called Belinda's home and there was no answer. He lay down on the day bed, which smelled of sand and sea, and he lifted the receiver to call the studio.

The phone was on a party line. It was busy now. He heard the voices of a woman and a man.

"That's all right, dear," said the woman.

"Well," said the man, "I haven't more than two dollars left. That'll just get me there."

"Don't worry," she said. "As long as you get here, that's all I care about."

"I bought a lot of stuff," he said. "Scotch, and some rum for the punch, and peas, bread and soupmix, some radishes, the salad greens, and butter. That comes to about twenty bucks."

She said, "That's fine, dear. I have some money left, and anyway Jack always takes us up to Chez Roland for dinner, so that takes care of one evening."

"For Christ's sake," said the man, "get that bathroom cleaned up . . . it's a mess . . . and the linen. I'll stop at the laundry and pick up the clean linen so you can take those sheets off—it's high time—"

The woman said sweetly, "Well, darling, it may not be ready. You know how laundries are now. . . . Oh, darling, I forgot to tell you, Mary and Bob called up. They want to come—"

"Oh, God," said the man, "they've been down now for the last two week ends and they always bring those damn dogs. You call them up and tell them you're awfully sorry but some unexpected people turned up and you couldn't say no—"

"Oh, darling, I hate to do that. They've been so nice to us, John."

"Well, do what you please," said John gruffly. "But you

know how it's going to end up again. There won't be enough
beds and Mary is going to sleep with you and I'll be in the
cold as usual. You've got to call them and tell them—"

"But, dear, it's already Thursday. I hate to do that. And
then maybe they'll take us to dinner and that takes care of
two evenings, and they always bring a bottle of something."

"But there won't be enough ice and beer, and the damned
dogs, and the beds—Christ, why don't you learn to say 'no'
just once in a while?"

"What time will you arrive, dear?" she asked pleasantly.

"I don't know. It depends on a pal of mine who is coming
down with me. Oh, you'll like him. You see, I sold the car—
I'm using the money for a deposit on a newer model. The
papers ought to be through by the first of the week."

"Well, that's nice," said the woman, "but isn't it going to
be hard to meet the installments, dear?"

"Listen, stop nagging, Margie. I got three weeks' work next
month, and after the agent and the tax is paid I'll have four
hundred a week clear."

"All right, dear. I was just thinking. You know best. Now,
that pal of yours—where is he going to stay?"

"Oh, on the couch—don't worry about him."

"Well, I guess I better get busy with the bathroom, dear.
Now, have you any idea what time you'll get here, John dear?"

"Oh, I think we might make it, say, about six, but it may be
eight or later."

"And when is your pal going to leave?"

"Oh, Tuesday or so."

"Well, that's a rather long week end, isn't it? I thought you
were just bringing him for dinner."

"Oh, it'll be all right. And listen, Margie—"

"Yes, dear?"

"Don't put all the food in the icebox. Leave some room—
I'm bringing a lot of ice."

"All right. Good-by, dear."

The conversation was ended. Cassard called the studio.

"Belinda," he said, "where are you?"

"Here at the studio, darling."

"What are you doing at the studio?" asked Maurice impatiently. "I thought they had stopped shooting."

"Maurice, they won't let me go. They won't let anybody go. It's awful!"

"Who won't let you go?"

"Moses Fable. He's found a pig."

"What!" screamed Cassard. "What kind of a pig?"

"Oh, a nice little pig. He's the size of Dirty Eddie."

"But that's terrible!"

"Don't worry, dear, so far he doesn't know a thing about acting. They can't use him," said Belinda.

"Why can't they?"

"Because he's white. They've got him over in make-up now trying to make him black. You have no idea what I'm going through—"

"I can imagine."

"They've tried everything, but it always comes off under the lights."

"Good!" said Cassard.

"I've had three changes of costume this afternoon on account of that black stuff. I even got it on my hands and face.

"Don't laugh—it's so awful. I wish you were here. We just got through with one shot. The pig had to go back to make-up and I had to go back to make-up myself and they are fixing us both up again. I'm not allowed to even powder my own face. That's the thing I hate the most—other men's hands in my face."

"Darling," said Cassard, "have patience. Those are the problems that only technicians understand."

"Yes, I know. But I feel sorry for the pig."

"Oh, they're mean and heartless!" said Cassard. . . . "I'm all alone, Belinda. Come as soon as you can."

"As soon as I get through with this," said Belinda, "I want to go home and take a bath and go to bed."

"Well, good-by." He hung up, thoroughly depressed.

He put on his jacket, muffler, and overcoat. He was freezing in the blue-gray loneliness. He stood alone before the little caviar boats in the icebox of the windy shack. He looked out of the window. Finally he called his agent.

"Arty," he said, "I am in need of an address. Do you know anybody?"

"Well, no," answered Arty Wildgans, "but I know somebody who has a number. You know, it's very hard these days. This town isn't what it used to be. They're all in defense work now. But I'll call you back. . . .

"Beverly is her name," said Arty Wildgans a while later, and gave a number to Cassard. "Call her now. She's waiting for your call. She don't take calls unless she knows who it is. She has a very small clientele—high class—and she's built like a rock."

Cassard called the number. The voice of a woman, gay and warm as the neighbor, answered. Cassard said:

"Mademoiselle, alors, I am a practical man."

She understood instantly. "It'll be thirty bucks, honey."

"But that's rather high," protested Cassard.

"Not for what you get. Besides, it's a long way out. Now tell me, dear, just how to get there."

That done, Cassard rearranged his emotions. He scraped the caviar out of the little boats and put some of it back into the can. He ate a good deal himself during this process and washed it down. He consoled himself. "It is all in the mind," he said, and he played on the rusty piano and sang ribald ditties.

He had lit the fire and a cigarette and sat watching the sea gulls outside in the soft rain. They were evenly spaced for taking off, their heads buried in their plumage. Through the unwashed windows they looked like round white stones.

Maurice heard a solid footstep on the planks that led from the road over the sandy lot, and he put on his coat and muffler to open the outer door.

"Maurice?" she asked.

"Yes," he answered.

"Well, all right," she said. "Hello!" She laughed. "You have a cute place here."

She walked into the house and took off a good wild-mink coat. Cassard cruised about her, astonished by the phenomenon of a very attractive woman on this errand.

"You *are* Beverly?" he asked, to make sure, and took her mink coat.

"I told you," she said, "that it was worth it."

"Vendeuse dans une laiterie," he said to himself, "with an apron of white and all things about her clean—bread, butter, milk, white tile, bright light. . . . Or someone you encounter in the children's department of a good department store on Fifth Avenue asking for a little boy's suit, and the saleslady says, 'How old?' and she says with a smile, 'Four.'"

The hair was genuinely blond, the cheeks glowing, her lips soft, and her eyes frank.

"Would you like a drink?" he asked, and twisted the cork on a bottle.

"Something happens to champagne out here," he said. "It gets that fatal, golden-reddish color. Anything older than ten years is completely spoiled, and even younger wines get it. It can't stand the traveling or the climate. Anyway, it's not particularly good, although a great ceremony is written around it. Everybody oh's and ah's about it."

"I can take it or leave it," she said. "I drink anything you give me—rye, beer, bourbon, Scotch . . ."

"You must forgive me," said Cassard, staring at her voluptuousness and beauty. "I can't get over it. I'm delighted with your visit. You are astonishing."

"Just wait," said Beverly, and emptied her glass.

She picked up her coat, and on the way through the kitchen of the bungalow she opened the icebox door.

"My, this place is cozy," she said. "You've got everything here. Let me come often, will you? They can keep their fancy joints. This is the way to live. You know what, Maurice? I'll cook us a snack—after. I'll make the best spaghetti you ever tasted." She opened the larder and inspected it. "You've got everything."

She came back. "Maurice, the blinds—" and she pointed to

the windows with a hand on which there were several good rings.

Cassard pulled down the blinds at the six windows.

Beverly wandered about, inspecting the house, went into the bedroom and came out again. She had undressed, let down her hair, and tied it with a little-girl bow. She had put on a femme fatale sculptured silken nightgown, and brought with her the forbidden fragrance of Tabu. The professional equipment of Beverly consisted of all the proper hills and roundings. She had a clean and good body and passed muster. She showed it with pride.

"I like to lay here and talk about the body," she said. "I mean—you know—as if it didn't belong to me at all. I love my body.

"I read a book the other day by a guy who complains that some things aren't in the right places—" She arched her back and stretched.

"I think everything is in the right places. I'm satisfied with it. I'd change a lot of things in this world, but the body I'd leave alone."

"You are so right," said Cassard.

She came toward him.

"You're cold, honey," she said. "Wait, I'll fix that fire."

She put on her mink coat and ran along the beach, with her hair blowing out into the wind, and came back with an armful of driftwood.

"Now," she said, "I'll make it cozy."

She piled the wood on the fire, nursed it, and poured herself some bourbon. Although she posed before the flames like an illustration from a privately printed book, the scene lacked only a stocking hung from the fireplace to make it a Christmas card.

"Now," she said, "you can take that coat off, and the muffler too, and stop freezing. . . . If we're just going to talk, we might as well be comfortable." She fixed the pillows for him. "Let me untie that tie for you, honey. Now relax." She spread her toes toward the flames.

"Mademoiselle," said Cassard, getting up, "I am delighted with your visit."

He had become strangely inarticulate, but to show her that he was a man of the world and not bewildered or a novice, and that the presence of a woman in a silk nightie was an everyday matter with him, he leaned forward and, in the manner in which one presses the button of a bell to ring for room service, he touched the pale orange bud on her right breast with his outstretched index finger. Then, saying, "Excuse me one moment," he went to get another bottle.

"Hey, Maurice," she shouted after him, "bring a cracker or something when you come back."

Maurice went back to the icebox. He brought the can and the boat-shaped pastry molds, and now he smeared the caviar back into them again.

"I liked your voice on the telephone," she said. "When I don't like a voice, I just hang up. A voice tells almost everything."

Cassard made himself comfortable beside her and looked into the fire.

"A voice tells everything about a guy," she repeated. "And you won't believe this, but I can even tell by the way the phone rings who it is."

"How interesting," said Cassard. "I know what you mean exactly."

"Well, anyway, one guy. I know it's him before I pick up the phone. And another one too. And that other one, when he rings, I haven't got sense enough to leave the phone on the hook."

"Who is that?" asked Cassard.

"The guy I can tell by the way the phone rings?"

"No, the one you haven't sense enough to leave it on the hook."

She held out her glass and he filled it.

"That's Big Ben," she said. "I'll tell you about Big Ben.

"As I was saying, the telephone rings and I'm too dumb not to answer it. I know it's Big Ben. I know that oily voice is on the other end, and when I pick it up it's Ben all right.

You can see his eyes when he talks to you over the phone. He sends them along with his voice. So it's Ben, and he says he's lonesome. Well, Ben couldn't be lonesome in a thousand years because he loves nobody but Ben. And he says would I come over, and I say okay, Ben. So I get to the house—and oh God, that house—and he's in bed and he's got a drink all ready for you, and it's a quart of champagne, on ice in a bucket that's standing next to the bed. And there he is, his hands folded over his belly, and he's a little drowsy. He's worked hard or chiseled hard, I don't know how he makes his money. Anyway, there he is in bed all ready to curl up, and while I have a drink and talk he gets even more sleepy, and then he turns the light out and I slip in bed with him. And you know, you wouldn't believe it—it's nice and quiet and comfy, and you just send him off to sleep. You done a good job, and sleep with him a couple of hours. Okay, I like that.

"Now, there's the next call. He's not so mellow on the phone this time. You see that big face and the voice is sharper. He sort of hisses. You know what I'm glad about then, Maurice? I'm glad that we're not Romans, in them old days, and that Big Ben isn't Nero, because your head would come off just like that if you said no. Well, he's in that mood and you say all right, Ben.

"You know, you always forget. You don't think it's as awful as it was, or ever can be that awful again, and you say to yourself maybe I'm wrong, maybe he's in low gear. Anyway, you go, and oh boy! He takes you over the jumps and you wish you'd never been near him—and you've got enough sport and ache to last you for a week. Wait a minute, that's not all . . .

"There's the third form of torture. He says listen, baby— now he's sort of between the mellow and the Nero—well, he says, I got a friend here who wants to meet you . . . just came in from New York, a swell guy, very important, an ex-president from South America, or an oil prospector, a colonel that's been in China six years—always a guy with a scenario. Well, you know what you're in for. So you go. Sometimes the guy hasn't ever been near a woman since he left the States. All

right, you don't mind that. There's not much fun, and sometimes they're nervous, and a little bashful, and sometimes
that's good and sometimes that's awful. Well, anyway, you
know that all this time Ben has been on his knees outside the
door, looking. And as soon as it's over—oh boy—there's a
knock on the door and Ben's head comes in. He looks like
Nero now all right, and then he doesn't give me any peace,
and, God, let him keep his God-damn dough—and you almost
cry—and he walks around the room complaining and calls
you a deadhead and knocks things around . . . that's when
your head would come off if you were one of them Romans,
or the lions would get you. You almost faint, and in the end
he's like dead . . . and you have to bring him his fountain pen
and the checkbook, and he writes out a check."

"But why do you go there?" asked Cassard.

"You know, that's what gets me. Every time I go there, I
swear I'll never go there again. And yet I go. I don't have
to—I got other customers—but I go. Can you tell me what
it is?"

"Ah," said Cassard. "I understand it very well. It's simple.
You enjoy it."

"I wonder," said Beverly. "I hate him—I could kill him.
But he's going to pay up one of these days . . ."

"Not that kind," said Maurice.

"Oh, yes. I'll tell you when he's going to pay up—when he
dies. You know, he's been able to beat everything, Ben has.
He's got friends in politics and others that are judges, and
women sleep with him one after the other—and he's got
money, and he fakes and lies his way through life. There's
a lot of things that would throw most guys if they only did
one of them. He's not even above murder and the black
market, and cheating people who work for him. And jealous
husbands and lovers, he handles all that beautifully. A guy
I know knew him in Paris and in Bucharest. Ben thrives anywhere, and it's as natural as here. One day, maybe, you see
him in Port Said—and he'll have a house and women and he'll
be able to show you a hell of a time and nobody knows how
it's done—and maybe, neither does he. He'll have another

name but whoever he is and wherever he is, he'll be where the money is and where the food is, and the beautiful women and the liquor.

"Funny thing about him, he never gets drunk—he's always neat. Now, he's got something to do with sewing machines and refrigerators that you or I can't buy, but he exports them to Turkey or someplace down there. He used to have a shipping line—he owns planes—he's clever. Well, that's all right. But when he dies, when he lies there and it begins to get grim . . . you know, when Big Ben knows that it's over and he can't do anything and he can't call up any pals to fix it up . . . that's when I'd like to get a call from him and come and sit on the edge of his bed . . . and if there is anything in what they teach you about the other side, oh boy, that's where I'd like to be, too, to see him come in with the oily voice. Boy, oh boy, can you imagine what they'll do to him? . . . Well, I wish they'd come to me and ask me—*I'd* tell them how to take Ben over the jumps."

"Ah," said Cassard, "that is all wishful thinking. However, it may console you to know that Mr. Big Ben, whoever he is, is not a happy man here on earth—"

"Well," said Beverly, "he's got a farm in the Valley with a beautiful house and a swimming pool and three servants and a walk-in deep-freeze."

"That is all nice and good. Still, it's not happiness . . ."

"Well, what is happiness then? Are you happy? Am I happy?"

"I could be very happy," said Cassard. "It is the simplest thing to be happy."

"I lie awake," said Beverly, "and I think what the hell is it all about, and the other day I thought to myself, when was I ever happy? And you know, I started to remember back, and I think that between four and eight I was happy.

"We were very poor. We were three little girls and we slept in one bed together. In the morning, my mother came and shook us and she said, get up, get up—and it was cold. And in the kitchen, on the table, was oatmeal and chocolate and home-made muffins, and outside the window was fog. And you dug in that oatmeal and put sugar on it and then poured the milk over it and you sat there together and then you rushed in and washed yourself. Then you put on your sweater and hat and you ran out and went to school, and the weeds were as high as you were, and they stood in the fog like plants in an aquarium. And you did this without thinking about anything, except what you did. And you were happy. . . .

"I'll cook us something. I'm hungry," she said at the end, and then asked him, "Do you like dogs? Well, then, while I warm up some soup, would you go out to the car, Maurice, and get my dog?"

On a special cover that the neat girl had placed over the back seat of the car sat patience and devotion in the shape of a fawn-colored cocker spaniel.

Beverly was dressed when he came back, and looking into the kitchen cabinet.

"I'll make chicken soup first. You like chicken soup?"

"Very much," said Cassard, "I make it myself occasionally. I make it perfectly. The basis is always a good consommé de volaille. The old way was to buy two chickens and you have the trouble of cooking them—it takes hours, it is tiresome. You know what I do? I buy Le Noodle Soup—I throw away the noodles. With the rest, I begin."

After this bit of householder's wisdom they began to warm pots, cooked, and sat and ate.

"I like this more and more," she said, and she gave a house-wifely performance during the entire meal.

"Have you ever thought of getting married?" he asked abruptly as she cleared away the dishes.

She came back to the table with milk and sugar for the coffee, never making a useless move.

"Well, yes, there's a couple of guys in this town that want to marry me in the worst way," she said, "but when I think of having to go to bed with them—well, I just can't imagine myself doing that. Do you know what I mean?"

She poured the coffee.

"Listen, Maurice. Tell me, how does a girl keep herself mysterious when you're a character like I am?

"I am in love with a guy and I want to tell him everything

about myself. I want to have somebody I can tell it to. You know, somebody like you."

"Oh, never, never do that if you value your happiness," said Cassard. "Imagine how much he would enjoy the stories you'd tell him . . ."

"I make believe I tell him when I lie next to him," said the girl, "and I make believe that he listens quietly, and I answer myself what he would say.

"I saw him walk to a cab yesterday. His back is just like Gary Cooper's when you see him slowly walking down the main street in a Western with his arms out ready for the draw —only my boy still has his baby fat around the jaw. I can see him from my window when he lopes into the drug store across the street. Who would think that I, Beverly, would stand at a window and watch a guy's back disappear into a drug store and feel inside like crying? Well, that's love, and what are you going to do about it!"

"Just don't tell him anything—not even on your deathbed," said Maurice.

"I guess he's just a bastard, too. He hit me the other day and he said that he didn't need me but that I needed him. . .

"I had big ambitions once," she went on. "One day I wanted to be an actress. The next I wanted to be the biggest whore in the world. Then I wanted a family, and especially a lot of kids, and a nice guy. I just couldn't make up my mind."

Cassard drank again. He came close to her and felt her shoulder—smooth, muscular, and soft—and smelled the clean hair. She leaned her head against his and reached inside his shirt and clawed him and pressed her body to his, and he started to kiss her.

"No, no," she said, "the lips are for the lover. I don't like to be kissed. Anything else, but not that. No kisses, Maurice."

"Belinda—I mean Beverly—in a fashion," he said, "you resemble a woman whom I dearly love. She also is impeded by principles.

"I am," he went on, "genuinely attracted to you."

He was drunk, and she pushed him gently away. He opened his mouth and wanted to say something brilliant, but his words were like the sea gulls that had sat in the soft rain along the beach in the late afternoon, unable or unwilling to move.

"I'm having a wonderful time," she said.

"And I'm very happy you came." He looked into her clear blue eyes.

"I've got to go," she said. "It's almost eleven."

After she had put her coat on, she said good-bye to him and he saw her to the door.

"Didn't you forget anything?" he asked.

"Never mind," she said. "I didn't do anything for it."

"But I insist," he said, and brought out his wallet. He undid the rubber band and searched in the back compartment. He snapped the bills and gave them to her.

"I'll give you a rain check for this. Well, good-bye," she said. "You have a cute place here—and call me again, won't you?" She whistled for the dog.

The starter whined in the neat black car, which was like the ones from the Wildgans Chase Agency, and then the motor fired and she drove away.

In the corner of the clothes closet Maurice found some old coat-hangers. He threw them on the fire, and while they slowly turned into black sticks and broke up he poured himself another drink.

He took the little wafer diary out of his coat pocket, and, in his sharp calligraphy, he entered the expenditure in the rubric of deductible items and put it down as "For research."

20. *Time and Money*

Next to Moses Fable, the suddenly idle pork-packers and manufacturers of weenies of the extended area of Los Angeles were most unhappy about the suspension of activity at Olympia. Like fond mothers who bring little girls to the casting offices, every owner of a pig came to the studio gates and presented his entry. The carillon was drowned out by the squealing of the applicants for the Dirty Eddie job, and the air-conditioning systems pulled the farmyard odor with which the region had become saturated into every cubic foot of studio space.

The auditions lasted late into the night, and there was no hope in any one of the thousands of candidates that were patiently tested. The one possibility was a pig called Belladonna, a professional, with some stage experience. Interrupting a vaudeville tour, Belladonna had been rushed to Hollywood by plane, and turned out to be a minor performer, able to do tricks, walk a tightrope, count, and push a wagon. It was the nearest thing, but Belladonna was difficult. She was used to a live audience, was camera-shy, and was totally lacking in dramatic talent.

The golden time ran through Moses Fable's fingers for another month. At the end, he held conferences that lasted almost all night. He even considered doing what he never had done before—abandoning the whole project. But when he was shown the fan mail that came in truckloads, and noticed the nationwide concern that had built up for Dirty Eddie, he realized that there was no way out except to settle.

"This God-damned pig," said Moses Fable, making some rough calculations, "is costing us an awful lot of Time and Money. I wish I'd never laid eyes on Dirty Eddie."

In the great agony before he made his final decision, he

consulted with Ma Gundel, and when she sided with him he summoned Arty Wildgans, whose client Dirty Eddie had become, and they were locked in a strangle hold for a week, which cost the studio an additional fortune.

It must be said here that once Moses Fable conceded defeat, he did so with good grace. Dirty Eddie came back to a fanfare of good will and a contract that any actor might well envy. He was guaranteed star billing; a seven-year contract with yearly increases and no layoff; a percentage of the gross; a waiver of the "force majeure" clause (in case of fire, strike, flood, or other acts of God, he was to be paid anyway); retention of radio and television rights; first-class transportation for any traveling; the right to choose his own stories, hire his own writers, directors, and producers; and the right to approve the cutting of the picture. There was a rider attached to the contract allowing him to do an outside picture a year.

Every provision that man could make against the wiles and chicaneries of a powerful corporation and against fate appeared neatly boiled down, paragraphed, attested, and initialed by the parties of both the first and second parts. The amateurs' hopes were dead, the lawyers' and agents' holiday was over. The carillon rang again in pure air, and Dirty Eddie sat in his dressing room with Belinda's arms around him. The signing of the peace was celebrated with a luncheon in the private dining room of Olympia.

"You sit over there, next to de Bourggraff," said Moses Fable to Cassard. "And you, Mr. Weatherbeat, next to me." On his other side Fable had placed a new protégé, an adorable creature who spoke little but pointed her lips sweetly and then smiled, and made eyes, and sounds, and wiggled when she was spoken to, or just giggled delightfully. Her soft little hand was next to Fable's knife and remained there for the executive to pat. With his other hand, Fable ate the French fried potatoes off of Weatherbeat's plate. That is how close they were to each other.

"What you tukking?" asked Ma Gundel, meaning what did Moses Fable want to drink. And he said:

"I want some of the milk of human kindness."

That was the only time he touched on the recent painful past. He kept his eyes mostly on Weatherbeat's face.

"You, gentlemen," he said, addressing Cassard and Weatherbeat, "are both geniuses. We know that. I am not a genius. I am just a simple business man in the business of entertaining.

"I welcome you to this organization," he said specifically to Weatherbeat. "I hope you are going to be with us for a long time. I will try and acquaint you with some of the elemental facts about this business.

"Gentlemen, the basic thing to remember, in the making of pictures, is that there is really nothing new under the sun. Conception still takes place where it took place one million years ago. That hasn't changed and it will never change. It isn't done in the ear, in the nose, or the throat. The baby still grows in the mother's womb. Woman loves man—man loves woman. That is why *Will You Marry Me?* is one of the greatest titles in the whole world. It is universal.

"We have two things here that are important to the making of great pictures. They are Time and Money.

"Now, this lovely child," he said, turning to the new find, "is going through her first tests—and they are not all they should be—" He patted her hand. "But there's nothing to worry about, my dear. All it takes is patience. Anybody can be taught to act. Animals have been taught to act, yes, even fleas have been taught to act!

"When I say that here at Olympia we have both Time and Money, I don't mean that we have them to waste. Large spectacles, and underwater pageants, Ziegfeld Follies, and such stuff—that costs five million and up. That I gladly leave to Louis B. Mayer and Arthur Freed. Political pictures and 'save-the-world-from-this-and-that' stuff I leave to those Kikes over there. We, here at Olympia, go in for simple entertainment—pure entertainment. And now, perhaps, you will understand when I tell you why I met your demands. I did because a property like Dirty Eddie is top entertainment, clean and wholesome. Who do you think brings in the biggest money at the box office? Gable? Garson? Lana Turner? No, gentlemen, not any of them, but a dog—an animal, ladies and gentlemen

—a dog named Lassie. Now, there are several dogs on the screen, but there is only one Dirty Eddie, and if we don't beat all records with that property, my name isn't Moses Fable."

He paused among admiring smiles and looked around and then he said, "There is one more thing I want to say." He looked at a director by the name of St. Clair, and kept looking at that specialist in religious subjects during the rest of his speech.

"Every year some son-of-a-bitch comes to me with an idea for a picture about Christ and insists on a new treatment . . . do it in modern dress, do it in a night club, do it with Negro actors, they say. And that's where I put my foot down.

"I don't know whether Christ ever lived, but I know that a story that's been good for nineteen hundred years is a good story and I don't want it changed. If we do it, gentlemen, we do it the way they did it originally, with the last scene on the cross. It's time again, now, for that story.

"I've just wasted several hours with that writer you sent to me," he said to de Bourggraff. "That Cape Cod pawnbroker with stars in his eyes and a new treatment, What's-his-name.

"When a man says to me, 'You know, Mr. Fable, money means nothing to me,' that's when I get really scared, because when we ask him what he wants, he names an astronomical figure, and we'll sit around for days trying to figure how we can pay it—because for that story you need a big name. Well, I admit, this is one of our biggest poets, but I wish they would stop making suits with large pockets on the inside: no matter what I mentioned to him, he reached into his pocket and pulled out papers and began reading from them—a poem he had started on this, or a play he has in mind on that. And when he had nothing on one particular subject I mentioned, he started to produce a general ode on the Universe. Well, I convinced him that if he wanted the money, he had to put away all his Ideals and Ideas, and write the story, the old story. And then I asked him what he really would work for and that was a little better than I expected even. So, all in all, it's been a good day, gentlemen.

"Mr. Weatherbeat, I'll show you to your office and I hope they treat you right around here. If they don't, you come and tell me."

The silent ingénue got up with many cute motions and walked with her set smile through the Commissary alongside her protector.

"Now run along, back to school," Moses Fable smiled benevolently. "And good luck to you."

"What's her name?" asked Cassard.

"Laura, Lena, Lorna, something like that." And Moses Fable walked off.

Your Sins Are Forgiven

In which we sit through a silent movie

and see a couple of kids get married

. . . and in which all goes wrong and

comes out happily in the end.

21. *Snowy Night in Malibu*

Betsy Allbright, the silent picture star, arranged the seating for her dinner party. Lieutenant Casey McMahon, her fourth husband, was busy playing along the beach, throwing pieces of driftwood for his giant black schnauzer to retrieve from the Malibu waves. The lieutenant was out of the Army only a week, and Betsy Allbright stopped occasionally and lifted her eyes from the table and looked out through the plate-glass window, watching his youthful leaps and runs, and the dives he did into the ocean.

"Tell him to come in and get dressed," she said to Auguste. "And here"—she handed the butler a large vase that was in the center of the table—"take these artificial flowers out of here. They make such awful noises."

The modern house was insulated against the sounds of the sea, and the soundproofing extended to the telephone, which did not ring but announced calls with a soft green light. Tom, the chauffeur, came down the stairs and told Betsy Allbright that Maurice Cassard was on the wire.

"Betsy darling," said Cassard, "I depend on you. I am bringing her down tonight—put in a good word for me. She is infatuated with that crêpe Suzette, Buddy van der Lynn; she has mentioned his name three times today already. Tell her about actors. . . ."

"Let me have a look at her first," said Betsy, "and then I'll do what's good for you."

Miss Allbright's secretary used a special typewriter with

letters large enough so that the old actress could read menus,
messages, and place cards without using glasses.

She put Cassard on her left and Belinda next to her husband.
Ludlow Mumm was on Belinda's left. An old admirer, Sir
Gerald Graveline, the distinguished actor, was seated on Betsy's
right.

"Now, go ahead and tell him to put away that God-damn
dog and get dressed. They'll all be on time tonight," she said.
"What time is it, Auguste?"

"I should say we're nearing seven, madame," replied the
butler.

She came down at eight-thirty, in gold lamé this time, her
hair wound like fresh bread in a yellow twist on top of her
head. She wore a broad emerald necklace, and from her wrist
to the floor hung a chiffon handkerchief to match her necklace.
Around her waist was a girdle of leopard skin and gold leaf.

The sun-tanned lieutenant had exchanged the uniform for
a dinner jacket. He was romantic and lithe. He moved about
as if he were on a set, playing the parts of several young men
at the same time, all of them keen and debonair, standing in
the four corners of the room.

"I've got to go to a funeral Thursday," said Betsy Allbright.
"I just found out that I've got nothing but beach wear and
evening dresses, so tomorrow remind me to get some things
sent out from Adrian's. . . . I told him to go to the Mayos,
or to the Walter Reed, but he had his own ideas. All the
good people are dying now," she said, looking over the table.

The young man walked back and forth and occasionally
mumbled by way of answering.

"We were just talking about poor Sam," said Betsy Allbright
to Cassard as he came into the room.

"Ah, yes," said Cassard. "Poor Sam. What a pity!"

"Six months ago, when he first told me what was wrong
with him, I said to him, go to the Mayo Clinic. There is a
doctor. He did this throat for me. You know, the Mayos,
what they said to me ten years ago? They said, you better
have that goiter out or your life won't be worth a nickel. So
they sent me to this man that I wanted to send Sam to, and

he took it out . . . you can hardly see the scar. And the Mayos, they operated on my leg." She shook with laughter. "When you see me here, Maurice, you see only half of me. I left most of it in clinics all over the world—and what isn't cut out is sewn up . . .

"Give him a cocktail," she said to the lieutenant, who was chewing his lip. He came forward and bowed to Belinda, pressing his neat mustache on her hand.

Sir Gerald arrived. He greeted the hostess and the lieutenant and then the other guests in proper sequence.

"The funniest thing is," said the hostess to Cassard, "that the poor bastard gave a couple of million dollars to build a wing on this God-damned hospital, just to die in it. That's gratitude!"

Cassard said hello to the host. The lieutenant, who had kept a British accent intact through two and a half years of service with the Canadians, slapped Cassard's back.

"You are glad to be back?" asked Cassard.

"Awfully," said the host. "Been playing on the sand with the dahg all afternoon."

"Are you in pictures?"

"I've been approached by several agents, and there is talk of giving me a part at Olympia."

"And what are you going to play?"

"Oh, something in Galilean homespun . . . But there," said the lieutenant, with raised voice, and holding his glass in the direction of Sir Gerald, "is the man who should play the lead, not—what's his name?"

"Thank you. Thank you very much, dear boy," said Sir Gerald, "but there are three roles in this world that I do not care to play. They are, in fact, not playable. They are: Christ, Shakespeare, and Jeeves. You start with six strikes against you when you try to portray any of them."

"Well, I dare say you'd be good—better than anyone else, anyway," Lady Graveline said. "He's so tired, the poor darling. All his activities—the radio, the screen, and all the things he does besides. I'm glad they didn't ask him. I'd hate to have him step out of *Monte Cristo* to do *The Mount*."

208 Your Sins Are Forgiven

"Well, that wouldn't be a serial," said Betsy Allbright.

Sir Gerald turned to get a drink.

"I don't know anything about pictures any more. I've got money in them—that's all," said Betsy Allbright. "I finance one or two a year and I look at one or two a year and I take a lot of trouble selecting them—more than the Academy Award people take."

Sir Gerald said to Mumm: "It's fatal for actors to come out here. Oh, how fatal this place is for talent!

"We have lived in Paris, in London, in Stockholm, and it's been wonderful, but you come out here and something happens to you. I wish I had the courage to leave and go back to the stage. Well, for me it's too late, but I pity the young ones. I don't have to tell you. You can see for yourself what happens to actors out here. God—I believe in a hard life for actors—to try and try again—to meet with misfortune—to walk into managers' offices and sit there and wait for a part and to have that a matter of life and death. Out of that, sir, came actors."

The lieutenant nodded gravely.

"The same holds true of your work, doesn't it, Mr. Mumm? A garret—turn-down—and misery—and try and try again?"

"That is true of all that is art," said Ludlow Mumm, stroking his beard.

"As far as actresses go—"

Sir Gerald held up both his hands. "Take that girl, that awfully silly girl. She's a new discovery and now she's a star. What's her name? Whether it rains or shines, whether the piece is happy or sad, she's always the same."

"Ah, but she has something," said the host.

"Well, all right. You mean she has breasts. Well, dear boy, acting is not done with the breasts, if you allow me."

When they had sat down to dinner, Mumm asked: "Did you all see that awful picture of Mussolini in today's paper?"

"I say, such a thing could never happen in England," said Lady Graveline. "I mean the girl hanging next to him, upside down."

"I wonder how they kept her skirts from falling down over her head," said Cassard.

"Rather good legs," said the lieutenant.

Sir Gerald occasionally absented himself in mind from the table; he frequently closed his eyes and dozed off. When he awoke he sat up and pulled open his eyelids, which were like a large bird's. He awoke now and leaned toward the hostess with blank eyes.

"We were just talking about Mussolini," she said loudly, as if she could thereby recall the entire conversation to him.

"Oh yes, good fellow—made the trains run on time."

There was loud laughter at the other end of the table. "Who's the silly ass?" Sir Gerald asked his hostess.

She kicked him in the side with her elbow.

"My new husband," she said.

"Oh, dear," said the great actor.

The ruddy lieutenant reached for the card that leaned against the candlestick and read the menu.

"Excellent dinner, darling," he said in a pause across the table. "May I congratulate you, particularly on the selection of the wine. Claret goes well with filet mignon, particularly a full-bodied claret like this—"

"You'll have to thank Dennis for that," said Betsy Allbright. "That's all I ever got out of my first marriage. He made me wine-conscious, and he taught me how to pronounce 'Auguste' in French—and a few other things."

Betsy Allbright moved the open-toed sandal on her right foot over to the buzzer and pressed down on it. "More wine, Auguste."

The butler carefully poured the claret from a crystal decanter. The host lifted his glass, held it against the light of the candle and slowly turned the stem between thumb and index finger, studying the color carefully. Overseas he had been stationed at a replacement center close to the Château Lafite, and he had made the study of French wines, and particularly of the local vintages, his concern.

"What year, Auguste?" he asked eventually, after sipping some of the wine and letting it roll over his tongue.

The butler, who had taken the menu card and was using it to scrape bread crumbs off the table, straightened up. He said: "No year, monsieur. Just Sonny Boy California Claret."

"Oh," said the lieutenant, and put the glass down. He turned to Belinda. "A kind of vin ordinaire," he said.

"Precisely, monsieur," said the butler over his shoulder, continuing with the crumbs.

"For that—not bad at all," said the lieutenant.

At that moment Betsy Allbright suffered an almost uncontrollable impulse to throw her glass of Sonny Boy California Claret into her husband's face, but she turned her head and looked out through the wide, plate-glass window at the sea.

"The war does funny things, even to wines," said the lieutenant. "No one would ever have thought of serving this before."

"I must say I've grown to like these wines," said Cassard. "I have this claret regularly with my meals, and I think it is getting better and better every year. I say to myself—perhaps the Américains are learning to make good wine after all."

"Na-a-ah," said the lieutenant, forgetting his accent. "You're wrong there, Maurice. It's because you've been away from home so long—you forget about good wine. Think back. Take a St. Emilion or a Pouilly—a Montrachet—or, better still, a Bâtard Montrachet. That's what I mean when I speak of good wine."

The butler placed one of his blue hands over the other and pressed both to his chest. He sighed.

"Ah, monsieur, vous avez bien raison."

"Cut out that foreign talk and get the coffee," said Betsy to the butler. "And the brandy," she shouted after him. "That special Santa Monica Brandy—from Thrifty's!"

The lieutenant returned to Belinda.

Sir Gerald was engaged in solving the color problem.

"I've given it a lot of thought, Mr. Mumm," he said, "and I have a theory of my own about it. I say the color question doesn't exist at all in America—not the way you people think it does—I mean, it isn't hopeless at all. We have some friends in Santa Barbara, the Barbarians, I call them—hahaha—and I go there frequently. I will tell you what I have observed there. These friends of ours run a large establishment and they employ Negro help. Now, these Negroes are married and they have children and the children are allowed about the grounds, and I have observed that the children are several degrees lighter than their parents—and that solves the problem. A few more generations, and these people will have bleached themselves completely and the question will no longer exist."

The hostess got up. There was conversation in the living room, and drinks, and most of the guests went into the card room. Betsy Allbright was alone with Belinda. "Why don't you marry him?" she asked.

"Maurice?"

"Hasn't he asked you?"

"He asks me every day."

"Well, you're crazy if you don't. You couldn't do better in this town," said Betsy Allbright. "At least he's got a mind. He's devoted to you—my God, he worships the ground you walk on—and for a Frenchman that's something. How long has it been going on? Four months, isn't it? Well, that's a long time. You don't find anybody like that again out here. You better grab him."

"I don't know," said Belinda.

"Anybody else?"

"Well," said Belinda, "sometimes I think I like Buddy van der Lynn—he's sweet."

"He's an actor. Listen to me, Belinda. Don't ever marry an actor."

"What's wrong with actors?"

"Everything. To begin with, I can't think of them as men. They're not men—they're boys—and then, suddenly, they get old."

Betsy Allbright half filled the inhaler with brandy. She warmed the body of the glass in the palm of her hand, rotating it with slow, expert motion.

"I'll tell you about actors, Belinda," she said, and turned to look for the butler. She scratched her abdomen and her scalp. She looked into the dining room.

"Hey, Auguste, leave the table alone and bring us a bucket

of champagne—bring us the Krug sans anné—the private cuve
that I keep for special occasions," she said to the butler, who
was blowing out candles.

"I'd like you to look at some pictures of happy married life
out here." Betsy Allbright was offering the family album,
enhanced in Hollywood fashion.

"Auguste," she screamed, "tell Tom to run off the picture."

"The old silent?" asked Auguste, who knew the moods of
bitter nostalgia that overcame his mistress on such evenings.

"Yes, the old silent," she said. "*Snowy Night.*"

Auguste drew the high curtains and shut out the moonlit
sea. Betsy's eyes were frozen on the spot where the screen
sank down from the ceiling at the far end of the room. The
butler moved a sofa into position and put a bucket with the
good champagne on the floor next to it, and a bottle of good
brandy and an ash tray near by, and helped her to establish
herself in comfort. She kicked the sandals off her feet and
waited. The lights went out. The projector started, and from
an opening in the wall behind a shaft of white light played
over her, searched the wall, and came to rest within the
confines of the screen.

In the spotted, flickering, and jumpy opening sequence
that showed the inside of a mountaineer's cabin, the young
and innocent Betsy Allbright, in a gingham dress and braids,
stood before the stove stirring something in a kettle. With a
sudden jerky motion of the head toward a door which appeared
at the left of the cabin, she indicated that she had heard someone knocking there. She dried her hands on her apron and
for a full second she stared at the audience with wide, clumsily-
mascaraed eyes. Then, in stilted, broken-up, rapid progression
she moved to the door. . . .

Betsy Allbright crushed the half-smoked cigarette into the
ash tray and took a long drink. She looked up at her young
self on the screen, and, as she always did when viewing
Snowy Night, she began to provide the silent two-reeler with
her own running comment.

As Betsy on the screen opened the cabin door, Betsy on

the sofa below said: "All right, you son-of-a-bitch, come in," and after that there was a curious change.

In the dark, as she spoke, Betsy Allbright's voice became the organ of another woman. The rasping toughness was gone, age went out of it. It seemed as if time in the room had turned back to the old film, and yet not to the mood of that day, for, curiously, what was said was alive.

It was the woman's lament that can be suffered only once in a lifetime and is sealed with the deepest dyes of memory, so that whenever it is uncovered and examined it is as brash and loud as on the day it was recorded.

It is a freakish thing—this malformed child of the past that runs alongside the present, singing in its cretin voice, inflicting its presence forever, and never offering forgiveness.

Dennis Calhoun carried his magnificent body through the cabin door and greeted the woodsy creature with a hasty smile. He pushed the door shut with his immense shoulders and knocked the snow from his feet. Even in galoshes, he was the man whose love no woman could hold. In a close-up, he carefully released a luxurious growth of wavy ebon hair as he took off his coonskin cap and, lifting his lips up over his white teeth, pressed them down on hers as if he were blowing a trumpet.

"What an idiot I was to fall for you!" said Betsy Allbright in the flesh.

Dennis lifted a new traveling bag to the table and, motioning with his head toward a sleigh that stood outside the window, made clear that he wanted her to come with him.

"The one thing I never will forgive him, that vulgar tramp, is his greediness. That bag up there was mine. I bought it myself in London—and he took it, along with all the good furniture, while I was away getting the divorce. I looked all over for it. I looked all through the house—I went into the garage—it wasn't there, but I found a stack of old pictures of Henrietta . . . He left them there for me, I know. That's another thing, his cheapness, his boasting, even after she was gone. He always talked of 'good taste'—why did he leave them around where everybody could see them? Why did he have to

have her around? She was twenty years older than I was, and
seven years older than he, and still I suffered by comparison
with her. . . .

"She was good for him, he said. It was just a friendship
with an older woman. She taught him the few things he knew,
he said. . . . That's another thing I don't forgive him, the way
he lied. He lied to everybody. He even lied to his secretary.
. . . And then, his greed again, when she died—the way he
went to the relatives to get back that emerald ring he had
given her, saying she wanted him to have it—and then he
gave it to me. How stupid I was! I should have known then
what a chiseler he was. . . . The other thing was the Rumanian
—God, how I hate Rumanians!—I even hate the letter 'R'—
they're all the same. They have a peculiar form of contempt
for women. That was nice, too, when I found out a week after
I married him that he had his little girls in the apartment of
the Rumanian. In my great innocence on the wedding night,
I found one of those ugly things made of rubber in the bathroom. And afterward I used to find them everywhere, in his
pockets, among his papers, in drawers, and in that bag. And
the names of call houses and first names of girls written
in his hand on pieces of paper and in his small telephone
book.

"There was a book out then with the title *Call House*. I
never could understand why he kept that book locked up—
was he afraid of spoiling my innocence? That infuriated me.
Particularly the fact that he kept it locked up. He could have
left it around, I read it anyway. And as I read it, I wondered
which of the characters he was. . . . It became so that I was
suspicious of every move he made. I became sick to death and
nervous at his coming and at his going. He used to say to me,
Betsy, I am going down to have my hair cut, and leave. And
he would be gone for three hours and come back and I'd look
and his hair would not be cut. He could have had some consideration. He could have had it cut too, in that time. Or, he
could have said, oh, I met my agent, or so-and-so, and went
to such-and-such a place with him and talked about my next
picture. It would have been kinder. I would have known

anyway whether he was speaking the truth or lying, but he didn't bother to lie well.

"Oh, how I hated that house! All the objects in it became connected with him and his lies. What I could never understand was that his sins fell on me. I suffered for them—I felt dirty—I trembled when we went to parties because of the eyes of women that were on him. They ignored me, although I stood at his side like a dumb little schoolgirl, and they said things which must have had meaning to them and him alone, a code with sly laughter mixed in. And, of course, to make the terror complete, there was always Henrietta. . . .

"There was a day I cried so terribly, a day I cried all day long, when I said to him that I knew what he was doing and he laughed his silly laugh and said that it was all in my mind and denied everything. And I believed him because I wanted to believe him. But then in the middle of the night he came and he said that if ever I did anything like that, the only thing to do was to deny it. And so he threw me back into doubting him. Do it and deny it, that's what he said, and then I knew that every word was a lie and that he was hopeless for me. . . .

"And the ring—when I put it on my finger, he gave me another lesson. He said—and I remember every word—whenever you get nervous, dearest, he said, and when you think that somebody in the room thinks something about me and any other woman, just take the ring and turn it slowly and say they don't know anything, it isn't true. And that almost killed me when I found out that it was Henrietta's ring. He had brought the dead woman out of her grave to help him.

"He had no respect for anything, no kindness, no honor. I was brought up to take marriage seriously, and so I ran away at last. And he came after me to New York and he promised that everything would be all right. And he said that all my fears were those of an hysterical child . . . he always treated me like a child, never like a woman. But in New York, the same things happened again after a week. The Rumanian was there, with the sly little winks and the laughter . . . there were other women's eyes and there were those again who hunted him and those he hunted, and my room and all the objects in it were soon sick with his presence. And how he prided himself on his little elegancies and the things he had learned from Henrietta!—his talks about tailors, his French phrases, his conversations with head waiters, his dinners, and his knowledge of vintages. . . . I stood for all of it, and I agreed to come back to him.

"I will always remember that day on the Chief. We were in the dining car, and he asked for a wine card and studied it. I looked at him and for the first time I dared to say to myself, he's not only stupid, he's a fake. Those were the miraculous words that set me free.

"He had a very learned conversation with the head waiter about wines, and finally he chose something. And then he turned to me and inquired what I was eating. I had ordered a mountain trout—the train had just gotten over the Rockies— and he said, and what wine goes with that? And dutifully I said, white wine. So he ordered it for me. And then with great ceremony, the wine came—a small bottle of Château something. . . . The red wine he had ordered for himself and the white wine for me—I will also always remember those two little bottles. He was always careful with his own money, and he made himself conspicuous adding up the bills.

"He checked up on the labels . . . I wasn't awfully smart but I said to myself, wine that rides back and forth on trains can't be any good at all—I remembered the lessons he had given me about sediments in wine . . . he poured it himself, and I can draw the label on that bottle now, that's how well I remember it, because it was my door to freedom. He held the glass against the light and sipped slowly and tasted it. And then he said, not bad, that was a good year, or some such wine-drinker's phrase.

"I looked at him and he looked fakier than ever. He was all lies and fake and no longer beautiful to me, and I said to him, Dennis, will you do something for me? It's very important. And he grinned and said yes. I took both my white wine glass and his red wine glass and I said, Dennis, close your eyes and turn your head and I will give you a glass of wine, and all I want to know from you is whether it is red or white.

"He laughed his smug, indulgent smile and he closed his eyes, but I didn't trust him any more and I made sure that he couldn't cheat. I got up and held the napkin over his eyes. All the people in the car were watching the scene. And then I handed him the glass and he drank and said, it's the white . . .

"But it was the red. . . .

"Well, that was that," said Betsy Allbright. She scratched her abdomen again, and also the scalp under her crown of golden hair.

"Hey, Auguste!" she yelled; "take out that bucket and the glasses and straighten up the room before anybody comes in."

The muffled projector stopped its soft humming, the lights went on, and the screen disappeared. With her arm around Belinda, the Queen, still blinking, walked toward the card room. The guests there were lost in their games; only Cassard sat bored in a corner.

"Betsy, alors," he said, struggling out of his chair, "we must go—you know the long ride home. Thank you for a wonderful evening." He took both her hands, bent down and kissed them.

"Betsy darling—you spoke to her? You have straightened it out?" he asked, while Belinda was wrapping herself.

"I fixed up everything. She's all right—you can't go wrong there," said the experienced Queen, with closed eyes.

Lately, Belinda and Maurice had driven close together, especially on nights such as this when it took the convertible a while to get warm. She would sit pressed against him on the clammy leather, and when it got warm her head would lean on his, while he sat stiffly supporting her. Then she would fall asleep, and from time to time he would carefully turn and kiss her cheek or mumble tender words into her ear.

Tonight the car again was cold, but Belinda sat pressed alone on her side of the car, as far away from Maurice as she could get. The windshield wipers smacked busily back and forth, the heater was going, and Maurice Cassard was bent forward over the steering wheel peering through the windshield at the fog-drenched road. The road fed the white line

into the fenders, then under the radiator and to the left and
right of the car, as Cassard tried to keep her on an even keel.
He wiped the inside of the windshield with the back of his
hand, a chore that Belinda usually took on. He took out his
handkerchief and wiped his forehead.

He passed Topango Beach and there was still silence.

"Tired, darling?"

She had to clear her throat before she could speak.

"No, I'm wide awake."

"What is wrong?"

"Nothing, but do me a favor, Maurice. . . ."

"Anything, my sweet."

"Don't ever again ask me to marry you," she said.

He glanced at her in surprise and drove on without answering. He turned into Sunset Boulevard, where the red neon sign
of the Friendship Café colored the fog. The rearview mirror
deflected the beams of the headlights of cars following them
so that they shone into his face. He tilted the mirror . . . and
then he suddenly sat up straight and laughed fiercely.

"Ah, alors," he said, "I know what it is."

"What?" asked Belinda.

"She has hit you over the head with that Grade B biography
—the obscene opus she calls *Snowy Night.*"

"That has nothing to do with it. I just don't want to marry
you or anyone else."

"How much in love she must still be with Dennis, to bother
tearing open those old bandages."

"You mean wounds."

"Yes, wounds, of course—most of them self-inflicted. . . .
While she was married to him, she had a knife in her hand
also, and she made his life hell on earth."

"That's just what I mean—why go through all that when
you don't have to?"

"I know, I know, I know, Belinda . . . but it is still better than
being lonesome. And you must admit that sometimes things
work out beautifully—for example, take your first marriage."

"That's another reason why I don't want to take another
chance."

"Believe me, Belinda, it's the picture and that awful house, and Betsy. How stupid of me! Most women, my darling— women like Betsy—have dark memories; they can see only black and white. Now if tonight, instead of going to Betsy's, we had gone to Dennis's house, and he had insisted on showing us his films, I am certain they would have been lighthearted, gay, and colorful. All he would ever have kept and remembered out of his marriage to Betsy would have been the sunny epochs, the happy moments. . . .

"Men are generous and kind with their memories. Man is devoted forever, like a dog. No matter how you kick a dog around and how badly you feed and treat him, he forgets it. Come back no matter when, open the door, and there he is— friendship in his eyes, tail wagging, and making all his motions of joy and sounds of pleasure—and he will do that until he dies.

"Women are otherwise, and even the best of them—those that profess to understand—never forgive."

"I agree with you," said Belinda.

"Besides, what has all this got to do with us? She married an actor—don't forget that."

Belinda had to clear her throat twice. Then she said, "Oh, what's the difference—it's all the same."

The light on Rodeo changed to red.

"Belinda," he said, slowing the car down, "I am a saint—the most patient man on earth—and I am kindness itself. But even for me there is a limit."

He looked at her while the car stood still. She stared straight ahead.

Five blocks farther on he said, "What are you thinking about?"

"Oh, just something you said the other day."

"Well, tell me what it was."

"We were driving along this same road and we came to that same light on Rodeo. There was a blind beggar trying to get across and you almost ran over him."

"They don't allow beggars in Beverly Hills. I don't remember anything like that."

"Oh yes, he even had his little tin cup and the pencils, and not even a dog, and afterward you said to me, 'I don't know why, but whenever I see a blind beggar like that, I have an almost uncontrollable impulse to kick him in the stomach.'"

He drove on. Eventually he said, "That doesn't mean anything. For example, I have also an uncontrollable impulse to kick a pregnant woman in the stomach—that is, provided she is young and beautiful."

"And you call that kind?"

"Ah yes, and it is also noble."

"Well, a lot of people I know will disagree violently with you. And I also know, for example, that with all his faults Buddy van der Lynn would never do a thing like that."

"Just a moment, Belinda. I did not say that I would do it. I merely stated that I had the impulse to do it. There's a great difference in that, and also an explanation for it."

"Well, maybe I'm dumb. I just think it's mean and brutal even to think such a thing."

"Let me try to explain. When you kick something, you try to get rid of it. When I have an impulse to kick the poor blind beggar, I voice thereby a subconscious complaint against a world that allows a man already sentenced to darkness to be further degraded by having to make an object of pity of himself and being forced to stand on street corners begging. In the case of the pregnant young woman, I proclaim my disgust with nature for allowing her lovely body to be bloated into the obscene and ugly evidence of her condition."

He slowed down the car and turned into Belinda's street. She picked up her gloves.

"I guess you could talk yourself out of anything, Maurice," she said, getting out of the car.

"You are very tired tonight, and I will not bore you with more talk. But one day, Belinda, I am going to ask you again to marry me and you will answer 'yes,' and then I shall have to lie down on my couch for half an hour, to get over the shock."

"Good night."

"Good night."

22. X'Isle

Ludlow Mumm had arranged a quiet luncheon in celebration of the marriage of Maurice Cassard and Belinda at the other good restaurant in Hollywood, a place called Chasen's. At this place, the prices are the same as at Romanoff's, the food is plain and good but served on larger plates, and the clientele is not disturbed by complicated seating arrangements.

In a small private dining room of Chasen's, twenty people celebrated the happy event. Moses Fable made a speech, during which he prophesied a brilliant career for Belinda and announced her next two pictures. He saluted Cassard as the most brilliant of writers and promised him a great future. Speaking of their romance, he used the words "These two kids," or he said, "Just like a couple of kids." He gave the kids his blessing and, on behalf of Olympia, a bonus.

A trio played appropriate music. Vanya Vashvily, who had given the bride away, discussed her next picture with Buddy van der Lynn. He suffered and had the leaning-into-the-wind expression on his face, with eyes half-closed, when he looked across the table.

After the cake was cut and they were ready to leave they went to the parking lot, where rice was thrown at a new car, a two-and-a-half litre Lagonda, which Belinda had given Cassard as a wedding present.

After Belinda had made herself comfortable in a new mink coat, a wedding gift from her new husband, they set out for the rancho of Moses Fable in Palm Springs, which he had lent them for their honeymoon.

Everybody waved after them. It was a lovely day, and the good wishes of all were genuine. In this town, births, birthdays, engagements, marriages, and sometimes anniversaries, are celebrated with an intensity seldom encountered elsewhere.

After a delay caused by photographers and autograph hunters, they drove on through the downtown section of the city. The traffic conditions in Los Angeles are, even for a good driver, hazardous, but Maurice, on this great day, steered the slim car calmly through the roughest traffic and came to the open country, past the center of Los Angeles, without damage. At this point there is a stretch of road as desolate as the passage from Newark to Hoboken, and after that there is good scenery all the way to Palm Springs.

The car hummed its peculiar foreign-muffler tune. They both sat silent and played the game as experts do—no false moves, no wrong words, no reveries, no regrets. A mood of happiness brought about on Belinda's side by good digestion, by sage decision, and by success, fortified by humor, courage, and sincere affection on Maurice's side—this mood was bolstered by an amalgam of love, passion, and sagacity.

Maurice had got some spots on his new gray suit made by upsetting a cup of turtle soup. That was, however, the only blot on their happiness.

Maurice whistled and sang and preached to himself a small silent sermon as he drove along. He held Belinda's hand and drove with the other, carefully, at less than the legal thirty-five miles an hour, and on the right side of the road. He could not have been calmer if he had taken drugs.

"Most fortunate," went his mute sermon, "is the man who, like myself, while still in his best years, alors, finds a mate young and yet experienced—one escaped from the fearful bondage of first love—a ripe, desirable woman like Belinda, not an upset maiden out of the dank dungeon in which they awaken from the fraudulent dreams of youth and innocence. Blessed is the man, like myself, who finds a woman like Belinda who, when her first wedding dress is shed, finds the courage to dress up anew and listen once more for the music." He looked at her sideways. "And how to be envied am I, who have found this woman of warmth and courage, of experience and humor, of intelligence and principle, who, besides, alors, is at the beginning of a great career and will earn no less than a hundred and fifty thousand dollars a picture! How unbelievable is my fortune, when I can say that on top of all this, she is beautiful and alluring off the screen as well as on! Alors, I am indeed a lucky man!"

After two hours of such gay melody and matching lyrics, he stopped the car. There was a little basket of sandwiches in the baggage compartment and a small bottle of wine. Under a tree, in a field, "just like a couple of kids," they enjoyed the repast. Cassard took pictures of his bride and then embraced her tenderly.

He whistled again as he drove. Belinda had placed her head on his shoulder and had gone off to sleep. He whistled a Spellbinder tune from *Will You Marry Me?*, a number called "Bird of Paradise," and he continued his silent essay on the pleasures of a second marriage.

"What fear, what uncertainty, what painful awkwardness ruins the wedding night of most young people! How often is this overrated moment turned into never-forgotten misery! How idiotic, alors, that when every other step in life is carefully prepared for and properly explained and rehearsed, this most important act is neglected and left to embarrassed fumbling! How otherwise and good with us!"

The wind brushed Belinda's sandalwood-colored hair against his cheek.

He continued the praise of his fortunate circumstances. "The wedding night," he said to himself, "alors, promises perfection." They both had experience and knowledge, and they both had rowed their boats through the troubled waters of uncertainty and beached them on the most desirable of islands.

"Darling," he said, "Palm Springs. Wake up!"

"If it just had a few really big hotels, like Atlantic City, it would be completely awful," he said, driving through the main street. He was overtaken by that disappointment that always goes with arrival in much-praised resorts, and began to see it for what it really is: A row of camera shops and souvenir and postal card emporiums, restaurants—none of them good—a Lanz dirndl store, several bars, an Indian mud bath, and extravagantly named small hotels. The excessively hot street.

The stucco bungalows, disfigured with air-conditioning equipment standing outside on stilts and looking like old-fashioned automobile radiators that have overflowed and left stains down the sides of the buildings. The usual natives who thrive on the visitor. And the California motorcycle policeman who, more shamelessly than anywhere else, hides in the side streets, in the shade of boarding houses, waiting for the traffic violator. . . .

At the end of the village, they passed a coconut-milk bar and the cement shack of the fire department, with a clock that doesn't work.

"Where is the rancho of Moses Fable?" asked Cassard of the motorcycle policeman who was hiding behind a palm tree.

The estate was on the outskirts of Palm Springs and the entrance was marked by a sign saying "X'Isle."

"Get it, darling?" asked Belinda. "It means 'Exile.'

"You better watch your pants," she said as they arrived at the house. The man who came down to get the bags was Vashvily's ex-butler, Walter.

"That is another thing about Hollywood and its environs," said Cassard. "You are always running into your own or other people's ex-servants."

The palatial villa had separate apartments for man and wife, and everything a honeymoon couple could desire. Beneath the shaded balcony, the length of the house, was a pool, mosaic-lined, with a springboard leading out from the master bedroom over water that seemed heavy and solid like quicksilver.

The male apartment offered a miniature gymnasium with mechanical horse, exercycle, and punching bag. The bed was somewhat narrower than that in the lady's wing, but supplied with a bedside dictaphone, bookshelf, an invalid's table for working, and a reading light like Cassard's own at home.

Like every well-run establishment in California, it was furnished with an assortment of bathing suits for the guests. Cassard searched for his size, and then, with his furious laugh, he went out on his spindly legs, which were covered with black hair. Holding his nose, he jumped into the pool below and swam up and down. Belinda swam with him. They were again "just like a couple of kids."

After swimming, they sat on the terrace. They had the appetites of passengers on the third day of an ocean voyage, and they waited impatiently for dinner.

The snake-and-lizard paradise stretched to the horizon. The skeleton and borax scenery, here and there relieved by the yellow flame of desert flora, the lava-like alkali land, lay trembling in heat. The sun's cemetery of dried bones and the lacy, dried, finlike leaves of cubaya plants and cacti, robbed of their colors and then lit up like a stage set, simmered on for a while and quivered.

Belinda and Cassard felt feverish. Omelettes could have been cooked on the tiled terrace. It was hot even under the umbrellas. The water was lukewarm. Around the pool stood broad deck-chairs designed by Raoul de Bourggraff, and on each one of them Moses Fable had left his imprint. He had lain there sweating and his form was stained into the center of every one of the russet sailcloth mattress covers. Cassard was warm for once, and he brushed the sweat off his body with his hand held flat. The air was like a Finnish bath.

"Mr. Fable loses ten pounds every day he comes here," said Walter. He brought a large jug of lemonade and then wet towels to put on Cassard's forehead. Suddenly the temperature changed, as if someone had come into a warm room from out of a winter's night and left the door open. The sun had gone past the summit of the slag-colored mountain range. It turned cold and the scene was for a moment purple, and then indigo.

The intimate bar was heated and they ate dinner and drank and sat and talked.

"I cannot play—what you call it?—'Jimmy run,'" said Cassard. "I am terribly sorry. I cannot play any game of cards. I should have told you before. I cannot keep my mind on it."

Belinda put the cards away and she said that she wanted to go to bed. Again all was proper and calm. He followed her in half an hour in a yellow dressing gown.

She brushed her hair. She was framed in six mirrors. He stood behind her and smoked a cigarette calmly. He talked quietly, all without haste, nervousness, or awkwardness, as if it had all been rehearsed and could not be otherwise.

The bedroom was softly lit, the satin sheets turned back. He held her small white well-formed foot in his hand, and, in that most limited dialogue that love allows, he said his small piece to her.

He loitered on the side of the bed and then bent over her. He engaged in the brief brutality of couching her to his advantage. The moon outside transformed the treeless, waterless wasteland into a sea that was like the quicksilver in the pool. In the bridal suite, his hands now under her strong shoulders, he pressed his face against hers and pushed her head back into the pillows. With half-closed eyes, in legitimate acquiescence, her unrouged lips half open, she was about to abandon her token resistance, when the telephone rang.

"Don't answer it," whispered Belinda; but the moment was ruined. The telephone rang again, and Cassard swept it from the night table.

Out of the instrument, up from the carpet, came the voice of Moses Fable.

Cassard put on his dressing gown and picked up the phone. "Yes?" he said.

"I will see to it, if it's the last thing I do," screamed the executive, with the voice of a knife-grinder, "I will see to it that as long as you live you will never get a job with me or any other studio."

"But what is wrong now?" asked Cassard.

"We can throw the whole picture away, that's what's wrong," cried Moses Fable. "Your God-damned pig has cost this company five millions."

"But why?"

"Dirty Eddie—" Fable started, and choked.

"But I thought he was wonderful," broke in Cassard.

"Yes, he's wonderful, all right. He's so wonderful he's ruined the whole show."

Belinda held Cassard's head as he listened.

"That's awful," said Cassard, "really awful," when Moses Fable had slammed down the receiver. He began visiting the four walls. He looked as if he were going to cry. "I don't know what to do. . . . For the first time, I don't know what to do!"

At that quiet, unworried, and completely happy moment a few hours back when Maurice and Belinda, pleasantly fatigued, had come in from the terrace and sat down to dinner, and Cassard, in high good humor, had looked out of the window and observed that the outlines of Moses Fable on the mattresses in the fading daylight were beginning to look like enormous gingerbread men, Moses Fable himself, back in Hollywood, was returning to the lot.

He worked in his office until they were ready for him at last, and then he went down to his private projection room. He entered in the highest spirits, with more hope than he had ever had for the success of the picture. He was about to see *Will You Marry Me?*, which had finally been cut and put together; and he and a handful of executives were to be the first to see the completed film run off.

He seated himself, surrounded by his executives. He passed out cigars and gave the signal to start.

Through the first part of the picture he laughed loudly and slapped his knee repeatedly. He was sure of several awards. . . . But suddenly he jumped up with a wild cry of pain that awoke all the others who sat around him. The lights were turned on and everybody asked him what was wrong.

"Haven't you got eyes?" he yelled. "What do I pay you for? Didn't you see?" He was beside himself.

"Run it once more," he said. "Look at it this time, for Christ's sake. In the meantime, I don't want anybody else to see this picture, or to hear about it. I don't want anybody to arrange a preview, even a sneak preview, or any showing whatsoever. I want this film and every foot of film we have taken locked up in the vault tonight and nobody is to see it—or discuss it with anybody!" Moses Fable watched for a while and screamed again at the same place, and then he ran out of the small theater.

The executives, now awake, saw it through to the end, and paralysis overtook them. They left in silence.

They found Fable up in his office, on the telephone to Palm Springs.

"Did you see what happens?" Fable shouted, slamming down the receiver. "I speak for millions of theater-goers, and for the stockholders of this corporation, when I say that this is the most inexcusable and sordid thing that I have ever experienced in my life—the most terrible thing that has ever happened out here. It makes the whole story pointless and injects an element of utter ridicule. The fine portrayal given by Belinda, the money lavishly spent on this production, is totally wasted. How in hell could a thing like this happen? Judas Priest! If I don't watch every detail myself, everything goes wrong. We can throw the whole God-damned picture away!"

"Mr. Fable," said Sandor Thrilling, "let's examine this quietly for a moment."

"All right. You examine it quietly. I can't."

"All right. What has happened?"

"I can tell you what has happened," said Fable. "A pig, which is one of the central characters of this story—and steals the show, incidentally—grows smaller and smaller as the story unfolds. Nothing, gentlemen, can be written or shown to explain that.

"Look, gentlemen. In the first scene"—Moses Fable showed a good-sized pig with his hands—"he is this big. Suddenly he shrinks to this size." With his hands he showed an animal a little bigger than a mouse.

"That was on account of the layoff," said Wolfgang Liebestod. "It happened while he was suspended. He grew in those two months."

"If he grew, that would be all right," said Fable, "but he shrinks."

"That," explained Sandor Thrilling, "is because we shot the end of the picture first—and the beginning afterward."

"Oh, God! Why doesn't somebody watch these things?" groaned Fable.

"Come to bed now, darling," said Belinda, out at "X'Isle." She sat beside him and looked at him worriedly. The unhappy writer was hunched over the dictaphone the way Hack, in moments of distress, bent over his typewriter.

She put a coat over him and he lit cigarettes again and stared out into the desert, concentrating on the moon as Mumm did on his ink spot.

"Good night," she said, but he did not hear her. He was thinking of the story problem.

"Come to bed now, darling," she said.

"No," said Cassard unhappily.

"Tonight I sleep alone," said Belinda again. And she went to her room to cry on her wedding night, as most brides do.

23. *It's Fishing Time Again*

The radio in Ludlow Mumm's workroom was on. He lay on the leather couch.

"In just a minute I'll be back with Ben Piazza, who is going to tell you how to get into the movies. In the meantime, Marvin Miller is going to tell you how to become more beautiful . . ." said the radio.

"They've just announced officially that Hitler is dead," said Mumm as Cassard came into the room, exhausted from the quick drive back. "And they've signed the Armistice in Berlin."

"Alors," said Cassard. "Congratulations! You have won the bet. It's not June yet. Alas, there will be no exchange of money —because I, too, have won my bet. You will recall that I said that Mussolini will be gone, Hitler will be gone, but we shall still be here. We are, alors, still here—that is, today. Tomorrow we shall be gone, for just now Mrs. Sinnot has smiled at me; and you will also recall, amigo, that I have said when Mrs. Sinnot smiles at us, that is the signal for our departure."

Cassard opened the drawer of the desk and took all the paper, the pencils, paper clips, and envelopes and put them in a brief case.

"I said some time ago when things became uncomfortable here—you will undoubtedly remember—I said that the moment had come when I would take over. Well, now the moment has come to let go. I step down. Now, Mr. Hack takes over—"

"Why?" asked Mumm, getting off his couch.

"Because the picture stinks—"

"How?" asked Mumm. "How does it stink?"

"It stinks like Liederkranz and castor oil mixed."

"And now what?" asked Mumm.

"Now the following happens. You, amigo, have just received a wire from a magazine. You must go to New York to do a profile on Moses Fable. That is the best rear-guard action we can employ."

"You mean—?"

"I mean that you will tell your chauffeur to drive you to the next train on which you can get tickets, and then fire him —not until then. Don't change your mode of living, amigo. That will be held against you, and the next time you come out here to do a picture, your agent will have trouble getting you an increase in salary."

Ludlow Mumm was stunned by the sudden change.

"What happens now—with the picture, I mean?"

"Let me explain," said Cassard, and sat down next to him. He was very calm.

"Moses Fable, alors, has not slept all night, and he is a very disagreeable man this morning. Mr. Hack, whom he has not seen for the last year, although he passes him a dozen times a day, is suddenly reinstated and given an amnesty. His coolie wages, a condition about which he has screamed for months, will be adjusted. He may even be asked to have lunch with Moses Fable.

"Moses Fable will say: 'Listen, Hack, I'm in a difficult spot and I count on you to extricate us.' In times of stress, they suddenly esteem the professional, the galley slave, the dreary carpenter, who is the regular screenwriter. 'Listen, Hack, we'll talk about that raise later,' Fable will say, 'but first, let me explain the problem . . .' And at the end he will say, 'Now, listen, Hack, I don't want you to lose any of that richness of the original . . .'

"Alors, amigo, the repairs must not cost too much and they must be made in a minimum of time."

"And Hack will be able to fix it?" asked Mumm.

"But of course, amigo. He will fix it so that it comes out right. He will stay within the budget and he will be not one day late. He is, and I say that with respect, a responsible and able man. Hack has the taste for hard work and the tremendous discipline of the interpretative artist. That is what people like him are. Some, even, are inspired, and work easily and well, and it makes for a good picture. Others, like Hack, are plodders and worriers, but none of them have the quick invention, the flash of wit, the creative facility, that you and I have. Alors, our work is done."

"But, if Hack doesn't want to do it, couldn't we fix it?"

"Of course we could fix it. I could fix it in half an hour, but why spoil Hack's moment of glory? As for him saying no, that word is not in his dictionary. If he said to Moses Fable—I go into the realm of pure fantasy now—if he said, 'Mr. Fable, this story can't be fixed' or just 'I don't care to do it,' then Moses Fable will say, 'Listen, Hack, I have six swimming pools, and if I close five of them I can still swim, but you have only one, and if I close that, you don't swim.'"

"How would you fix the story?"

"Alors, the problem is simple. Eddie in the last half of the film abruptly fades away to one third of the size he appears in the first part. An unforeseen disaster, which occurred because the end of the story was filmed first and the beginning after an interval of several months in which he was allowed to grow. Not your fault, not my fault, an act of God, and due to the rapacity of Moses Fable, who can do almost anything except keep the world and time from advancing. The solution is simple. There are many solutions for this oversight. The most evident is to inject a small scene in the middle of the picture in which Dirty Eddie falls in love with and proposes in his inimitable fashion to another pig, say, Belladonna, and marries. In another scene that can follow right after, their proud son is shown in a bassinet, and then we continue with Dirty Eddie playing his own son at the end of the picture. Very cute. The audience will love it. It's been done a thousand times with people, and it works. That is the simplest way possible. There are others, but I shall not bore you, amigo."

"I think that's brilliant, and a wonderful solution," said Mumm. "Don't you think you could tell Hack quietly?"

"He would only resent it. He is going to drag himself to his typewriter. He is now in a state of grace. His faith in humanity has returned. He loves Moses Fable, who has given him a raise and promised him two weeks' vacation with pay so he can take his ulcers and his wife and four children to Santa Barbara. Now, he only looks sadder than ever. He is slowly dying, folded over his typewriter. He is giving birth with blood and carefully examining his dirty fingernails and every possibility with which to straighten out the story—and he and his tribe, amigo, detest free and creative artists like us: believe me. As for them, I shy away from them completely."

They heard Hack's voice out in the hall. He was speaking to Vashvily. The collaborators crept to the door and listened.

"But heavens, Hack! You can't do that in the middle of a picture," said Vashvily.

"Listen, Vanya—please," said Hack. "There's no other way."

"It lacks unction," said Vashvily.

"You've just gone sour, Vanya," said Hack.

Cassard opened the door slowly, just enough to hear better.

"Oh," cried Vanya with real anguish. "This ruins the whole thing for me. You have upset the whole mood. Do that and she has lost all emotional isolation. You demolish the picture right there. You end up by having nothing, but nothing. You rupture the whole construction."

"Listen, Vanya, I'll guarantee you that nothing will be lost.

I'll pull it through, believe me. Now, just let me show you how I'm going to do it. Nothing will be lost."

"I wish I'd never seen or heard of that God-damned pig!" cried Vashvily.

Their voices faded away. Cassard closed the door carefully.

"Did you hear? He is now St. Christopher, to whom the script has been entrusted. He shines with an inner light as he carries it through the swirling waters and over the rocks safely to the box office."

There was silence for a while and then Mumm said: "I spoke to a Russian the other day, to a man who has been there and seen for himself how it really is, and I believe him. He said that a people's artist, a dancer, an actor, a singer, or a writer, retires for the rest of his life with the amount of money he made when he was at the top of his art. In other words, you and I would retire now at three thousand dollars a week for life—special privileges, like a box at the opera, and a car, a house in town and a nice dacha in the country, and no taxes—"

"Alors," said Cassard. "Amigo, I always fancy that I would have been happier if born in another century. The fault with this speculation is that one always assumes that in that other century one would have been a man of outstanding position— if not the emperor, at least at the court. I, for example, see myself as Voltaire, but in somewhat less frantic circumstances and in properly heated rooms. Yet, if I were transported back, I might find myself Jean Calas, or, worse, an anonymous member of the police department with my beat in the suburbs or in the most malodorous section of Paris. Also, consider, amigo, that if we were to find ourselves in Russia, as writers, and we find that Vashvily is the Commissar, and that he can do with the knout what he does now with his small and insidious intrigues, we would not be very happy. Or imagine for a moment that perhaps, on account of his idiocy and cowardice, he is shelved, and Mrs. Sinnot becomes the Commissar, and you have to bring in your twenty pages of dialogue a day to her. Oh, no, amigo, since we must earn our bread with our labor, I prefer the United States. Incidentally, on

this day of remembrance, you will think back about what I
said about the General Staff of the United States and how right
I was about that. They have acquitted themselves mag-
nificently.

"Now that we have come to the end, amigo, there is something I have wanted to tell you from the moment I met you,
and I must get that off my chest. It is about the Russians.
First, let me tell you that I have never met an individual
Russian whom I have not liked, but as a nation I think they
should be left to themselves for the next hundred years until
they have caught up with what you call democracy. As for
people like us talking about Russia, I have this to say: If,
alors, a coal miner comes out of his shaft in a dirty, sweaty
shirt into a dirty town, spitting blood, and finds that he
will die before his time, unable to rescue his children from
his own fate, in spite of all the increases in pay—if that man
lifts his black hands to heaven and, coughing his anger, says,
'I wish the Russians would take over,' I say, right, and good
logic.

"But you and the other Stork Club communists who go out,
dressed for dinner, to the houses of the rich every evening,
who spend your week ends at millionaires' estates and sit at
the best tables of the best restaurants, munching caviar, washing it down with vintage champagne, and inhaling the
fragrance of twelve-inch Havanas . . . you who travel in
drawing rooms on the Superchief, and change women the
way you do shirts, and pay abortionists a thousand dollars a
throw . . . when I reflect that people like you hire tax specialists
to cheat your own Government out of money—and I admit
that I do the same—when you say that you wish the Russians
would take over, and accuse everyone who is not in full
agreement with you of being a fascist, when it is really you
and the Russians who have taken over the methods of the
fascists . . . then, cher ami, when I think of that, I feel like
taking your hat and vomiting in it."

"I beg your pardon—I never—" began Mumm.

"Ah, I cross that out. I know you have never paid a thousand
dollars to an abortionist, but the rest remains."

"People like me," said Mumm mildly, "have a conscience—and when you spoke about the miner, you put your finger on it. We write and talk on his behalf because he is without representation and inarticulate—"

"Amigo," said Cassard, "liberals, alors, are the most intolerant people in this world. I am sorry I spoke. We shall get nowhere. It was a pleasure to work with you. Let us not mar our beautiful friendship with the ugly temper of the times. I embrace you with affection, and I thank you."

"What will happen to this office?" asked Mumm as they were about to say good-by to their secretary.

"Tomorrow, amigo, you will not know the place. It will be dismantled and perhaps set up on Stage Eight, because Hack, in his insane fits of jealousy, and in an attempt to save money for Olympia, will most probably write the scene for the marriage of the pigs into this hotel room. He is low enough to do that."

"Don't we say good-by to Vashvily?" asked Mumm in the corridor.

"Ah, non," said Cassard, and he took Mumm's arm to head him in the other direction. "Belinda has arranged a luncheon at Romanoff's tomorrow. All this must be done carefully and without loss of face for anyone. I must ask you to turn back again to my sermon on the word 'great.' If, instead of the hard, back-breaking sweat and toil we have put into this story, we had written one half a typewritten page and handed it to Vashvily, he would still be committed to saying that we were 'great,' and that we had written 'a great story' for him, and that *Will You Marry Me?* was the greatest picture that Vanya Vashvily has produced up to now. Alors, we must let him down easy—gaiety, a bottle of champagne. I have arranged for Belinda to give a luncheon, as I said, tomorrow at Romanoff's, and casually, during the coffee and cigars, Vashvily will thank us for the good work we have done, and that is the termination of the contract."

"We go half and half," said Mumm.

"No, alors, permit me," said Cassard. "I have enjoyed our

collaboration, and anyway, Belinda and I have a tax problem—
the clause which allows California couples to split their
incomes does not do us any good, since we both earn considerable sums, and this luncheon is a welcome item, since
it is deductible from the income tax."

In the entrance hall they met Mrs. Sinnot, who smiled at
both of them again. And, as the carillon began to ring, they
saw Hack going toward the Commissary. Moses Fable had
his arm around him and was talking to him. Hack leaned over
and tilted his head down, smiling.

"Before they had so much time and money, here at Olympia,"
said Cassard, "things were simpler. The function of people
like Jerome Hack was carried out by a small Japanese who
sat in a ramshackle old building that since has been torn down.
This Japanese was a miniature-painter, and once there was a
complaint about a picture, about a scene in which an actor
walked about with his suspenders hanging down. The small
Japanese then licked his brush and painted the suspenders
out in each of the thousand little pictures of the film. After
a while he didn't like the expression on the actor's face, and
he changed that too and improved the picture a great deal
thereby.

"I will see you there tomorrow. At one, then, at Romanoff's,"
said Cassard as he stepped into his car and drove off.

"I have always wanted to have lunch at the Farmer's Market
and to take a look at the La Brea tar pits," Ludlow Mumm
said to himself. "I better look at them before I leave." And he
asked George to take him to these tourist attractions.

24. *Come Rain, Come Shine*

Mumm and Cassard were going in to lunch.

"When something like this happens," said Cassard, "they spray embalming fluid all over the place. When something goes wrong, the people in this village can hear you think. They come and stand next to you, and they know. It's like dogs that can smell whether you're afraid of them or not, and they bite you if you are afraid. They can smell whether your option has been taken up, or whether a big deal has fallen through. They know by looking at you that your picture is a failure, and they cool off instantly. You will notice that they don't shake hands with you. They take your hand to push you away."

The cool reception of the man who opened the door at Romanoff's bore out this truth. He used to trumpet a nasal greeting, saying: "And how are you today, Mr. Cassard? And how do you do, Mr. Mumm?" Today he just said "Hello." And inside the reception was very formal and they were demoted and taken through the length of the restaurant to where the discarded wives of producers sit, and where the minute steak takes an hour. The good waiter from the front, Mr. Reinhardt, came back and looked at them with some sympathy, but he said he was sorry he could not wait on them. He seemed to look at them out of a shattered mirror, so broken with worry was his face.

"You're only as good as your last picture, here," said Cassard.

The ever-placid Mumm looked around and saw people he had never seen before. It was as if he were in another restaurant. And Cassard looked up as a girl smiled at him. She had a man with her.

"May I present my husband?" she said. "Mr. Copfee."

They got up and shook hands.

"Who is that?" asked Mumm.

"That," said Cassard, "was a call girl a month ago. She came once to visit me. Her price was thirty dollars and worth it. She came to my beach house. Alors, she is now a respectably married woman!"

Mrs. Copfee went about from table to table, introducing the new husband, and everybody smiled.

"She seems to have had a large clientele," said Cassard. "And very solid!"

"You must admit," said Mumm, "that they are tolerant here. Now, in no other city could a woman like that who decides to get married—I mean, in a small town like this—suddenly change her life and face the community and be accepted. I think it's very nice and very tolerant."

"Alors," said Cassard. "If they weren't tolerant out here, where would they be? They'd have no one to talk to."

"We were talking about tolerance," said Cassard as Vashvily and Belinda came in.

"God!" said Belinda. "You have to be tolerant in this world, but out here you have to be especially tolerant or you choke with hate. Gee, it's easy to hate these guys, if you let yourself. They're so awful. Every one a heel, every one a procurer, every one a talker! Look at them. I told a story to Moses Fable—we stopped at his table to say hello. You know, the silly jerk didn't listen to me at all. For the first part, he was watching the door, and when I came to the second, he turned that fishface of his and listened to a conversation on our right. At the end he laughed, but he was looking past me—trying to read the lips of some guy who had just come in and was talking to Vanya . . ."

"Somebody just offered me a job," said Vashvily, "thinking this would be a good time." He patted her hand. "Well, don't let it get you," he said. "If he doesn't take up your option, somebody else will."

They ordered.

"Mr. Mumm is leaving. He is going to New York to do a profile on Moses Fable," said Cassard to an assistant director of Olympia who stopped. "And then he is going to write a novel."

"Well, that's nice," said the assistant director. "Good luck, Mr. Mumm, and a nice trip east."

They had to pass Moses Fable's table as they left, but there were no greetings. Fable was suddenly interested in a large slab of mocha cake, and the others looked straight ahead.

Mumm drove back to the hotel. He dragged his traveling bag out of the closet. The valet had become lax.

"Your tickets are here," said Miss Princip, dabbing at her eyes. She was typing out several unbelievable checks to the Collector of Internal Revenue; and when they were added up, together with the hotel bill, the last tips, and the check he had told her to make out for herself, they left Ludlow Mumm a shocking balance in only three figures.

Mumm signed the checks and spent the rest of the day winding up his business.

The next day, when he was ready to leave for the train, Mumm walked to the cigar counter in the lobby to buy supplies for his trip. His finger moved slowly from the Cuban corner back to the Robert Burns Panatelas. The surprised girl had the box in her hand and was ready to bring it up out of the glass case when Ludlow Mumm felt himself tapped on the shoulder by a bellboy.

"Call for you, Mr. Mumm," he said. And Mumm thought he heard the old respectful ring in the boy's voice. "Will you take it in the booth?" he asked. Now with an unmistakable upswing in his voice: "It's the Wildgans Chase Agency," he said, folding back the door of the telephone booth and handing the instrument to the writer.

"Mr. Mumm," said the cheerful girl with ecstasy, "let me be the first to congratulate you—"

"On what?" asked Mumm.

"It will be in tomorrow's *Reporter*. Haven't you heard? They had a sneak preview of *Will You Marry Me?*—Just a moment, Mr. Wildgans wants to tell you himself."

"Well, it's in the bag, Mumm," said Arty Wildgans. "Listen! The audience was in stitches. They rolled in the aisles. They stamped and whistled. It's great, and everybody is talking about it. I just had Moses Fable on the phone. He's crying. He wants to offer you a straight contract for seven years— anything you want—and double what you're getting now. But we'll make it tough for him—real tough!"

The girl took over again. "Mr. Mumm," she said, "you're having lunch with Mr. Wildgans at Romanoff's. The car will be under the porte-cochere of your hotel in fifteen minutes!"